# The Journey of Gamel and Lidya

## Michelle Warren

ISBN 978-0-473-25995-2

# CONTENTS

# PART ONE

## THE HEARTLAND

CHAPTER ONE: Gamel and Lidya

Raventown was sleeping. A quiet township of six thousand, she was the crown of the Heartland. Built on the western shore of the Blue Lake, and along the edge of the Dandes River, she stood charming and inviting, surrounded by the majestic mountains of the North and South.

All was still.

A small figure hid amidst the roots of an oak tree. He gazed out across Raventown's oak and pine cottages, seen quite clearly by moonlight and starlight, and smiled. Then, suddenly, he moved – gathering his cloak about him, racing as if against an unknown friend, kicking his legs against the tall grass, until he collapsed at the side of the Dandes River.

Moonlight now reflected his own face, in the peaceful waters: bright blue eyes, wide and young, a smooth face older than his eyes, and long brown curls beating against his high cheeks with each breath.

"Behold, Raventown!" he declared to an unseen audience. "The second prince has come of age!"

He drew himself to his feet, ran along the edge of the Dandes, and then thrust himself up the side of Raven Hill.

The path was well known to him – weaving through grass, amongst pine trees and fallen maple leaves. Even the new moons and starless nights could not hinder him, for the darkness was always his ally – but now the night was easing to a deep blue sky.

Gamel emerged, gazing expectantly east – to find Altenhine spread out before him. Below his feet, at the foot of the hill, was the still dark water of the Blue Lake – then, beyond the lake's distant shore, up the remote Eastern Ridge emerged the deep blood red beginnings of sunrise. To his left and right beckoned the mountains of the North and South: majestic peaks, lit with the faintest hint of pink as the new day began to dawn.

Gamel drew in a deep breath, drinking in the pure delight of the land. Chest full, heart pounding, he stood – and then he released his breath, and turned.

A slim figure sat on a flat rock, a few feet from him: her face hidden in a hood and cloak, also turned to the view.

Gamel smiled. "Lidya!"

Now she turned to him: her face young and white, as his, framed by black curls dropping down to her waist. She had the same high cheeks, and blue eyes: they were wide, smiling at him.

"Happy birthday!" Gamel said, reaching to grasp her hands – lifting her to her feet. "Twenty-three, Lidi! We have waited a long time for this day!"

She hugged him – and then he drew back to find her face again: to search for any change in her gaze revealing her new adulthood. Her eyes still sparkled with a joy that mirrored his.

"Congratulations, my dear brother!" she said. "You have become a man!"

Her words somehow brought tears to his eyes: tears of gratitude, and release.

"And you!" he quickly replied. "Congratulations, Lidi – for you also have come of age!"

She tipped her head slightly, with a gentle smile – beauty and sophistication seeming as natural to her as they were unnatural to him. For a moment he saw in her a queen – dignity, and grace, defining her rule. But then that moment was gone.

Gamel grasped her hand again. "I have a birthday gift for you, Lidi!"

"A gift?" she exclaimed, and quickly her dignity melted into childlike glee. Gamel reached into his pocket and pulled out a special wooden box, tied with white ribbon.

"Here!"

She received it between her fine fingers, poked lovingly at the bow, and then gently tugged at the ribbon.

Gamel watched her face as she peered inquisitively at the object inside – and then reached to lift out the pendant, hanging on a fine white cord.

"It is gold!" she said, drawing a finger around the yellow edge. "Gold, Gamel – where did you find it?"

Gamel cleared his throat, and grinned.

"A Southerner?" Lidya asked. "Gamel! You spoke with one? King Maki forbids contact..."

"...of Heartlanders with those from the North and South," Gamel said, "I know. I just...stumbled across him one day. At the Southern foothills, beyond the valley..."

"How did you...?"

"I went out at night, of course – with a lantern. And some money. And a horse."

Lidya stared at him – and then she laughed. "Gamel! No one else would dare!"

He smirked back at her – and then looked back to the pendant.

"So smooth, their craftsmanship – do you like it?"

She followed his gaze. "A solid circle?"

"He said it meant never-ending loyalty." Gamel smiled. "I thought it was quite fitting: what about you?"

"Yes," she replied, "Couldn't be more fitting for a twin." And she quickly tied it around her own neck.

"Strange, though," Gamel mused to himself for a moment. "It was almost as though he knew who I was..."

Fear flitted into Lidya's eyes – Gamel saw it, before she smiled it away.

"Don't worry," he said, "He was kind – he gave me the pendant off his own chest. A second prince is no use to anybody – and no threat."

She nodded silently – and then she tugged on his sleeve.

6

"I also have a gift for you!"

"Truly?" He grinned. "You also have been riding beyond our borders? Perhaps you bought me something from the North."

"Nothing so extravagant! I made this myself."

And she pulled out a small paper package.

Gamel took her gift, and gingerly opened it. Inside was an embroidered handkerchief – his name stitched in small dark red letters across the top right corner. Below his name were two embroidered lanterns, and beneath this the day of their birth.

He drew his thumb over her stitching – it was perfect work – and smiled.

"Thank you, Lidi – I will keep this on me always. And I will never use it."

She laughed again – and then she pulled on his shoulder.

"Gamel."

The warning in her tone seized his attention. He quickly looked up to see the sun had risen well over the Eastern Ridge.

"Oh…"

"Time to go."

"Yes: time to go."

And quickly, grasping again for her hand, Gamel moved back to the path to descend Raven Hill.

They emerged off Raven Hill into the grounds of the Palace. The grey stone of their home could not be seen from Gamel's lookout on Raven Hill, and was easily avoided in the great expanse of the Valley: yet here, now, after sunrise, it was unavoidable.

Three levels of the Palace towered over the Heartland Valley – the windows like eyes of sovereignty. But the rear of the Palace faced the Blue Lake – and so this was Gamel's favourite entrance by far. A guard Jamel, slim and fully dressed in black, with a sword by his side, stood attentively in the internal hallway – but Gamel was used to avoiding his gaze. Quickly and quietly he led Lidya to a window, and soon they were returning, each to their own private chamber.

Gamel quickly kicked off his old shoes under his white feather duvet bed, grabbed another pair, and dragged off his robe, before reappearing in the hall. Lidya stood quietly, now also without the robe, her peach silk dress flowing down to a few inches above her ankles. The walk had somehow not unsettled her clothes, but apparently his hair was untidy: Lidya's fingers were now working over his head.

Sighing, he endured it, and glanced down to straighten his own dark brown jacket, vest and trousers.

"How do I even move in these clothes, much less get up a hill? Anyhow, enough!" He pushed her hand away. "Time to go!"

And they moved, again, past Jamel and on to the Dining Chamber.

They were the first to arrive. Gamel heard Lidya's muffled sigh of relief, as they moved toward the large oval oak table in the centre of the grey marble floor. He ignored his own relief, and instead dragged out an oak chair for Lidya.

"All is well," he chimed, and dumped himself on another chair alongside.

A servant came, dressed in white – to set knives and forks before them.

"Thank you, Tadi," Gamel responded. Then the King appeared. Quickly Gamel rose to his feet, reaching instinctively for Lidya to rise with him.

King Maki stood tall, with full chest and large hands. His penetrating blue gaze was framed by short neat black hair. The royal robe, purple satin, sat easily on his broad shoulders, over black jacket and trousers.

*That robe*, Gamel pondered, *It's always there! Any time of day, even for breakfast!*

There was no time that Maki ceased to be King.

"Good morning," Maki said – his voice deep and resonant.

"Good morning, father," Gamel and Lidya replied, in unison. Then all sat – Maki at the top end of the table.

After a few moments of silence the Queen arrived: Tali. Gamel glanced quickly at her – she looked a little flustered, her grey silk dress not quite straight, and her short brown curls not properly clipped back.

"Good morning, mother," Lidya's voice offered, though no-one arose, and Tali stopped next to her.

"Good morning, child."

For a moment Tali's green eyes lit, her face breaking into a rare smile – but then, as usual, her light faded as she moved to sit next to Maki.

Breakfast was served. Gamel looked down hungrily to the plate before him: egg, sweetbread, and strips of lamb – all his favourites, picked by the chef Frodin. Happily he indulged, and out of the corner of his eye he knew his sister was picking at her favourite: hot sweetbread. Their mother was not eating. Maki's plate was heaped with lamb and plain bread, and he steadily worked his way through the meal.

No mention was made of their Coming of Age. Gamel had expected this, and yet now he felt a growing heaviness. He looked at his father to see kingly distraction: he looked at his mother to see another form of distraction entirely. And then...

Gamel looked sharply back at Tali. "Where is Friedrich?" He asked. Friedrich was the oldest Prince, next in line to the Throne: Gamel's older brother. Friedrich would not have forgotten their Coming of Age!

Tali glanced quickly at Maki, who fixed onto her eyes with steadfast silence, and then Tali looked back to Gamel.

"Friedrich is still sleeping."

"Sleeping?" Gamel laughed. "That's not like him."

"He is tired, after his training."

Perplexed, Gamel stared at him. Sleeping? Surely not: not today!

"But..."

Maki's dark eyes fixed on him. Gamel held them, reaching to grasp the edge of his chair. Now mild surprise crossed his father's face: before this day Gamel would have looked away.

"The duties of a sovereign are arduous," Maki commented. "This you would not understand."

Gamel grimaced slightly. "So be it," he said. "I am happy with my fate."

"A second prince," Maki continued. "What use is there for such a position, but to play like a child, even at twenty-three?"

Intense pain now struck Gamel, unexpectedly – deep in his chest. His father had remembered his birthday, after all: only to acknowledge it with an insult. And what of his sister? Was she to be ignored?

"Life can be purpose enough," he countered, though Lidya's hand prodded his knee under the table. "Such freedom cannot be overvalued."

Maki's eyes narrowed, and his fist clenched. "Maturity demands responsibility."

"Yet must adulthood conquer joy?" Gamel challenged. "I am free to explore otherwise."

Now Maki rose briskly to his feet, his form seeming to enlarge before Gamel's eyes, towering over him. Heart pounding, Gamel instinctively rose as well – but now Lidya was by his side again.

"Gamel means no harm, father," she said gently and smoothly.

"Indeed," Maki conceded, sitting again. "Such wishful thinking propels the infant, but degrades an adult into a common fool."

Gamel sat, tears pricking his eyes, anger swelling in his heart.

"May I be excused?" he asked, and Maki nodded curtly. Then Gamel strode quickly out of the Dining Chamber.

In the hallway Gamel lingered, caught for a moment between the King and the guard. Stairs were before him – and so he took them, up to the second level: to the lounge. A woven rug covered the grey marble floor, with oak armchairs surrounding a small oak table – but Gamel gravitated straight to the large windows, framed by greystone. There, beyond, was the Heartland Valley: plush green farmland, bush, and in the distance the Highland Elevation, bound on either side by the towering snow-clad mountains of North and South.

"A king or a fool," he muttered. "Is there not some fate, some purpose, which lies between these?"

A hand came to his shoulder, and his sister's voice drifted over him.

"Don't let Father's words trouble you."

"That I am a child?" Gamel laughed sadly. "This we already know. But today, my dear sister, I am also an adult."

"He knows it: he doesn't know how to respond."

"No...but am I a fool?" Gamel closed his eyes tightly for a moment. "How does one answer such a question?"

"With truth."

Gamel opened his eyes, and swayed slightly before the Heartland. "Truth..." he whispered. And then he turned to her concerned eyes.

"There is only one truth I know, Lidi: we were born together – and together we shall remain."

Her face broke into a gentle smile – and he could see tears in her eyes.

"I know," she whispered – and as her hand reached into a small pocket in her dress, he also reached into his own pocket: and both drew out their gifts.

"Here!" he offered, passing the handkerchief over – and she laughed again, vigorously shaking her head.

"Never! Otherwise you must wear this!" And she passed the pendant over.

Gamel entertained her for a moment, tying the pendant around his own neck. "Good enough for a Southern warrior…" Then he removed it, handing it back.

"Loyalty forever," he repeated, pressing the pendant into her palm. "That is my promise to you, Lidya – whatever happens."

"And that is also my promise to you, Gamel," she responded in kind.

"Loyalty from birth."

"Happy birthday, Gamel."

Gamel paused for a moment, in that place, remembering the light of her expression, and then he finally responded.

"Happy birthday, my dear sister: happy Coming of Age to us both."

CHAPTER TWO: A Hidden Threat

It was Endweek.

Gamel lounged back on a chair, glad for the seclusion of his Bedchamber. Before him, on a thick oak desk, was a game: carved wooden pieces moving across engraved circles with each turn. Gamel eyed his sister's gaze, wandering across the board, and then reached over to nudge her.

"Do you know?" he explored. "The people in the valley play this too."

"Oh, yes?" she muttered, a slight frown of concentration clouding her response.

"I've seen them, late at night in Endweek. I see, by the light of the lanterns in their cottages: they seem happier then."

Lidya moved a piece, and then looked up. "Why?" she asked. "Are they unhappy during the week?"

"I don't know," Gamel said, pondering his own move. "There's something about them. I don't see, during the day – I'm always here. I'm sure they are working. At night during the week: there is no time, it seems – no time to play."

"Father's officials collect the royal taxes during the week."

"Yes: they seem…strained, with the load."

"The courts are closed on Endweek."

"Yes."

"But the guards, Gamel: don't they watch every day, patrolling the streets? How do you get beyond them?"

An opening was before him on the board. Swiftly he took it, and smiled as she scowled.

"I have my ways."

Yet Lidya's response was as swift: taking his piece from an unexpected move from the left.

"You are not invincible, Gamel," she insisted, "Only human. You have almost made your home in the valley, at night, amongst the grass and trees, and yet you are never seen or missed. How is it you are not caught?"

Gamel swallowed, hesitating – seeking to preserve her. And then he replied.

"I think Father already knows, Lidi."

Her hand jerked – and knocked over the piece she had just moved. Gamel watched a familiar fear fill her face, her eyes penetrating and suddenly intense.

"Gamel: he cannot know."

"Why, Lidi? What do you think he would do?"

"It's not him."

"Then what? Who?"

"I can't explain it. Something else: something more than him."

"That doesn't make any sense."

"But neither does this! The guards have been ordered to let you be?"

Gamel studied her, frowning with his own confusion.

"I…don't know," he replied. "At first I believed I was eluding them: they were guarding against the North and South, and the town – not against the Palace. I came from behind their backs. But now – even the North and South know what I am doing, Lidya: I have met a Northern warrior, too, patrolling the Northern foothills. I can't believe Father does not know."

She tilted her head, her frown deepening. "But how can that be?"

"I don't know." Gamel shifted awkwardly in his seat. "This hasn't happened before."

"He's always been so – strict."

"Yes. I would expect a beating, and yet nothing comes. And now, in adulthood: he still does nothing?" Fear twisted his own heart. "Somehow the beating would be easier."

Lidya stretched her hand to his in comfort. "Maybe he is preserving you?"

"Or maybe ignoring me." His teeth ground together. "Yes – I think that must be it. He thinks me a fool – why bother disciplining a fool? He releases me to whatever my fate may be."

"Gamel…" Her hand tightened over his, and he feigned a smile for her sake.

"Don't worry, Lidya," he persevered, "it is a gift! Freedom! I have been given something so rare, so precious: I should make the most of it."

She saw through his partial truth, to the pain beneath.

"Gamel…" she murmured again, and her gentle feminine care suddenly made him want to weep. Vigorously he fought back the tears, threw her hand away – and then, suddenly, raised voices were over their heads.

Lidya's face paled as she stared up to the ceiling. "Father and mother," she whispered.

"Arguing again," he sighed.

"Yes, but this time – it's different…"

Tilting his head, Gamel strained to hear – but the voices were too muffled.

"What do you mean 'different'?"

But now, suddenly, she was gone – escaped, out of the bedchamber, into the washing room alongside.

Perplexed, Gamel wandered out of his room. Lidya was there, to his right, now in the washing room – burying herself amidst clothes, water and soap. It was so odd, the way she would do that: suddenly run away. Why? Why such great fear, so repeated in her face, at the thought of their father? What did she see, or hear, that he could not perceive? There was something paradoxical in her: a love for their father, and yet an intense fear also – and now she was speaking of someone else?

Lost in thought, he wandered aimlessly straight past Jamel, who now halted him.

"Prince Gamel, the lounge is not yet free."

Gamel glanced over Jamel's black robe and hood, and the sword by his side, starting slightly at his own lapse of concentration.

"Apologies," he stuttered. "Please inform me when it is free, Jamel – I will be eating."

"Very well."

And Gamel turned right into the Dining Chamber.

12

Frodin had left some baking on the table. Gamel lingered, reaching to try a small raisin cookie, comforted by the taste – yet his instinct was drawing him elsewhere. Dare he act? Dare he confront a secret he could so easily avoid?

He vacillated, bouncing slightly on the balls of his feet – but then, swiftly, he decided. Abandoning his food, he strode out of the chamber and halfway up the stairs toward the lounge: out of sight from both levels.

His parents' voices now were clear.

"He can't do it!" Tali cried, and Gamel shuddered, though he did not know why.

"He will do it!" Maki thundered back.

"Don't you see? It's too much for him!"

"Do you think he is the first? Kings have borne this burden from the time of Hemin! It is his fate!"

"It is his curse!"

Now Gamel heard a slap, and a gasp, and Tali's voice was silenced.

"You knew what you were getting into, woman," Maki whispered, his voice clear and dark. "This is the burden we all must bear."

Gamel's fists tightened and he longed to run up the stairs – but somehow the memory of Lidya's fear held him back. Sobs echoed down the stairs – and Gamel groaned, from deep within, wrapping his arms around himself.

"Mother…"

Maki's voice was lowering, now – softer. Gamel was surprised to hear comfort in his tone. But then, suddenly, something changed.

The air turned cold. Gamel's skin pricked, his hair standing on end: and he strained to see, inching closer toward the lounge. The next staircase, above his head – something was happening! The forbidden Throne Room – entrance given only to Maki, and now to Friedrich, in training…

There were no voices – only a figure, slim, collapsing down the stairs, caught against the larger chest and strong arms of Maki.

"Get it off him!" Tali's voice pleaded, and, amazingly, Maki seemed to obey – jerking something away, from around Friedrich's neck, placing it over his own head instead. Friedrich's slim body seemed to wane in Maki's arms.

"You see?" Tali whispered. "He can't bear it."

"Perhaps he is not ready…"

"Not ready, at twenty-five? He's a grown man!"

"A grown man – reduced to a child…"

Gamel heard sorrow in his father's voice – another tone he had never heard before – but quickly it was surpassed by the familiar curt sovereignty.

"He must bear it, Tali – it is our destiny: we are the royal line."

"And if he cannot?"

Maki shifted slightly, and his voice lowered. "If not Friedrich, the kingship will pass to Gamel."

Now utter terror seized Gamel's heart. The fear! The fear he had seen so repeatedly in Lidya's face – the threat she had never put to words! Now it was his! Now it consumed him!

13

He shrank away from the lounge, and stumbled down the stairs – forgetting again to avoid Jamel.

"Prince Gamel!" Jamel exclaimed. "Were you...?"

"I was not," Gamel whispered – and he rushed toward his room, swiftly closing the door behind him.

There was a knock, and now Lidya's voice – Gamel threw his door open, though he could not meet her eyes.

"What happened?"

"I..." He wrapped his arms around himself. "I..."

"You went up?"

"Only half way up! To the lounge..."

"When Jamel said..."

"Yes...But..."

"But, what?"

He stared desperately at her, and then looked away. "It was only the lounge!" he pleaded. "I heard them arguing – about Friedrich, and becoming king. He fell! From the Throne Room! It was so cold, and...father said it might have to come to me..."

Now he dared to meet her eyes directly: they were wide, fixed on him – revealing the full fear he now was sharing.

"It can't fall on you," she whispered. "You are second in line."

"I don't want the kingship."

"No."

"It changes people! It corrupts them – even destroys them!"

Lidya was white. "Some forces are stronger than we are," she whispered.

Gamel swallowed hard, holding her gaze. "You would have me stay away from all of this."

"Yes!" Distress consumed her.

"But I must find out what's going on!"

"I know." Her voice was suddenly weak, and tremulous.

"I can't stay away."

His hands clenched into fists – his nails digging into his palms. Not stay away? What foolishness was this? Who was he, against the power of a Throne of centuries: against the expectations of the valley, and the requirements of the North and South? Tears threatened him again – and again he fought them.

Lidya's hand came to his shoulder, her chest expanding with a deep and costly breath.

"I know you can't ignore this any longer, Gamel: I know who you are."

Her understanding uncovered his weakness: he began to tremble under her hand.

"I was reduced to a child too, Lidya! I can't explain it..."

"I know."

"The answers are up there, in the Throne Room."

Her jaw tightened. "Yes."

"What would you have me do?"

14

Lidya paused, frowning with deep sadness. And then she spoke. "Gamel, I would keep you safe! I would have you live!"

Caught, he stared at her. "Live?" he breathed. "Run? Live my life in the valley, alone and hidden? Run away?"

Now Lidya closed her eyes tightly. Gamel's tears took him, overwhelming his defences as his life's plight was suddenly and unexpectedly revealed. "Run?" he choked. "Keep running, even now, while my brother collapses, my mother wastes away, and my sister…"

Her eyes snapped open, now, and he suddenly understood the sacrifice she had been contemplating. If all else failed, might she protect him? Might she become queen?

"No!" he cried out, all of his instinct now to protect her. "No! No! No!"

He reached for her handkerchief in his pocket: reached for his pendant around her neck. A circle of gold: loyalty! Loyalty…

"I can't ignore this anymore, Lidi! I have to face it! I have to face it, for all our sakes."

She grasped his shoulders, her eyes fervently holding his gaze.

"Wisdom!" she insisted clearly. "Wisdom, Gamel! Don't just rush in – think, first! Think!"

"Think what?" he asked.

"Who knows what you don't yet know? Who knows the truth, Gamel?"

Confused, panicking, Gamel stared at her – and tried to shake his head clear.

"Friedrich?" he cried. "Friedrich!"

A single sob escaped from him.

*We have known of this trouble all along! All along. Why did I leave it so late?*

"I must act," he whispered. "I must find the truth."

"Yes," Lidya admitted. "You must."

"The Throne room."

Now Lidya choked. "Gamel, it is dangerous."

"I'll be careful."

"Friedrich…ask Friedrich."

"He will not speak."

"Try him first – he may prepare you."

Shivering, Gamel nodded. Yes; Friedrich. First he would need to face his brother, before the threat itself: face his own possible fate in his brother's eyes.

"All right," he finally whispered. "I will talk with Friedrich first."

CHAPTER THREE: The Threat is Revealed

It was breakfast.

Gamel stared hard down at his plate. Crumbs of sweetbread spotted his fingers, beaten egg and strips of lamb lying neglected beneath his face. Beside him, to his left, Lidya steadily and slowly ate her warm cake.

He had not returned to the Valley – not since that Endweek when…when he had heard the argument. Neither had he led Lidya up Raven Hill. They had remained in the Palace, entrapped: imprisoned.

He had told her he would talk to Friedrich: he had not yet found the courage. Lidya was leaning toward him now: unusual, for her, in front of their parents.

"Eat," she whispered. "You will need your strength."

Strength for what? For who? Shifting slightly, he obliged – and then lifted his eyes to look at his father.

Maki was eating, as always, heartily, within purple royal robes. His chest was free of the thing Gamel had glimpsed before, up the stairs – the thing his father had taken from his brother's chest.

Gamel stared at him, took a long breath – and then set his jaw.

"Where is Friedrich, Father?" he asked.

Maki calmly met his eyes. "Sleeping," he replied.

"Why does he no longer join us at breakfast?"

Tali shifted with discomfort, at Maki's right side – eyes also down, staring into her plate: ever silent.

"Is he sick?" Gamel pressed, throat constricting slightly, and Maki's eyes narrowed again.

"Yes," he now answered. "Friedrich is sick. You should stay away from him, or you may catch his illness."

Anger took Gamel: suddenly invigorating, and empowering, though he also felt its danger. He clenched his fists again, under the table, seizing control – yet somehow, at the same time, he strangely discerned his father was trying to protect him.

"May he get better soon," Gamel said, intending to finish – but now his mother's gaze lifted to him. Her face was weary, grey shadows of sleepless nights under her green haunted eyes.

"I do not believe he will recover."

Her statement, so bold, so resigned – so unexpected, amidst her loud silence – stunned him.

"What?" he breathed, and her face contorted.

"You heard me, Gamel." Some kind of new purpose was girding her voice.

"But – there must be a cure!"

Maki's curt tone intervened. "There is no cure – only strength and weakness."

Fury flooded Gamel: his temples were throbbing! Desperately he forced the feeling down.

"I cannot believe that!" he insisted. "Friedrich was never weak!"

Now, before his eyes, Gamel sore vividly a memory of his brother: tall, slim, up a tree – laughing, hanging upside down; blonde curls beating against his face.

*"Here, Gamel!"* The young voice cried. *"Take my hand! You can do it!"*

*"Not yet, Friedie! I'm not big enough!"*

*"Yes you are! Now, Gamel: don't be scared!"*

The hand lifted him – soon Gamel was swinging on the branch next to him, laughing.

Tears misted Gamel's vision.

"He was not weak."

Maki's blue gaze fixed on him. "He is weak now."

Gamel's teeth gritted together as Lidya's silent warning grip took his hand under the table.

*You have made him weak!* He longed to yell at him. *You have made him this way! You should have protected him!*

But he chose silence, like mother and sister, and began to despise himself.

Breakfast dragged, on and on – and finally came to an end. Gamel sat still, waiting until Maki and Tali first left the Dining Chamber. Then, shoulders sagging, he looked at Lidya.

"Go to Friedrich," she said. "Go now."

"I am afraid."

"Go – and find the truth."

Trembling, he rose to his feet, set his jaw, clenched his fists – and strode out of the Dining Chamber.

Friedrich's Bedchamber was to the right. Glancing to his left, to Jamel facing the other way, Gamel quickly moved to the oak door, opened it, and closed it swiftly behind him.

Now he stood within Friedrich's Bedchamber.

Friedrich lay on his bed – thin and curled up, his head of blonde curls hidden in his arms. Heart twisting, Gamel stared at him – and then wandered over to the bed.

"Friedrich…"

The figure groaned – and Gamel fleetingly closed his eyes.

"What is it?" he breathed. "What's wrong?"

"Can't…" Friedrich gasped. "Can't…"

Friedrich's white shirt was loose around his wasting body, his black trousers loose around his waist. Gamel reached out to lay a hand on his head.

"Can't what?"

"Can't…do anything!"

He sobbed, now – lifting his face from his arms, his eyes erratic, searching for Gamel.

"I'm here," Gamel whispered, reaching for his hand, sitting alongside him on the bed. The eyes found him – green, as their mother's: haunted. Gamel swallowed, but continued to hold his brother's gaze.

"What has happened to you?"

"Can't go back there…"

17

"Where?"

"To the Throne Room!" He choked. "Can't! Don't make me…"

His body shuddered, shaking the entire bed – and Gamel tightened his grip on Friedrich's hand.

"Tell me what happened to you."

"Can't!" Friedrich cried. "Can't!"

With tears Gamel held him. "How can I help you?" he breathed, half to himself. "How can I help you?"

"Get him off me."

"Father?"

"Get him off me."

Perplexed, Gamel gazed at the wretched trembling figure before him – and then stroked his face, as he would a child.

"Rest, now," he murmured to him. "Rest."

But now the strained eyes were fixed on him. "Rest?" he cried. "For me there will never be any rest!"

And he pushed Gamel's hand away, shoved his feet under his brown blankets, and hid his body deep within his bed.

Gamel rose to his feet, staring at him – dismayed. Then he backed away, turned, and left the Bedchamber.

For a few moments Gamel stood, caught once again outside Friedrich's door. Jamel was pacing backwards and forwards, guarding the door to the Palace – Gamel watched him for a moment, feeling no threat from him. Upstairs was the true threat – but was it in his parents' room? Was it his parents themselves? No: they no longer threatened him – he was no longer a child. There seemed something deeper – something darker, beyond the second level: above his parents, stronger than they were.

Should he act?

*Courage*, His sister's voice whispered to him. *Courage.*

He moved – up the steps to the second level, and now beyond: up the steps – into the Throne Room.

Stretched out before Gamel's eyes was the Heartland – Raventown close at hand, her charming cottages, her people dutifully at work, and beyond the beautiful green Heartland Valley, of grass farmland and bush. The Highland Elevation was further beyond, a natural boundary to the Valley – but also, from this level, Gamel could see the clear magnificence of the mountains: the full beauty of the South, to the left, and the North.

Gamel had never seen this view before – unhindered by greystone: a single wide, expansive window, from the single most strategic site in all of Altenhine.

*I will give you all of this.*

His heart pounded hard at the thought: the Heartland! All he had yearned for – ownership! Freedom. Even, dare he admit it, strength to control…?

The Throne sat in the middle of the room, facing outward – claiming all he saw: seeking to rule all.

18

A stone lay over the head of the Throne – a uniquely carved stone, unlike anything Gamel had ever seen. He leaned closer to look. It was shiny and black, a serpent, with small garnets for eyes. Out of its head came a cord, to be worn around the neck: the stone pendant to be laid on the chest.

*Friedrich is weak, but you will be strong.*

The eyes seemed very bright – inviting, almost glowing...

"Gamel!"

Gasping, he jerked his body away from the Throne. He had been reaching, somehow! Reaching for the stone...

His sister's face was before him – her strangled whisper bringing him back: her face pale, the blue eyes boring into him.

"What are you doing?"

"I...I wanted to know."

*And now you do know.*

"Why are you here?" Gamel asked Lidya desperately.

"I felt danger – I knew you were here."

"I...I found this."

He reached to lift the stone by his cord, but Lidya stopped his hand.

"Don't touch it."

"It..." Struggling, he made himself confess. "I...wanted it."

Now he wanted to writhe, but Lidya pulled him away.

"Look, Gamel."

He followed her gaze – and turned to his right. To the southern end of the room was a folded door, left slightly open – key in the door. Gamel walked toward it, Lidya behind his back – he opened the folded door wide, to find rolled parchments within.

"Our history," he whispered. "Written by the kings themselves..."

But now Lidya was pulling at his hand again.

He turned, looking to the northern end of the room – and there, another folded door also left unlocked and wide open, was a shrine. It was laid with gold – also from the mines of the south and north – table, plate, knife, napkin, cup, and wall behind, from table to ceiling. In the cup was...

"Blood," Lidya whispered, and Gamel suddenly cupped both hands over his mouth.

"Whose blood?" He gagged, his voice muffled. "For what?"

Lidya was reaching back – now she carried one of the parchments, and was reading: her voice tremulous.

"Soutar."

"What?"

"Worship. Offering. Sacrifice."

"I don't understand..."

*Do you not?*

Gamel swayed, staring at the stone. "That thing," he whispered.

"The Kings have written things here. 'We must appease him! Always appease him.'"

"Who?"

"Soutar!"

"But what is 'Soutar'?"

"Spirit…"

Now Gamel frowned at her. "What do you mean 'spirit'?"

Lidya was shaking. Afraid, Gamel grasped her hand. "What is it?"

"We have to get out."

"Yes – but why? Why are we afraid?"

"Have to get out!"

She was gripping the parchment tightly. He took it from her, and read.

"The firstborn son must be offered, to reign – never the second-born, and never a daughter, unless death intervenes."

Gamel froze. Lidya's face now was deathly white.

"You know what I fear," she whispered. "You know what it says."

"I know nothing!" he desperately insisted. "Lidya!"

"The parchment…"

"We decide our own fates, Lidi – not some parchment!"

"Can't you see it, Gamel?" she pleaded. "Some forces are stronger than we are!"

"No!"

"Gamel – you must face the truth! There is more to our lives than just us!"

Gamel fell back a step, away from her. The stone was there – the Stone of Soutar – lying over the Throne. The garnet eyes were now dead.

"This is madness," he whispered. "Our own fears, taking a hold – even leading to this!" He waved his hand toward the shrine. "Did Friedrich do this? Madness!"

He turned toward the parchments behind – and waved his hand over the writings.

"What if we painted history differently, Lidya?" he asked. "What if we rewrote it without 'spirit' – what if we wrote that it was only ourselves?"

Tears filled Lidya's eyes. "I wish that was true, Gamel!' she cried. "But I cannot believe it! Look at father! Look at Friedrich!"

"No more fear, Lidi! No bloody sacrifice to appease! Just us! Just us, trying to make it through each day. We help our neighbours in the North and South, because we want to help them – not because we are made to."

"Some forces are stronger than we are!"

"I don't believe that, Lidi! Not as Friedrich believes it. Not as all the Kings before were made to believe it. We are our own worst enemies."

And now his father was before him.

Gamel held Maki's gaze – standing tall and strong. Initial anger on his father's face melted away to surprise.

"Now you know."

"Yes – now I know."

"It is our fate."

"I don't believe that."

"Then you are mistaken."

Gamel shifted a little on his feet. "Perhaps," he replied. "But we shall see."

He reached for Lidya's hand, and moved toward the steps – but now Maki tapped him on the shoulder.

"Tell me, Gamel," he enquired. "Do you really think that your 'rewriting' of history actually changes the reality of how things are?"

A shiver tracked down Gamel's spine. Spirit? No – it could not be.

"I can't change spirit, father," he sighed heavily, "Whether or not it exists. But we might be able to change something of ourselves – and this all looks like madness to me."

Lidya pulled on his hand. "Also, the parchment says that Soutar cannot reign without the Prince's active choice."

Gamel studied her eyes. She had found peace again – trust, in her brother's control.

"Then perhaps we can all be happy," he concluded, glancing back at the Stone. "Whatever Soutar is, I will not let him reign."

Maki's face was drawn in a strange smile of cynicism. "Five hundred years of history," he declared, "Five hundred years of appeasement to secure peace for Altenhine, and you believe, with one foul sweep of change of thought, that you can stop Soutar's influence?"

"It is written!" Gamel proclaimed, grasping the parchment from Lidya's hands. "The Prince must invite him in."

"There are many things written, Gamel," Maki quickly replied. "Do you know them all? Do you know anything of them? Anything at all of Soutar?"

Gamel shrugged, and passed the Parchment now into Maki's hands.

"I do not know," he replied, "And I am happy to continue not to know. I will not invite him in – and I will not reign."

Gamel thrust himself down the stairs – yet the words of his father still came drifting over his head.

"May it be as you proclaim, Gamel!" Maki declared. "But this will not be your decision."

Even so, walking down the steps, away from his father and the Throne Room, Gamel felt a curious confirmation of adulthood.

## CHAPTER FOUR: Crisis

Gamel stood outside the Palace.

In the rear gardens, the Blue Lake was before him: glistening in the mid-morning sun – extending out east, toward the centre of the Navigar continent. Behind its furthest most shores rose up the Eastern Ridge: from this route came the Travellers, to the Officials in Raventown, bearing the life-giving fertilizer and other supplies for those in the North and South.

Sighing, Gamel reached down to grasp a stone – and he threw it, skipping, across the calm surface of the water. Circular waves spread out, disrupting the calm with every collision – the stone itself eventually sinking into the depths, engulfed and silenced.

Death. Somehow the theme was always close to his heart now. He feared for his brother's life: the 'sickness' that seemed to be sapping away his strength and very will to live. What was that thing – that stone that had so thoroughly claimed Friedrich's soul? How had his brother concealed the cuts, that day, on his bed? How had he, Gamel, failed to notice them?

Tears filled his eyes, a single sob escaping his lips – but then came the all too familiar anger. Maki knew! Surely Maki had led Friedrich to this fate! Surely Maki had given him the stone: sacrificed his own son to that…that *sickness*…

A touch came to his shoulder – and he knew, before he turned, who it was.

"Lidi…"

She relieved him, somehow: her presence calmed his fury.

"It is not Father's fault."

"How can it not be his fault?"

"He…" Lidya shifted slightly on her small feet, her gentle face tilted with the effort of understanding. "He is trying to protect the people."

"By sacrificing our brother?" Fury took him again – his temples throbbing again. "Don't you care about him? Didn't you see him?"

Tears filled Lidya's eyes – and his anger swiftly disappeared.

"I'm sorry," he quickly whispered. "Of course you care."

"You don't understand."

"Explain it to me!"

"Soutar…"

Now he turned his back to her – staring again across the lake. There was someone there, now – a figure in the distance, along the northern shore. Strange – no-one was allowed on that land.

Gamel dragged his thoughts back to his sister.

"What is this 'Soutar,' Lidi?" he asked fervently, "What is it, but the fear in our own hearts? What is this stone, but the wretchedness of our own desires?"

"There is more!"

"No, Lidya! No!"

He turned, and stared hard at her, willing her to silence – she stepped back one step, with tears, yet she remained.

"Father believes Soutar exists."

He writhed, yet remained. "Yes. All right."

"He believes we must appease him."

"Or what?"

"Or...or war again, Gamel. You know the history..."

"Yes: that there was war I believe."

"The Northerners and Southerners, fighting over the Heartland for hundreds of years – fighting for control, to get the fertilizer from the east: never stopping..."

"Yes, I can see the truth there."

"The writings say – it was only when King Hemin submitted to Soutar, and wore the Stone, that Soutar enforced peace. He had the power, when we did not."

Now Gamel swallowed. "He had the power to control all of Altenhine: the Heartland, the North and the South – everyone, through the Heartland..."

"We couldn't do it ourselves! The Heartlanders were slaughtered – dominated by our neighbours: we were never warriors..."

"So we submitted to that thing?" Gamel jabbed his finger toward the top level of the Palace. "Even if it was real, Lidi: that thing? That was our solution?"

"We asked him in."

Gamel swayed on his feet. "Our family..." He shook his head in dismayed realization. "Our ancestor did it, Hemin: that is how we came to be the 'royal' line."

"Soutar gave Hemin his own power..."

"...if Hemin submitted to him. 'Appeased' him. But for what?"

Lidya frowned at him. "What do you mean?"

"What does this Soutar want from us? Our blood?" He shook his head. "It makes no sense."

"Our worship, Gamel," Lidya insisted. "He wants our worship."

"Why – does it make him feel good?" He laughed satirically. "Spiritual power playing with us, as pieces on a game board? Is this the price of our peace? This is no true peace at all, Lidi – not worthy of our brother's sacrifice!"

He stormed back toward the Palace – then stood, helpless, staring at the door with Jamel pacing within.

"And yet, how can I stop it?" he demanded of his sister. "My whole family shares in the madness: all believe he must die!"

"Gamel..." Again, her touch to his shoulder – but now he shook it off.

"We must save him!"

"We cannot!"

"Soutar doesn't exist!"

"He does, Gamel: at least in Friedrich's heart and mind."

Gamel looked at her – at her imploring gaze. "Only in his mind?"

"I don't believe that," she replied, her voice gentle and preserving. "But you do."

"How do we save him from his own mind?"

His eyes drifted up to the Throne Room, towering above: wide windows also looking out toward the Blue Lake. Then he started – Friedrich was there! Looking down – looking at him.

"He's there," Gamel breathed, "There again! The stone, again…"
And now, suddenly, he moved.

Instinctively, without thought, Gamel ran into the Palace. Jamel was in front of him, physically restraining him – Gamel shoved a hand into his face, forcing him aside. Lidya was behind him, crying out for him to stop – but Gamel could not listen. He thrust himself up the steps to the second level.

Jamel's voice loudly announced his rebellion over his head – and Maki and Tali were before him on the second level.

"Stop!" Maki ordered, his eyes intense and penetrating.

"No," Gamel responded, darting around him.

"Gamel!" Tali screamed after him, as he ascended the final steps to the third level. "Take the stone now and you will die!"

Gamel thrust himself up – and now he was in the Throne Room.

Friedrich was before him: pale, staggering – bleeding. The knife was in his hand, the stone on his chest.

"Friedrich," Gamel whispered desperately, his body shaking with his brother's pain. "Give me the knife."

Friedrich's face was contorted – his green eyes haunted, erratic as Gamel willed him to meet his gaze.

"I…can't…" Friedrich groaned.

"He's crushing you," Gamel whispered, joining his brother. "Take off the stone."

Terror filled Friedrich's eyes. "Can't!" He pleaded. "Mustn't!"

"I will wear it for you."

Gamel tried to keep his own eyes fixed on Friedrich's face – but now he noticed the garnet eyes of the stone were glowing bright red.

"Imagination!" he muttered to himself. "My mind playing tricks!"

He dragged his gaze back to his distraught brother, and reached out his hand.

"Give me the stone."

Friedrich shuddered, staring at him.

"It can't be yours unless I'm dead," he gasped.

"I do not believe that," Gamel quietly replied. "I will take it from you."

"The stone is linked to the Throne!" Friedrich pleaded. "You can't have one without the other!"

"Father still lives."

"Father cannot save you!"

"He cannot save you, but I can, Friedrich."

Gamel reached for the serpent – reached to grasp his hand around its head, to lift it free…but now the knife was between them.

"Don't!"

Fire was in Friedrich's eyes.

Shocked, Gamel stared at him. His face was different, now – unrecognisable: drawn, angry – even…evil.

24

"Put that down!" Gamel demanded instinctively. Maki was alongside, stretching out a hand.

"Soutar..."

Gamel shook his head vigorously. "Friedrich!" he pleaded. "I am your brother."

Friedrich's face grimaced, and laughed. "I am not your brother."

The air was cold – Gamel's skin was pricking. Still he struggled for reason.

"Enough!" he cried "Enough of this!"

And he reached to jerk the pendant off his brother's chest.

Friedrich screamed – strangled, tormented. Gamel shook hard at the sound, yet continued – hand around the pendant, burning, jerking at the cord. His father's arms were around his chest, squeezing his breath from him – but Gamel had the pendant!

"Reject him!" Gamel cried. "Reject him! Reject him!"

Friedrich's eyes were red. And then, suddenly, the knife turned inwards. With dismay Gamel watched, one agonized moment at a time, as the knife was plunged into his brother's chest.

Friedrich's body collapsed, dead, to the ground. Maki fell to his knees, as if a dead weight. Tali was there, somewhere, screaming.

The stone was burning into Gamel's hand. He was the next in line.

"I hate you," Gamel whispered to the serpent. "You are a lie, and I reject you."

He moved to place the cord around his own neck – to wilfully reject Soutar, mind and spirit, and conquer him – but then, suddenly, his sister was knocking his body to the side.

"No!" she cried, grasping the stone out of his fingers. And now she placed the stone over her own heart.

Rigidly Gamel watched: longing to have her demonstrate some similar proof – longing to have the threat of the stone at last undone. But it was not to be.

Horror filled the previous beauty of her blue gaze – the contortions of her face chilling him to the bone. Her body jerked, as if controlled by another, collapsing her to the ground. She screamed. And then she was silent.

Wordlessly Gamel reached to lift the stone from her neck. The eyes, glowing bright red, now rapidly faded. Her eyes also had faded – staring upward, not blinking, though she still breathed.

Gamel sank heavily to the ground. To his left lay his dead brother, the knife still in his chest. Numb, Gamel pulled the knife free. To his right lay his sister, all but dead. In front was his father, now weeping – finally stripped bare, with no strength remaining. Still standing was his mother: pale – shocked.

In his hand was the Stone of Soutar.

"I am the next in line," he whispered, in utter shock.

"You must obey Soutar," Maki groaned, "Or we will all die."

"I...cannot believe..."

"Death is all around you, Gamel," Tali now pleaded. "You cannot betray him."

"I cannot accept him."

"He will force you to submit, Gamel," Maki's blue eyes now met Gamel's own. "Do you think you are the first to resist?"

Distraught, Gamel stared at him. "You?" he sobbed. "You resisted him?"

Maki's eyes misted. "I tried," he whispered. "I did not succeed."

Gamel staggered to his feet – turned, and leaned heavily against the Throne. The Heartland was before him – the Highland Elevation beyond.

"I'll take it away," he whispered. "I'll take the stone far away where no one can ever find it again."

"There is no place to hide it!" Maki's voice insisted from behind. "Don't be a fool!"

"It's mine now – it's mine. No one else can bear it."

Silence confirmed his thoughts.

"I'll take it to the coast, and…and find a way to destroy it. He can't come in unless I bid it – isn't it true, Father? Isn't it true?"

He turned – to find Maki pale.

"Gamel…" And yet the man, once so overpowering, now seemed defeated.

Gamel placed the stone in his right trouser pocket. The shrine room was open! Grimacing, he placed the bloody knife back on the golden table, and closed the shrine – locking the door and placing the key in his left trouser pocket. He moved to the southern end of the Throne room – rolled up the parchments, placed them away, and locked this door also: placing the key with its twin in his left pocket. Then he turned.

Friedrich was dead. Weeping, Gamel knelt next to him – and laid a hand over his face.

"Farewell, my dear brother."

But Lidya…Lidya still lived.

Troubled, Gamel knelt next to her. Her chest rose and fell – her eyes, haunted, staring out.

"Lidi…" He shivered. The illness! The illness…

"Gamel…" It was his mother's voice. Surprised, he looked up at her – the only one still standing. Her face had changed into an expression he had not seen in her for a long time. Could it be hope?

"There are whispers…"

"Whispers?"

"From far away, across the sea. Across the Sea of Yerim…"

"What do you mean?"

"Whispers of healings…"

Gamel stared at her, and then at his sister's face.

"I don't believe in healings, Lidi," he whispered, suddenly clenching a fist. "I don't believe in them! But you do! You do – and I can't leave you here…"

Tears spilt down Lidya's cheeks – she had heard! Somehow she had heard.

Gamel rose to his feet. His father, now, was rising again to his full stature – blue eyes forged again.

"You must lead," Gamel suddenly realized. "You still live."

"Yes."

"But I will take the stone."

26

Reluctance filled Maki's expression – yet he nodded.

"Very well. Except, Gamel…"

"Yes?"

"When you return, be prepared for war."

Gamel shivered. Rule without Soutar – for five hundred years kings had appeased him, for fear of war. Now that fear was to be put to the test.

"From the North and the South?"

"Yes – Soutar will stir them."

"Separate from our own minds? Our own sphere of influence?"

"Soutar exists separate from our minds. He is a spirit – he stirs up the worst in all of us."

"The worst…"

"Do not underestimate him, Gamel! He will seek to entice you – he will seek to draw you to his own ways. The stone is his tool, and there are others, North and South – but he needs our wills also. We live in a physical world."

"Physical…"

Wryly Gamel held his gaze. "Is not the physical world all that there is?"

"Why must it be so?" Maki quickly replied, "Simply because we are physical? Is all reality really limited to what we ourselves can sense or see?"

Gamel frowned. And then he shrugged. Yet then he looked at Lidya.

"I don't have the answers, Father," he sighed heavily. "And yet for Lidi's sake I must search for something I don't necessarily believe in: someone else who might."

Lidya shifted slightly. Quietly Gamel reached down and lifted her in his arms.

"I have no idea where we're going, Lidi!" he whispered to her, exposed as he carried her down from the Throne Room. "A healer? Spirit? I know nothing of these things! But I do know this, my precious sister: we have to try! And we have to leave, for we can't survive here any longer."

# PART TWO

## TAKING FLIGHT

CHAPTER FIVE: Lost

Gamel stumbled out of the Palace.

The bright sun of mid-day struck him – making him squint. Never had he been in the front gardens of the Palace before in the light of day: never had he been so directly exposed.

In his haste, he had not paused to gather anything for their departure: all he had was the clothes he wore, shirt, vest, trousers – no food, no drink, no map…

For a moment, now, he hesitated. Should he go back, to order supplies? Return to the home where his brother had just died?

*No*, he shuddered. *Forward. I have to go forward.*

"Spare me," he pleaded into the air. "Help me."

The Stone of Soutar rested in his right trouser pocket: he felt warmth penetrating into his thigh, which broke his body into a cold sweat. The keys to the shrine of the throne room and the parchment cupboard jangled together in his left pocket.

In his arms lay his sister.

Her blue eyes, once so vibrant, were now vacant – staring through him. Her body, limp, was dressed in a cream silk dress: suitable for a princess of the palace, and almost useless for travel.

He awkwardly shifted her weight in his arms, girded himself, and then set off – through the Palace gardens and out of the Palace gate, past four guards in black uniform and robes, who said and did nothing.

Gamel was now in Raventown – on Main Road.

Dust promptly smothered his good black leather shoes – and now eyes were upon him. Heartlanders whose faces he recognised, when he had watched them from a distance at night with keen interest, did not recognise his face – and yet, as their gazes swept up and down his fine clothes, they knew he must be the Second Prince.

He stared at them – some of the men were dirty, surely from work in the farms: loose linen trousers, cotton shirt sleeves rolled up to elbows. The women wore blouses and long skirts – again, cotton, for silk was expensive, traded from the east.

They stared back, seeming confused: surprised. Gamel realized they might be awaiting an order from him – as Maki patrolled the streets, dictating conditions and collecting taxes. Why the Second Prince, now? Why the Princess, in his arms? Gamel felt a sudden danger: what if they perceived disruption to the Throne? What might they do? And what might follow, from North and South?

*When you return, be prepared for war.*

28

Soutar had enforced rule: enforced obedience. Maki had continued the show of authority. Gamel understood now – he could show no vulnerability: he could divulge the truth to no one.

How clear it was to him, for the first time, just how fragile the Heartland was: wide open to attack, and so wide open to manipulation. Truly the Heartlanders had no defence of their own.

Lidya groaned, and Gamel tightened his embrace of her – then met the onlookers' gaze.

"The Princess has fallen ill," he explained. "Our Physician has prescribed her mountain air – he is confident she will recover soon. Do not concern yourselves – and…have a good day."

Eyebrows went up – but soon the novelty was over. The people dispersed, heading in both directions down Main Road. Gamel took a deep breath – but then discovered there was one who remained.

The young woman stood still, her head slightly tilted as she held his gaze. Her cream blouse was slightly dishevelled, the rolled up sleeves falling slightly down again, alongside her slim brown long linen skirt.

She bowed her brown curls to him.

"Prince Gamel."

Lidya's weight was pressing into his arms: still Gamel maintained his dignity, nodding his head in acknowledgement.

"Greetings to you."

"Can…" She hesitated for a moment – and then continued. "Can I help you?"

Caution filled him – and yet so did the reality of their predicament.

"Help?" he muttered nonchalantly, and the woman smiled ever so slightly. There was something about the warmth of her brown eyes – something somehow trustworthy…

*Dare I?* Gamel's heart pounded in his chest with need. *Dare I?*

"You have not visited Raventown often."

"No." Gamel smiled to himself with irony. "Not really."

"Pleased to meet you."

"Thank you."

Her eyes now cast over Lidya's face – and Gamel felt his grip tighten involuntarily.

"I am sorry to see the Princess is unwell."

Her face seemed to show genuine compassion – a rare find, in Gamel's experience.

"She is unwell," he replied. "But the Palace's Physician is certain that she will recover."

"Of course."

"We must go now."

"Yes, my Lord."

Again, she bowed her head, and her words sent a chill up Gamel's spine. *My Lord…*

Gamel turned left, carrying Lidya down Main Street – and noticed the market of Raventown up a street to the right: Market Lane. Here merchants from the east sometimes visited, after gaining permission from the King's Officials – and occasionally even Northerners and Southerners might trade here, alongside Heartlanders selling lamb, bread, cakes, clothes... He needed food! And drink. Yet how would it look for a Prince to trade as a Commoner?

Impossible. And so, Gamel avoided the busiest dirt roads – and instead travelled all the way down Main Street to the very end: where the road disappeared into paddock.

There, away from prying eyes, Gamel lowered Lidya down into the long grass, sank down next to her, and cried. The Palace was behind his back – he could not return there. The township was to his right: he could not belong there. The path he must take was before him – through fields, farms, up the Highland Elevation, and beyond, into terrain he had never seen...and then beyond, even over the Sea? To find some Healer his mother had heard of only in whispers?

If his fate had been only his own, he would have chosen then what he had always longed for: a quiet, secluded, private life – a life amongst trees, along the Dandes River, upon Raven Hill; a life alone. But his fate was not only his own. Before him, lying now in restless sleep, was his sister. Her face was drawn, as if in a perpetual nightmare – she had put herself in harm's way to protect him from the stone, and now...now...

A hard shudder passed through his body. What was she feeling? What kind of pain, and battle, was she wrestling within that he himself had reached for to claim? What had she spared him from?

What was this 'Soutar'?

"You cannot stay here."

"I know," Gamel moaned, as if to himself. "I must find her way to healing."

Then, startled, he looked up. Someone had been there! Someone who had spoken straight to his heart...

But that figure was gone. And now, instead, there was a sheep: white, grubby – looking at him.

The sheep baaed. He defecated. And Gamel sighed.

"All right, all right!" he said to the beast. "I get the message! Time for me to move on."

He rose to his feet, amidst grass and sheep droppings, quickly removed his vest, rolled up his own sleeves – and then reached to lift his sister.

For a long time Gamel struggled – pressing west through the long grass, south of Raventown: his sister, in cream silk, draped over his left shoulder. Then he stopped, and heard a familiar voice.

"Prince Gamel."

Quickly he turned, to find the same woman. Her brown eyes were lit with a curious kind of altruism – she was pushing a cart. It was lined with straw.

Lidya's weight pressed hard into his shoulder, pulling at his neck. Gamel eyed the cart, fighting himself. Lay her in that thing: the Princess of the Heartland? He himself would not have hesitated to travel by cart, or by any means necessary, but this was his sister. He resisted, despising himself in his own struggle – but the woman remained.

"What is your name?" he finally succumbed.

"Hana"

"Are you following me?"

"No, Sir – you have stumbled into my farm."

Now he blushed hard – stuttering out an apology. But she smiled again – and again her warmth set him at ease.

"Have you arranged lodging for tonight?"

"I have not," he readily admitted.

"Where are you headed?"

"West."

"Not north or south? For the mountains?"

He looked at her – at her growing insight. 'Mountain air,' he had said – and she had recalled it well.

"No," he responded, in truth. "We will not be travelling north or south."

She looked perplexed, now. "Why would you travel west?" she asked. "What is there to find there?"

"What indeed?" Gamel sighed heavily. "Yet I know this is where I must go."

"Why?" she enquired.

"You have not heard the whispers?"

"Whispers?" Now she looked intrigued.

Gamel found himself suddenly liking her, though he could not explain exactly why.

"Whispers," he played with her. "Whispers of a magical land, across the sea – of a magician, with special powers…"

Scepticism filled her countenance, and he loved her for it: for this was the response he himself desired – but then her expression shifted.

"Actually, yes, Prince Gamel: I have heard whispers."

Now Gamel's heart almost stopped dead. "You have?"

"The townsfolk speak of something…something of this kind."

"Of what do they speak?"

"Something – I forget. Something beyond. Something big."

The idea frightened him – for she was, in that moment, clearly serious.

"What do you mean 'big'?"

She looked straight at him. "Big."

"Bigger than a prince?" He smirked at her, and she smiled.

"Yes, my Lord: bigger than a prince."

"Bigger than a king?"

Now hope began to entice him – yet, even as it did, he felt the Stone of Soutar pressing hard into his right leg.

Hana watched him, her smile easing into a more serious exploration.

"Yes – they whisper of something bigger than a king."

Gamel searched her – this was a serious admission, to the Second Prince of the Heartland!

"Do you wish for such a thing?" he asked, and her eyebrows rose.

31

"If I did, I would not have mentioned it so readily, my Lord."

"Indeed not." She was certainly sharp of mind. "Then…you do not wish for it?"

"I feel no such need."

Gamel felt a strong sense of admiration for her. This young woman owned a farm, and co-existed with the Throne in peace – he began to envy her, but then resisted the temptation: his path could not be as hers.

His shoulder ached under Lidya – and now he swayed slightly, feeling dizzy.

"Forgive me," he whispered. "I suddenly feel tired…"

Her hands now were outstretched to him – lifting Lidya from him, toward the cart.

*Stay here!* A voice breathed. *Stay with Hana. Live on her farm.*

"Can't!" he whispered to the unseen voice. "Can't!"

His legs collapsed under him, and now Hana was reaching to support him – to gesture him also toward the cart.

"Are you ill, Sir?"

"Sorry!" he gasped, desperately trying to regain his stature. "Sorry."

He was standing again. Hana's face was clouded with concern.

"Are you also catching your sister's illness?"

Gritting his teeth, Gamel stared at her – and then leaned against the cart, even as his sister slept within it.

"Thank you for your help, Hana," he replied. "Could we possibly stay with you tonight? Only for the one night then we must be moving on."

"Yes, Prince Gamel," Hana immediately replied. "I would be honoured to have you both stay. Please let me prepare you some food also for your journey to come."

Humbled at her service, Gamel allowed Hana to push the cart – and he stumbled alongside, grasping onto the edge.

He reached the oak cottage – simple, small, home-like: and was relieved to finally collapse onto a bed.

# CHAPTER SIX: Fear and Girding

*"Gamel! Gamel..."*

*Friedrich's young voice drew Gamel – he twisted around to see his brother carrying a long stick, wielding it as a sword against him.*

*"Fight, Gamel!" Friedrich laughed. "Fight!"*

*Friedrich's young blonde curls beat against his flushed face – green eyes lit with delight.*

*"Fight me, Gamel: you can do it!"*

*Gamel searched around himself – find a stick, in the well-kept rear garden of the Palace? He raced to a tree, picked up a fallen solid bough, and struggled to lift it: five-year-old arms eager but still lean.*

*Friedrich was in front of him: he tapped Gamel's bough gently. "Here, see?" he laughed. "This is how you fight! Hit me, Gamel: hit me!"*

*Gamel channelled all his strength into a swing – he hit Friedrich square on the branch and Friedrich stumbled and fell onto his bottom: astonishment written all over his seven-year-old face.*

*Now Gamel laughed, jabbing his finger at him. "You said I could do it!" he shouted with glee, and began to dance on his toes. "Look, Lidi: I beat Friedrich! I beat Friedrich!"*

*Lidya's vigorous clapping filled his ears from behind – Friedrich's face broke into a wide grin. Gamel reached out his young hand to pull his brother up...but now his face was melting into adulthood. The serpent stone lay on his chest, red eyes glowing: and now Friedrich's cheeks were drawn, his green eyes angry, piercing him with evil...*

*"Reject him!" Gamel cried. "Reject him, reject him, reject him!"*

*But the knife was in Friedrich's hand, turning inward – plunging into his chest...*

Gamel cried out. "Friedrich!" he shrieked. "No!"

His body jerked up, inside an unfamiliar bed. Desperately he reached out to grasp a hold of the cotton duvet cover: to grasp where he was. He was still fully clothed, under the bedclothes – still in his Prince clothes. The Stone! He felt it, again, hot against his right thigh – shuddering, he dragged it out of his pocket and threw it on top of the duvet. The serpent eyes – the garnets: weren't they alive? Just a hint of a glow in blood red?

Lidya was there. Astonished, Gamel looked at her: she was awake! Sitting by his side. Her cream silk dress was gone – her long black curls were tied back, and now she wore a cotton buttoned shirt and a loose long black cotton skirt. Her hand lay near his on the bed – she moved it now to rest over his hand.

"Nightmare?" she murmured, and wordlessly he nodded.

"It's the Stone," he finally choked.

"Not just the Stone," her gentle voice challenged, and he began to shake.

"No," he said. "Not just the Stone."

Her arms came around him – and there, hiding his face in her shoulder, he wept. Friedrich was dead! He was dead. How could this have happened? How could a stone do all of this?

Lidya also was crying – he felt her shaking, and tightened his embrace to comfort her.

"What happened to you?" he asked, "When you put the stone on, what happened? Are you better now?"

She pulled back from him, and he searched her face. There was life back in her eyes! Light! And yet, also, something else – some deep threat she was trying to conceal: some haunted knowledge…

"I felt him," she whispered – and Gamel shuddered hard.

"I…don't want to know," he pleaded.

"I know," she replied, eyes filling with affectionate sorrow. "My dear brother, I know."

Her words eased his heart. He gazed at her – black curls escaping a little from their tie, pink lips smirking a little: he reached to touch her white face. This was his sister – the one he loved more than all.

"I thought…"

She shivered. "I am back now."

"Yes, but…"

And now, as one, both looked at the Stone.

It lay on top of the white duvet – dead black stone. Its eyes were silent now.

"What are we going to do?"


There was a movement at the door. Gamel glanced up to see Hana now standing there. Her face, tanned and slightly hardened, Gamel realized, with working outdoors, was warm with compassion.

"How long have I been asleep?" he found himself asking her.

"A long time," she gently replied. "All of yesterday afternoon, and the night. This is a new day."

Gamel pulled himself out of the bed. He was in a little room – a small pine table stood across from the bed: he quickly scooped the Stone onto it. Then he moved to the window, and, leaning against its frame, gazed outside.

The sun had just risen – its early morning yellow light filling the paddock outside. Sheep grazed – he could hear their bleating voices. To the left Gamel could see the southern cottages of Raventown. Further away, toward the east, he could see the water of the Blue Lake: reflecting sparkles of the sun.

"I love it here," he said to Hana. "Couldn't I help? Couldn't I stay? I would work my way – hard enough for Lidya and I to live…"

It was a dream – how readily he spoke from his heart to this stranger! She stood next to him, now – also gazing out of the window.

"You don't want to remain a Prince?"

Gamel closed his eyes. He was a fool, exposing himself so freely – and yet…

"No," he whispered. "I have no desire to remain a prince."

"Yet a prince you remain."

34

Her words struck him. He twisted, now, on his toe – turned to stare at the Stone on the table.

"Only because of that thing!" he insisted, jabbing his finger. "That wretched thing! I would bury it! I would destroy it! I would undo history – I would overturn the fate of my family!"

"Then you would also overturn the Heartland, and all of Altenhine, in your desire to be free."

Gamel stared at her. Her face was plain to him – nothing attracted him to her. And yet her words were so astute: so painfully true.

"How can it be that the security of Altenhine would rest on my shoulders? How can it be?"

"Fate?" she offered. "A higher purpose? I don't know, Prince Gamel, but I can see this: you must continue to travel west – that much is obvious."

"Obvious?"

"Everything in you points that way, does it not?"

Gamel shuddered now. To travel west meant to enter into utter solitude with the stone – to face whatever horrors it might still hold for him away from the valley, away from any semblance of home: walking a terrain he could not yet begin to see.

"Naked," he whispered to himself. "To go there would be to strip myself bare…"

His eyes lifted to his sister – he felt her vulnerability, now: her shoulders lifted slightly, her brow creviced into a frown.

"If I try this," he said, "If I keep travelling west, with the stone, you must remain here,"

She rose to her feet. "No," she answered, and Gamel's heart twisted.

"You must remain, Lidya – you're better now! I'll take this thing away from you – I won't expose you!"

She tugged on the white cord around her neck: she revealed the golden circle.

"I cannot remain, Gamel."

Distraught, he shook his head. "That pendant was supposed to mean my loyalty for you, Lidi!" he cried. "Not some curse of your obligation to me! This stone is my responsibility now – I can't escape it: I have to carry it. But not you, Lidi! Not you!"

She approached him: she stood before him. Her face was before his face: her eyes before his eyes.

"This burden was never intended for you to carry alone."

Tears welled up in his eyes – he blinked them away, but they kept coming.

"Lidi…"

"As surely as this stone is your responsibility, you are my responsibility."

"No," he whispered. "No."

She poked at his pocket – he pulled out the handkerchief she had made, and she showed him again.

"Two lanterns, Gamel, see? Under your name: two lanterns, and our birthday…"

"I can't do this!" he cried. "I can't do this with you."

"Loyalty from birth, Gamel: this is not your choice to make."

Stunned into silence, Gamel stared down at the handkerchief in his hands. His name! But two lanterns. She might not be seen; her name might never be known – but her part would be vital.

And yet he knew, in that moment: she was also the most vulnerable part of himself.

This was not his decision to make.

Sighing, he yielded to her – taking the handkerchief back into his trouser pocket. And now he turned to Hana.

"Where should we go?"

Hana smiled. "I am familiar with the valley – I will show you a good route up to the Highland Elevation."

"How did you come to be so familiar?" Gamel enquired, suddenly grinning. "And, for that matter – how is it you own your own farm?"

"It was my father's – he had no son."

"No?"

"He showed me the farm – and the valley. He taught me to ride."

"I too can ride."

"A prince must ride to survey his own land."

"Hmmm."

Friedrich was the one who had been taught: the one who had been raised to be King. Gamel had taught himself, in secret – painstakingly around the Blue Lake, at night by moonlight, helped by a horse from the Palace Stables.

"There is a stable just west of Raventown, in the valley," Gamel explored.

"Yes," Hana replied. "My uncle and aunt own that stable."

"They loaned me a horse once – could they do it again, for a longer trip?"

Hana paused thoughtfully. "I could explain it to them."

"Explain?"

"A reason for a prince and princess leaving the Heartland Valley – requiring a horse for a long journey."

"Yes…What reason?"

Hana looked at him. "They will not need a reason," she replied. "I will borrow the horse: that will suffice."

With gratitude Gamel nodded. "Let us depart, then: before I change my mind."

"Your clothes and food…"

"Yes – do you…?"

"You may use my father's," she said.

"Too big?"

"He was short also."

"And the stone?"

Lidya's voice penetrated his plans. He turned again – looked at the stone, sitting on the table. He gritted his teeth – and then scooped up the stone and placed it again in his trouser pocket.

"Let's move!" He said. "Quickly! Get me out of the Valley."

And, as one, they gathered themselves, and prepared to depart.

CHAPTER SEVEN: Traversing the Heartland

Gamel stood outside the Raventown stable.

Before him was the entrance – a wide pine gate, and fence: a large paddock, with horses roaming. The stable building stood to the left, close to the gate. Hana was inside now, talking with her uncle and aunt – Gamel could just hear their voices.

He was wearing Hana's father's clothes, now: a grey woollen jacket, white linen shirt, and grey linen trousers. The stone rested in an inside pocket of the jacket – but he fidgeted, feeling the hard surface banging against his chest whenever he moved.

Lidya was watching him. Her head was tilted a little, the black curl pony tail falling across her green linen shirt.

"It's good of Hana to do this."

"Yes."

"Will we ride together?"

"Yes, Lidi: only one horse."

"Good – because I have no idea how to ride."

She screwed up her face, and Gamel laughed. Then he turned to his left – to glance over the western boundary of Raventown. Many yards from them were the last cottages: he could see a few figures through windows, but guessed they would not recognise them. A raven cry filled his ears – he saw flapping black wings to the north, near the Dandes River.

"What are we doing, Lidi?" he asked. "Where can I take this thing where it will be safe?"

He shoved at the stone, and Lidya smiled sadly.

"I don't know, Gamel," she replied, "But we can't leave it here."

"It can't stay in our family – it can't stay in our land."

"No."

"Maybe…maybe we'll destroy it, or something: somewhere far away, where no-one knows of it – where no one will react to it."

"Maybe." But Gamel could see the doubt in her eyes.

He turned back to the Stable – and now Hana was before him, smiling.

"Behold: a horse for the Prince and Princess."

"You said nothing of us?"

"Nothing."

Gamel looked at the beast. He was a brown stallion, rather similar in appearance to the horse Friedrich had ridden: his head bowed a little with Hana's hold on the rein.

"His name is Brena."

"Brena." Gamel reached out to stroke his head, murmuring to him. "I don't know where I'm leading you, boy, but I'm grateful for your help."

Hana now was placing carrot in his hand – and Gamel quickly offered the carrot to Brena. The horse nibbled, and shook his head a little – he neighed. And then he nuzzled his nose into Gamel's hand.

"You're a natural," Hana commented. "Now go, before my family sees you."

Gamel drew Brena aside, nodded his head to Hana, and then pulled himself up onto the saddle. Lidya stood alongside, looking dubious – the same half amused half scared look on her face.

"Come," Gamel murmured to her – and he lifted her up onto the horse's back. She pressed into his back from behind, and he heard her gasp.

"I've never…"

"I know."

"He's lovely!"

"Yes."

Gamel looked down at Hana. She was smiling again, with reassurance on her face as she loaded Brena with two leather bags of supplies.

"Farewell, Prince Gamel: and may all go well with you."

"Thank you, Hana – I will not forget your kindness."

"I expect recompense when you return."

He laughed, and allowed himself for a moment the certainty she had implied.

"Recompense indeed," he replied, "But what kind of reward?"

"We shall discuss that on your return: go! Go."

He nodded, and tugged on the reins – Brena turned, away from Raventown. And as Brena began to walk and then progressed to a trot, heading west, Gamel took in a deep breath. Wind sped past him, lifting his curls – and he felt Lydia's face buried in his back. Raventown was lost to him now, behind. And before him was the Heartland Valley, on and on: grass, and farmland, flooding past.

"May I return," he whispered. "May I return, and find you still as I leave you."

Fear filled him: the threat of war – of disaster, because of his choice not to submit to the stone. Yet he continued.

The Heartland Valley extended for thirty miles west of Raventown. Gamel could see in the distance the olive green brush of the Highland Elevation – their first goal. Brena's trot was easy for Gamel – he suspended himself on the stirrups with the natural bounce on Brena's saddle – but Lydia, behind him, was bouncing directly on Brena's back. Gamel persevered, perhaps for twenty minutes – then he pulled on the reins, and Brena settled to a walk.

Gamel twisted to look at Lidya. Her face was a bit flushed, as she shifted awkwardly.

"Ouch!" she proclaimed, smirking, and Gamel grinned.

"Sorry."

"Something you need to tell me?"

"Yes. You sit in the saddle, and I'll sit behind."

"Think that will help?"

"Yes. That, and…" He reached into one of their leather bags, and drew out a pair of trousers. "These."

Lidya's eyebrows shot up. "You want me to wear Hana's father's trousers?"

Now Gamel erupted into laughter again. "Unheard of!" he declared.

"From silk to linen, and now to trousers?" Her extreme mock indignation delighted him.

"Go on!" he chided. "Show me how it looks!"

"Very well!" She replied. "Stop the horse!"

Again he drew on the reins, and Brena came to a stop. Gamel lowered himself to the ground first – and then Lidya, with great dramatic flair, lifted her leg across the back of Brena, and virtually fell into Gamel's arms getting off.

"You're not making this easy for us!" Gamel chided her again, smiling, and she hit his shoulder – then, grasping the trousers, she launched herself in the direction of an outcropping of rock, to change behind it.

When she emerged, Gamel stared at her. The trousers, brown linen, sat well on her! Lidya herself stared down at them, patting the fabric.

"I..."

"I don't think they belonged to Hana's father," Gamel pondered.

"You mean they are hers?"

"You are her size, too: she obviously meant them for you."

Lidya brightened at this thought. "Meant for me." And now, with renewed purpose, she pulled on the rein to lift herself up on Brena's back. The first time she slipped down again, laughed, and tried again: again she slipped.

Brena shook his head – but now Gamel grasped his rein.

"Again," he instructed his sister, and as she tugged herself up and he pushed her, she was seated in the saddle.

Gamel quickly pulled himself up behind her – and now tugged on the reins. Brena began to walk – and Gamel passed the reins to Lidya.

"Here."

She took them, her knuckles white with the grip.

"Easy," Gamel murmured, reaching across her hands to the reins. "Like this."

She eased her grip – and then, suddenly, Gamel flicked the reins: and Brena was trotting.

Lidya gasped – and then laughed.

"Like this!" Gamel called out, suspending himself up and down, holding on the back of the saddle. "Push down on the stirrups!"

She followed him – and soon she was directing Brena, bouncing on her toes, grinning into the wind.

Gamel sat back a little, even letting himself bounce, watching his sister's joy – happy to let her lead for a while. Sadness beckoned to him: the stone bouncing hard now against his chest from inside his inner jacket pocket. Only yesterday she had been overcome. But for now she grinned: and for this he was very grateful.

Like this they rode, for over three hours. Gamel pulled on the right rein a little, to draw them closer to the Dandes River – the northern border of the valley. They passed farms of wheat, and sheep, and cattle – sometimes they came close to little villages, much smaller than Raventown, but kept their distance. Then, finally, they reached the Highland Elevation.

Here the ground sloped up before them, on a gentle gradient. The Dandes River was there now, to their right: and behind this the much steeper foothills of the Northland, rising progressively to the Northern mountains.

Lidya pulled Brena to a stop, and Gamel helped his sister down before lowering himself to the ground. He stretched his legs, and reached down to feel the rough olive green brush with his fingers. Brena wandered a few steps away – Gamel let him, and watched him graze on some grass on the flat valley ground. Then Gamel, with his back to the elevation, looked out across the Heartland Valley.

"This is it," he muttered to himself. "I am actually leaving."

Tears pricked at his eyes – but he pushed them away, and now turned to look up the slope of the Highland Elevation. In the distance, about thirty-five miles away, was the next change of terrain: the darker green of the Highland Forrest.

"Do you want to try for there?" Lidya asked him, at his side, and Gamel smiled sadly.

"There is still time," he said quietly. "And we will be under cover for night-time."

Lidya looked a little afraid now. "Where will we sleep?"

"Where we must."

"Who might be around?"

"I don't know, Lidya."

Gamel felt a fool again, in that moment, looking at her: a fool for agreeing that she might come, a fool for even making this attempt to achieve what he could not comprehend. Yet his sister's face reminded him also of all that had taken place the day before: of the threat of the stone, a threat that seemed now somehow simultaneously both surreal and chillingly real – there, where they were, on the very edge of home, pressing on into the unknown.

"Rest, my sister," he murmured to her. "Rest."

She wandered a little, after Brena, and Gamel watched her. But he, himself, withdrew. Closing his eyes, reaching for the stone to hold it, he backed away: into a cave he had seen, into which the Dandes darted, between foothill and elevation.

"Rest..." he whispered, shrinking up against the cool of the stone wall, wrapping his arms around himself. "Rest..."

"You cannot rest here."

Shocked, Gamel jerked his eyes open – to find a Northern warrior standing before him, blocking the entrance of the cave. Stocky in build, with dark curls and a dark face, the warrior's sword was drawn – and, for a moment, Gamel believed his life was over. The stone again was burning into his hand – he sank to his knees, closing his eyes again in readiness: but now he heard the sound of the sword being sheathed.

The warrior extended a strong hand to him. Shaking, perplexed, Gamel took the hand – and now he was being lifted up to his feet.

"My name is Koram," he said, his voice low. Gamel searched his brown face – his dark brown eyes.

"You are from the North."

41

"Yes."

"If I have stumbled upon your land, I apologize."

Now the eyes were studying him.

"You are at the very border of our land – but I think you already know this, Prince Gamel."

Fear struck Gamel. This man knew who he was? How? In these common clothes – how could he have guessed?

"You...have been tracking me." Quickly he pocketed the stone into his right trouser pocket.

Koram smiled, and Gamel feared he might go mad. How? Why?

"Lidya," he whispered, and now he ran out of the cave.

Lidya was still there, outside, with Brena – but now there was another. Astonished, Gamel stared at him: this was the Southerner from whom he had purchased Lidya's gold pendant! Lidya stood still, head lifted, talking with this warrior – her curiosity obvious, and, strangely, her caution absent.

Gamel rushed to her side, to engage him.

"Sir," he began quickly. "I know you."

The Southern warrior bowed his head slightly: long blonde plaits tilted. He was tall, and slight – a hand breadth above Gamel, who was indeed short for a Heartland man. His sword remained sheathed at his side.

"And I know you, Prince Gamel."

Again, his identity was known. Frowning, Gamel searched his white face.

"How do you know me? I never told you my name."

"It is our business to know," the Northern voice called out from behind him: and now Koram stood alongside. "Taierre and I patrol the borders of our lands."

Astonished, Gamel looked at Koram again. "That is your purpose?"

"Yes."

"Does...does King Maki know?"

Now Koram smirked. "The Prince is asking a Northerner what his own father knows?"

Gamel blushed, and looked away – but now Lidya's voice saved him.

"Gamel is the Second Prince: these affairs do not rest with him."

The warriors seemed to accept her response, and instead turned to her.

"You are Princess Lidya?" Koram asked.

Gamel watched her face blush slightly at their recognition. "I am."

"And what brings you and your brother out to the very borders of our lands?"

Now Lidya was silent – but Gamel spoke up, looking to the Southerner.

"Sir Taierre knows I am inclined to explore, you see? My sister wears his pendant."

Gamel reached over to lift the gold circle from Lidya's chest – and Taierre smiled.

"Yes: it is so," he confirmed. "I remember the trade well."

"Loyalty," Gamel quoted the Southerner. "The endless circle. A gift befitting my sister."

"Indeed."

"And so you are set next to explore the Highland Elevation?" Koram's voice interjected – and Gamel swallowed.

"Yes," he declared, knowing full well he could not conceal their path from these scouts. "That is our course."

Koram fell silent – Gamel noticed his gaze shift to that of Taierre. Gamel reached out to stroke Brena, seeking distraction – but now Taierre was shifting to confront him.

"Why are you travelling up the Highland Elevation?"

"Is not our business our own?" Gamel met the Southerner's eyes: they were green, and beginning to intensify.

"A prince seldom has such luxuries: your throne has a bearing on all our lands."

"The fertilizer still reaches you, does it not?"

"It does – for now."

"Then why fear this changing?"

"We do not fear, Prince Gamel: we guard. We watch – and we have been observing some strange happenings of late."

Gamel shifted uncomfortably between his feet. He shot a glimpse at Lidya, whose face was rigid, looked at Koram, and then returned to Taierre.

"I don't know to what you are referring."

"The Second Prince of the Heartland, rushing from the Palace with his sick sister in his arms – fleeing Raventown, changing into clothes as a commoner, acquiring a horse not from the Palace but from the Heartland Valley, in secret, and riding west, where neither he nor any member of his family, or indeed his Valley, have ever sought to tread."

Gamel flushed – astounded to hear that all of their movements had been watched. Koram's voice now sounded again, but a different surprising tone.

"Taierre..."

"We must know the truth, Koram!"

"Yes – but there is something more in him."

Gamel turned and stared down at the grass of the Valley, both warriors behind his back.

"Have you never seen a family argument before?" he asked, gritting his teeth, angry tears squeezing at his eyes. He could tell them nothing more – must tell them nothing more. And he resented being forced to tell them what he longed to keep to himself.

"A family argument?" Taierre pressed, and Koram again spoke up.

"Enough."

"We must know!"

"Enough! Enough for now, Taierre – let him be."

Taierre lapsed into silence – and Gamel fleetingly closed his eyes. Then Koram spoke again.

"The Highland Elevation contains some dangers, Prince Gamel."

"Indeed..." Gamel muttered.

"If you and your sister were to fall prey to some unfortunate incident, it would not bode well on any of our lands."

43

Gamel stared at him – and then, in an outpouring of nervous irony, laughed. "Surely you are not offering to protect us!"

Koram grimaced – and Taierre shifted, clearly disgruntled. Gamel realized he had insulted them – and yet still could not, in that moment, fully grasp what he was beginning to understand.

"You *do* mean to protect us…"

"Woe to all of us if a family dispute should be allowed to end in war."

His words, so accurate, so precise in their depiction, made Gamel shiver.

"Forgive me," he quickly offered. "I wholly misunderstood your purpose."

"Misunderstanding is inevitable," Koram replied, "when new alliances are being forged."

*New alliances…* Troubled, Gamel looked at Koram. This man was a complete stranger – a Northern warrior. And whilst his colleague, Taierre, of the South, was known to Gamel, it was only as a mere acquaintance. How could he possibly trust either one? He could not. And yet he knew he had no choice. His movements had been tracked – they would still be tracked. He and Lidya were defenceless, in truth: he knew anyone who had the inclination could take their lives at any time.

Koram had found him in the cave! He had found him, weak, even on his knees – waiting to die…

*You could have killed me, yet did not.*

Gamel glanced at Lidya, who looked at Koram.

"Tell me, Sirs Koram and Taierre," she enquired. "Why not take our lives now, and seek to conquer the Palace?"

Gamel almost choked at her boldness – yet this was the very question at hand.

Koram took a deep breath – and then sighed. Gamel studied him: he was perhaps in his late forties, surely with a family himself? Taierre, much younger, looked in his late twenties. He shifted awkwardly – but it was Koram who answered.

"Young princess," he said quietly, "I have no desire to kill you. War is sometimes a necessary evil – but only at the very last turn, when all other paths are blocked."

Now he turned face on to Gamel.

"Tell me, young Prince Gamel, Second Prince of the Heartland: are all other paths blocked?"

Gamel held his gaze, astonished: finally seeing him – seeing his honesty. Then he rose up straight, shoulders back: for the first time bearing full responsibility as the First Prince.

"No, Sir Koram," he replied. "There is still an open path for all of us: but for Lidya and me its direction is pointing west."

Koram's eyes passed over his face. West – was this not a mere flight? Perhaps even an escape from certain carnage to come? Gamel could read his thoughts – and yet Koram also seemed to settle on trust: seemed also satisfied by what he saw in Gamel's expression.

"Very well," the Northerner concluded. "Let us both protect you, Prince Gamel and Princess Lidya: let North and South gird your steps."

Surprised, Gamel watched him – and then finally nodded himself.

"Very well," he said. "Protect us – and make our path secure."

CHAPTER EIGHT: The Highland Forest

The sun was dipping behind the Highland Elevation, casting the Valley into shadow, when the four reached the Highland Forest.

Gamel looked at the trees before him: pine, rising high up over their heads, oak interspersed, and the afternoon shadow cooling the warmth in which they had ridden.

Koram was in front, on a black stallion – Tenith. Taierre was behind, on a grey mare Stiar. Lidya was leaning heavily against Gamel's back, sore, he was sure, as Gamel slowed Brena to a walk – and as they followed Tenith slowly between the trees.

Koram seemed to know where he was going. Gamel admired his apparent sense of direction through the forest – and soon, sure enough, they came to a clearing.

"We will camp here tonight," Koram directed, and Gamel readily followed. He brought Brena to a halt, lowered himself to the ground and then lowered Lidya after him.

Koram quickly set up camp – with Taierre joining him. Surprised, Gamel watched the two warriors erect leather tents.

"Do you do this often?" he enquired.

"This is our shelter," Taierre replied, "When we are far from home."

Home. Silently Gamel looked at the tents – and then moved a little apart, to the other side of the clearing, and sat with Lidya.

Soon the light and the temperature began to drop. Shivering, Gamel went back to Brena, his reins tied around a tree, and reached for the bags. Hana had packed more clothes for them both – and, yes, there also was a tent! Shaking his head, Gamel gathered all in his arms and wandered back over to Lidya.

"That Hana," he muttered to her, as she reached for a brown woollen jersey, "she seems to know everything we need."

"Well – not everything…"

Gamel looked up to his sister's eyes – the sudden seriousness in her expression – and grimaced. Then he laid out the tent on the ground and, glancing over his shoulder at Koram and Taierre, worked out the plan. Wooden sticks were needed – he searched around the clearing, and found branches fallen from bare maple trees. Grasping his own knife from his left trouser pocket, he trimmed the branches – and then erected the tent.

It was simple – but somehow, in that moment, exhilarating. With a grin he gestured to his sister – and Lidya crawled inside. Gamel grabbed her, and tickled her – they laughed, as they had done in childhood. But he knew the warriors were waiting – and so, reluctantly, Gamel succumbed to adulthood, and drew Lidya back out of the tent.

Taierre was making a fire. Gamel wandered over, watching his method – dry leaves, wood on wood: a spark, a wisp of smoke. Koram was gone, but now he returned – with two dead squirrels in his hands.

"Oh…" Lidya's voice cracked slightly, and Gamel grinned.

46

"Dinner!" he proclaimed, and Lidya hit him.

"Never!""

"It's either this or berries!"

"I'll stick with Hana's bread!" Lidya replied, her face turning a shade of green – and Gamel let her be.

A stream trickled nearby – Gamel could hear the water. Koram also had filled two clay jars, for drink. The four gathered around the warmth of the fire, cooked, ate, and drank – night fell, until the only light was from the flames and the stars above. All were silent – Gamel often met the exploring gaze of Koram and Taierre over the fire, but no conversation flowed. And then it was time for sleep.

Gamel and Lidya crawled into their tent – and now curled up, face to face, on the ground sheet. Hana had packed some blankets – Gamel shoved a blanket in the direction of his sister. It was the first time they had slept in the same place for many years – and yet, somehow, it remained familiar and natural to them as twins. He passed another jersey to her, to rest her head on, while he lay on the firm ground.

Weariness took him. His head lolled against the cold ground, but then he jerked awake again. Lidya was sleeping now – he could hear her regular breathing, and vaguely make out her face in the dark. The fire outside still cast shadows across their tent and some light within – but now he could just hear soft voices.

"What are we doing here, Koram?" It was Taierre – his voice a quiet yet strained mutter. "We would be better placed keeping watch in the Valley."

"The others will bring us warning if we are needed," Koram's voice, deeper, replied. "This is the Prince."

"The Second Prince."

"No longer second, Taierre – you know what we saw."

"I am not so certain, Koram."

"It was Prince Friedrich: buried in the rear Palace garden."

Gamel frowned. Friedrich, buried in the garden? And they saw? How could they know – did they have spies everywhere? They knew he was now the First Prince? This changed everything...

"Why did they not bury him in the Valley Cemetery – in the Kings' corner?" Koram's voice continued. "The royal family is hiding something, Taierre – something is very wrong."

"Perhaps," Taierre said, "but this path is blind, Koram. Where are we going, and for what purpose? We are blind."

"We follow the young Prince..."

"...blindly, while all of our fates may be hanging in the balance."

Gamel shifted, wrapping his arms around himself, shivering.

"Our fates rest on his shoulders," Koram replied. "You know this, Taierre – I need not remind you."

"I know it – but I cannot comprehend it, Koram. Look at him! He plays with his sister as though he is still a child."

Gamel closed his eyes tightly – the image of his father was before him: the expression of disdain. *Fool!*

"He is not only a child, Taierre."

"I have no time for children."

"You must make time for the future King of the Heartland."

Now Gamel reached to cover his ears – but the stone was pressing into his chest again, on the hard ground. He lapsed into sleep, and saw Friedrich again: face hard, eyes piercing.

"I am not your brother!" he hissed, and Gamel writhed.

"I know!" he pleaded. "I know..."

*Soon I will have you too, son of Maki, son of Hemin: soon you will be mine!*

The Stone was burning now into his chest. Groaning, Gamel clutched at it, but he could not get it away. His head lolled on the hard ground – caught between sleep and wakefulness, weak, without defence. Then, somehow, sleep took him again – and later he awoke.

It was morning. The tent was illuminated with yellow sun pouring in from the east, between the trees from the Valley. He had slept – how? Somehow the troubled sleep had subsided. But now he saw his sister, face close to his, eyes squeezed tightly shut – gasping in her sleep. Her hand was clutching something – and with chills Gamel knew what it was.

"Give it to me," he whispered, reaching for her hand: trying to pry open her fingers.

Lidya's arms fought him, in sleep. "Stop!" she cried. "Stop.

He shook her now, to awaken her – and her body jerked in his hands, her eyes starting open: her gaze shocked, and afraid, staring at him.

"Soutar!" she cried. "Soutar!"

But, as her gaze came to see him, the tension in her body eased.

"Gamel..."

Her hand relaxed under his, and he opened her fingers and removed the stone.

The serpent stared at him – the garnet eyes faintly luminous. He laid the black stone down on the ground between them, and sank back.

Lidya was shaking. "I saw him," she whispered. "In my sleep."

"I know," Gamel heavily replied.

"He...he wants you."

Gamel's jaw tightened, his teeth clenching. "I know."

"I tried to save you." Now her eyes intensified, with tears. "In sleep, Gamel: do you understand? You were clutching the stone..."

Gamel's body shuddered hard. *"Soon you will be mine!"*

"He can't have me unless I invite him in!"

"In sleep..."

"I was resisting him!"

"I know, Gamel, but – what if you stop? What if you give in?"

Gamel wanted to vomit – he shook the sensation off.

48

"I will not give in!" he whispered intensely – and now footsteps were at the door of their tent, with the sound of swords unsheathed.

"Is all well, Prince Gamel?" Koram's voice called – and Gamel stared at Lidya.

"All is well!" he declared – and now he swept the pendant back into his right trouser pocket.

"I should keep it," Lidya whispered – but Gamel curtly shook his head and thrust himself out of the tent.

The clearing was lit with sunlight filtering through the leaves of the trees. Gamel turned to peer between the trees – he saw the yellow warmth of the Heartland Valley spread out before him, at the bottom of the Highland Elevation. He longed to return – he knew he could not.

Koram and Taierre were before him. Gamel held their gaze and grimaced.

"Tell me," he began. "What is your purpose here?"

"We might ask you the same thing," Taierre quickly responded.

"Indeed you might – but I am free to roam about my land, Sir Taierre: it surprises me to learn that you also feel free to roam the Heartland."

The two were silenced – studying him. Then Koram spoke.

"The security of our lands requires…"

"Yes, yes," Gamel curtly replied. "I understand that: but what of the security of my land?"

*I will make your land secure.*

Gamel clenched his jaw, and persevered. "I cannot cater for the North and South if my own land is not first protected."

"You are now speaking as a King."

Taierre was openly challenging him. Gamel met his gaze and nodded.

"You are correct," he stated. "The First Prince is dead: I am now next in line."

Koram's eyebrows shot up, even as Taierre stared hard at him. Gamel saw Lidya, out of the corner of his eye, to his right – her mouth opening in protestation and then quickly closing again.

"Prince Friedrich is dead?" Taierre exclaimed.

"Yes."

"How?"

"He became ill, and succumbed."

"Your sister also fell ill?" Koram was frowning, now – searching him: studying closely.

"Yes," Gamel snapped back at him, "But she has recovered."

"And you," Koram explored. "Do you carry the same illness?"

Gamel met him face to face, and did not allow himself to flinch.

"I am well, Sir Koram," he said. "My sister needs fresh air, and I am exploring the land."

"A worthy task for the First Prince of the Heartland."

"Indeed."

49

The conversation lapsed into silence. Gamel glanced again over the valley – over his home – and felt himself watched. Taierre moved away, toward the camp – probably to pack up the tent. But Koram lingered.

Gamel avoided his gaze now – yet the warrior remained. And now his voice changed – became quieter.

"I see something else in you, First Prince Gamel of the Heartland," Koram said, "Some kind of trouble."

"You need not fear trouble from me," Gamel replied, resting his eyes on a tiny village surrounded by sheep farms.

"That is not the kind of trouble I mean."

For a moment, Gamel dared to look – and now, in Koram's dark brown eyes, he saw something else: compassion, insight – even some kind of fatherly concern…

Shuddering, Gamel looked away: gritting his teeth.

"There is no trouble, Koram," he stated, "Only exploration. I thank you for your help, and respect your decision if you should leave."

"No," Koram replied quietly. "We shall remain, Prince Gamel, for now: we shall remain in your service."

Gamel was relieved for their presence, somehow: relieved by their older skill, and insight, even while he could not trust them. Koram moved away, and Gamel finally breathed deeply.

"You shall stay?" he whispered to himself. "Very well, Koram of the North, and Taierre of the South: stay. And we shall all see together where this ridiculous journey may lead."

CHAPTER NINE: The Ice Lake

It was time to depart. The tents were packed, and the clearing left clean –
undisturbed.

Koram, seated on Tenith, again was in the lead. He glanced back to Gamel,
who nodded – and then set off between the pine and oak trees, up the Highland
Elevation.

Lidya shifted behind Gamel, on Brena.

"I'm not sure about all this riding," she muttered into his ear. "Even with
trousers, I'm not sure I was made for this."

"You're doing well," Gamel murmured back to her in gratitude.

"My backside!" She shifted again, but then laughed at herself – and Gamel's
mind was set at ease. For now she was persevering.

Taierre followed behind, on Stiar – and Gamel felt his gaze on his back.
Koram seemed to be warming to him, but Taierre? Gamel could see no such
orientation. He was a warrior, through and through: his thought was only for the
security of his own land.

And in this, Gamel could not blame him. He also felt a growing concern for
the Heartland: what might be her fate? How could he secure her boundaries?

*I will secure them from within you.*

*No!*

*It is your fate, son of Hemin: for five hundred years I have protected your
land, through the rule of your ancestors! Give yourself to me.*

*Leave me!*

*You have no claim to the Throne without me.*

Gamel shook the voice off – and glanced to his right, to see Taierre, now
alongside, peering at him.

"Are you all right, Prince Gamel?"

"Yes!" he quickly replied. "Onward, up the slope!"

And on they rode, darting over roots and between trunks, higher and higher
up the Highland Elevation.

After a few further hours of riding, they came to a stop. The valley behind
their backs had dropped substantially away – and the air was now crisp. Gamel's
breath turned to mist, and he shivered – reaching again for more layers for
himself and Lidya.

"The Ice Lake," Koram announced – and there, before them, was indeed a
vast lake solidified into ice. Pine trees surrounded the lake, with tufts of snow
like icing sugar scattered on the pines.

Gamel had never seen anything like it. In wonder he dismounted from Brena
– ensuring Lidya also was dismounted and warm.

*All this I will give to you.*

*This is not mine to take.*

*It can be, Gamel: all of it can be yours. The heights of the mountains,
Gamel: the strength of the world. I will give you all of Altenhine.*

51

Gamel's heart yearned: Altenhine! Strength, and such beauty! His to own: his to rule...

*You will never run again.*

The words enticed him – their hold terrifying to his heart. He found his hand reaching, into his right trouser pocket – but then Lidya's hand flicked his arm. Her eyes penetrated him, now: deeply, knowingly – exposing him. In that moment he hated her – and yet somehow, at the same time, loved her: he still knew her – still agreed with her.

"Give me the stone."

His body shook. His heart resisted. He struggled – and then he complied. His hand was in her palm, surrendering the stone. And then he turned away from her – away from all.

Koram and Taierre had erected the tents alongside the Lake – even that of Gamel and Lidya. They had lit a fire. But Gamel kept well away from them, now. He wandered a little distance into the trees, and sank against one. He began to crave.

The Stone was with Lidya. Where had she hidden it? He did not know. But he felt it somewhere nearby, drawing him – whispering fulfilment. If he took this thing, he knew his struggle would be over. Soutar, whatever he was, would have his way – and the fate of the Heartland would be decided. Yet, at the same time, he knew he could not willingly surrender: for he knew he would lose himself – and then, he knew, he would never return to who he was.

His back slid against the trunk of a pine tree to the frozen ground, amidst snow – his head lolled back against the trunk.

"Why...?" he breathed into the cold air. "Why is this happening? What did I do? I don't understand..."

He closed his eyes – but then sensed movement. Gasping, he looked up – to find a man standing alongside him. Gamel stared at him: what was he doing there, next to the Ice Lake?

The man looked like a Heartlander: white skin, light brown curls, linen clothes; a woollen black coat. But there was something different about him. There was no horse – no *anything*.

"Who are you?" Gamel breathed, and the man smiled slightly.

"My name is Michel."

"Michel? That is an odd name for a Heartlander."

"I am not from the Heartland."

Gamel cast his eyes back over the man's face, hair and clothes. "You look familiar..."

"You saw me, once, alongside the Blue Lake."

Astonished, Gamel nodded! "Yes, that's right! Just before...before..."

And now a sob erupted from within in. Friedrich! Friedrich...

The man's hands were on his shoulders: his touch strange – warmth flowing into Gamel's body greater than a man's usual touch.

"You are not from around here at all," Gamel whispered, trembling, and a hand now lay on his back.

"You are right, Gamel: I am not."

His name, without the title: somehow Michel's familiar approach comforted Gamel.

"Where…?"

"That is not for you to know."

"Then why…?"

"Don't be afraid, Gamel: you are right to travel west. You are still on the right path."

Bewildered, Gamel stared at him. His was the voice he had heard in the paddock, instructing him that he could not remain – an instruction that had propelled him toward Hana.

"I have questions…"

"All your questions will be answered at the right time."

Michel's face broke into a radiant smile. Gamel gazed at him, captivated – and then, before his eyes, he disappeared.

There was warmth residing within Gamel's chest. He took some deep breaths, rose to his feet, and then he wandered back to the edge of the Lake, where Koram, Taierre and Lidya sat around a fire, between two tents.

Silently Gamel lowered himself onto a rug next to Lidya.

"What happened to you?" she asked, leaning close to him: out of earshot of the others.

Gamel stared into the flames of the fire. What to say? How to explain?

"I…saw someone," he began hesitantly. "Just over there."

He gestured in the general direction between the trees. Lidya shifted with concern.

"A warrior? We should tell…"

"No," he quickly interrupted. "Don't tell them." He avoided Lidya's gaze as he tried to continue. "It wasn't a warrior."

"Then who?"

"I…don't know." Frowning, he continued to study the flames. "But he was good."

"'Good'?"

Her scepticism struck him as highly ironic, given her response to the stone.

"As Soutar is bad, this man is good."

Now he looked at her. She seemed puzzled – and yet also open. Her eyebrows went up, and then settled.

"Soutar is not a man," she commented.

"No," Gamel agreed, rather enjoying her confusion.

"So this one you saw? A man?"

Gamel left her question in the air: he knew he could not answer it adequately. She shoved him slightly in frustration, he shrugged – and then he lifted himself to sit next to Koram.

The Northern warrior made room for him. For a few moments Gamel again stared into the flames. Then he spoke.

53

"Sir Koram," he began, "What do you know of the history of the Heartland five hundred years ago, with the establishment of King Hemin?"

Koram's eyes were on him – and then, Gamel saw out of the corner of his eye, on the flames.

"Our ancestors passed on to each generation the history of what took place, Prince Gamel," Koram replied.

"And what did they say?"

"You do not know?"

"I would like to hear the Northern perspective."

Gamel glanced at him – Koram was smiling slightly now, for some reason. The brown eyes met his easily.

"And why would you like to hear our perspective, Prince Gamel?"

"Gamel will do."

"Indeed?"

"A wider perspective is always worthwhile."

"Always?"

Koram's eyes were dancing for a moment – before his expression settled into a more serious gaze. He glanced at Taierre – and Gamel also looked, to find the Southerner silently attentive. Then Koram's eyes returned to the flames.

"Our people struggled, Gamel, before Hemin. It was the same with those in the South." Taierre nodded his assent while Koram continued.

"The mountains are not gracious for food. We have 'valleys' in lower altitude, but nothing like the Heartland Valley. A harvest is only possible once a year, due to frosts."

"We store food," Taierre added, "To last the entire year."

"Both North and South plant seed only two weeks of the year." Koram continued. "For that seed to be given the chance to take root, in such a short period of opportunity, the soil must be fertile. Without the fertilizer from the East, our crops would fail – and our people would die."

Gamel frowned into the flames. "I understand, Koram," he murmured.

"Before Hemin, there was no agreement with the Heartland," Koram explained.

"We had to meet the merchants in the Heartland, either way," Taierre said. "We had to carry vast amounts of fertilizer to our lands."

"The merchants were reluctant to come," Koram continued. "They feared attack – and many times had their fertilizer stolen. Northern and Southern warriors fought over the bounty. The merchants bonded with the Heartland, and the Heartland sought to protect the merchants – but they had no defence."

Taierre now was on his feet, drawing his sword, and he laid the tip of the blade to Gamel's neck. Gamel froze, feeling his skin slightly pricked.

"You see?" Taierre proclaimed. "No defence – no swords." He lifted his sword away, sheathing it, and Gamel swallowed.

"In our desperation, we fought," Koram continued. "Warrior to warrior – and then more warriors, and then armies: all converging on the Heartland – all wanting the Heartland, with her easy harvest and easy access to the East.

"Our ancestors overcame – and then the South rose up, and overcame us. Many Heartlanders died caught between our great nations."

"So it was, Prince Gamel, until King Hemin."

"And what happened with him?" Gamel looked at him, and, again, Koram smiled.

"Our records are a little vague, Gamel," he said. "Hemin found a way: stood up and ruled. He wielded some ancient power in the Valley: a power that kept the Heartland shielded from attack."

"A power?"

"Legend, Prince Gamel – even myth." Taierre's voice and face showed his scepticism. "The story keeps us under control."

"And yet," Koram now interjected, "the history of our lands changed at that point. Since Hemin there has been no war. Since Hemin the fertilizer continues to flow to our lands."

"We built him the Palace," Taierre said. "It was clear to North and South that the Heartland must govern the fertilizer: providing safe and easy passage for the merchants and for each representative of our lands."

"Yes…" Gamel explored. "I can see that also."

"A Throne was necessary," Taierre said.

"Yes."

"But the Throne also needed power," Koram said, and Taierre grimaced.

"Only the appearance of power."

Koram smiled across the flames to his Southern colleague. "Would appearances alone appease you, my friend?"

Taierre's white face flushed a little. "No," he said quietly. "But I was not there."

Gamel glanced between them, and broke into a grin.

"I see now why mediation was necessary!" he declared, and Koram laughed while Taierre grimaced.

"Different people," Koram said, "With different thinking, yet the same need. And now here we are. So, Prince Gamel: give us the Heartland version of the happenings of King Hemin."

Gamel stared at him – and now blushed hard himself.

"Well, ah…" He grasped for a response. "Hemin, as you know, is my ancestor."

"Yes."

"And, as you say, the Throne was built for the purpose of establishing peace."

"Yes."

"I hope to achieve the same end: to maintain peace."

"Yes, Gamel," Koram said, "but the nature of the power?"

Gamel looked him straight in the face. He had walked into this exposure with his own curiosity! And yet it was suddenly clear to him that he need not oblige.

"Would a true sovereign reveal the source of his power?" he asked, and Koram smiled.

"Perhaps not," he admitted.

"Yet I cannot blame you for trying."

Gamel grinned again, and Koram nodded in acknowledgement, while Taierre seemed to be stifling a slight scowl. And now Gamel began to contemplate. So the history was true! War in the Heartland – repeated battling. The Throne built to secure peace.

The only aspect uncertain was the nature of the Stone: the nature of that very power that was enticing Gamel. Was Soutar a powerful force, unknown to North and South? The basis of the shift in history?

The kings had written their accounts in the parchment room in the Throne Room – the key to the cabinet rested in Gamel's left pocket. What had they seen? What had they done? Gamel wished now he had paid more attention to the history of his ancestors – wished he could gain from their prior knowledge of Soutar.

He glanced at Lidya. Ironically, he had sought the information he needed from strangers – when, in fact, it was his sister who carried now a kind of knowledge, from parchment and from experience, that he needed.

She held his gaze – he saw her determination. She had hidden the stone – but she was willing to share with him her knowledge, always.

Yet now it was time to rest.

Gladly Gamel laid his head back against the trunk of a pine-tree, and closed his eyes. The cool air began to penetrate – but sleep was the stronger force.

CHAPTER TEN: Attack

Gamel awoke – to find night having descended on the Ice Lake.

The fire had burnt out. Koram lay on the ground to his left, sleeping. Lidya was gone – but Gamel could see the shadow of her form lying in their tent. And Taierre – Gamel hastily searched for him, and saw his slim agile form between the trees, under starlight: he was guarding their campsite.

A blanket had been laid over him, but Gamel felt the cold penetrating into his body. He rose to his feet, shaking his legs, rubbing his hands together – they were numb. Why had he delayed? Why had he not pressed on to the top of the Highland Elevation, and beyond? Now another day was gone.

The Heartland Valley still lay beyond the trees. Gamel wandered over, a little apart from Taierre, between the pines. There, in the moonlight and starlight, far away and low down, was the Heartland.

Gamel thought he could just make out a faint haze of the lights of Raventown. He smiled sadly to himself. All was still – all was quiet. For now there was peace – and yet an uneasy peace: uncertain, insecure. He dwelt on her past – a past Koram and Taierre had confirmed: bloodshed. He dwelt on her present. He felt pained at the thought of the Throne – at the thought of King Hemin, with Soutar: and of his father with the stone.

The Heartland's fate had been tossed in the hands and choices of those not her own, until Hemin had submitted to Soutar. Would Gamel have her tossed again? Uncertain, unstable, wide open for war? And yet, would he choose evil to secure safety? What kind of safety could this be?

Michel's face was before him, now, in his mind's eye: to all appearances a Heartlander! And yet, not. What was he? Who was he? Somehow to engender trust – some kind of creature, some kind of being, unknown to him: alien to all. And yet, not alien: and yet, familiar, as if already known.

*You are on the right path.*

But where was this path leading?

Troubled, Gamel raised his eyes to look at the stars. There, in their light, was beauty, and mystery. Was there some kind of help to be found: some kind of knowledge beyond what he could see? He wondered – but then, suddenly, there was a movement.

Gamel found himself on his face, pressed into leaves on the ground. A burly Northern warrior was sitting upon him, his sword to Gamel's throat. But then, as quickly as Gamel had been overcome, the warrior was off his back. Swords were sounding – Gamel twisted around to see Taierre fighting the Northerner, sword against sword, forcing him to stumble backwards.

The Northern warrior fell – and now lay beneath Taierre's sword. Taierre's fine fingers tightened on the hilt of the sword in preparation to kill, but Gamel cried out.

"No!"

Koram appeared, standing at his fellow countryman's head. "Who are you?"

The Northerner clenched his teeth. "I don't know you!" he hissed, and chills went up Gamel's spine. Soutar…?

57

"Speak your name!" Koram said. "Are you a scout?"

"Speak or die!" Taierre insisted, and Gamel strode closer.

"Don't kill him!"

"Are you Northern resistance?" Koram asked. "In defiance to our Northern King?"

"I have no king!"

And now, suddenly, Taierre thrust his sword into the prisoner's chest.

"No!"

Gamel stared at the blood oozing from the Northerner's chest. Friedrich was before him, now: knife turning inwards – thrusting inwards to death…

"No!"

Now, seized from within, Gamel strode up to Taierre, grasped the sword out of his hand, and threw it to the side. Then, in fury, he slapped his face. "No, no, no!"

Taierre stared at him, stunned: taken by surprise. But now his hand stiffened, and he slapped back hard – throwing Gamel to the ground.

"Enough!" Koram's voice resounded. "Enough."

Taierre stood over Gamel, shaking his head – scowling.

"You are pathetic!" he proclaimed. "Have you never seen death? You, the proposed next King of the Heartland?"

"I have seen death!" Gamel spat at him, thrusting himself back to his feet. "I will not tolerate murder!"

"Not tolerate murder?" Taierre laughed. "What do you think war is, Prince Gamel: a walk in your Heartland pastures? Open your eyes! That Northerner was set to kill you!"

Shaking, Gamel held his gaze. "I do not believe that."

"Then you are naïve, silly boy! Give the Throne to someone else!"

Tears stung Gamel's eyes. "I am not naïve!" He protested. "You have no idea who I am! You have no idea what I know!"

Taierre seized the sword from the fallen Northerner, and now thrust the hilt into Gamel's hand.

"I know this, young man: you must learn to use this, or you will surely die."

Gamel stared at him. His hand instinctively wrapped around the hilt of the sword. The weight was heavy – awkward in his grip. Taierre stepped back, and stooped to grasp his own sword, fallen from where Gamel left it – and now touched his blade to that of Gamel.

"Fight me."

"No," Gamel whispered, shaking.

"Fight me!" Taierre hit his sword harder.

"No!"

Now Taierre threw him bodily back, almost knocking him over. Gamel stumbled, found his footing – and found his pain. With a loud cry he attacked Taierre, beat after beat bearing down on his sword with his own – forcing Taierre to his knees. Then, seeing the shock in Taierre's eyes – seeing the potency of his own domination – Gamel staggered back, again throwing the sword away.

"Gamel!" Lidya's voice cried out – he looked, to see her holding up the Stone of Soutar. The garnet eyes were glowing intense red – eerie, in the moonlit dark.

"Oh…" Gamel gasped. "Oh…" And he sank down heavily to his knees.

For a long moment all was silent. Gamel knelt hunched over, arms wrapped around himself – staring at the ground. He glanced up to see Taierre also remaining on his knees – watching Gamel. Lidya stood far away from Gamel – he knew she was keeping the stone away. And Koram stood still, at the head of his dead countryman.

Gamel closed his eyes tightly. What had just happened? What might have happened? He lifted his heavy weight to his feet, walked over to the Northern warrior, and sank down next to him.

The man's face was white – the blood gone. Gamel reached out a tentative hand to touch the blood soaking his leather tunic – he could not stop his fingers shaking.

"Who was he, Koram?" Gamel whispered to the man standing over him. "Your countryman?"

"I don't know who he was, Prince Gamel," Koram's gentle voice replied.

"Do you grieve for your brother?"

"He is a stranger…"

"But doesn't he belong to your land? To our lands?"

Koram's voice fell silent. Gamel felt Koram's hand to his shoulder, now – and tears blurred his vision.

"How can he grieve for one set to kill him?" asked Taierre's voice, from a distance.

"The Heartland is not like our lands, Taierre," Koram's older, wiser voice explained. "Do not try to make him into being as yourself."

"He needs a different answer."

Lidya was behind him, now – her hands on his shoulders, her words authoritative. Gamel turned to her.

"Did you see?" he pleaded, and her hands tightened on him.

"I saw."

"Taierre was just like…"

"Friedrich. I know."

"The stone – it did it! It did it…"

"Yes."

"And I…" Now Gamel writhed. "I…"

He desperately looked for her eyes – found her serious warmth.

"You almost succumbed."

The truth was painful. She stated it in the utmost of love – she stated it to warn him. He could have hated her for it    but he did not. Rather, he remained with her.

"What should I do?"

She smiled sadly. "You know what you must do, Gamel."

"Tell me."

"Fight it. Fight it, with all your strength – with all your determination."

"But what if all my strength, and all my determination, is not enough?"

The question was left unanswered: hanging in the air.

Gamel rose to his feet over the Northern warrior.

"Bury him," he said, and Koram stilled Taierre's protestations.

"Very well," he replied. "But there is one other matter we must discuss."

Gamel clenched his teeth. "What?"

"What is the stone?"

Fear took Gamel. Koram was before him, now – Taierre alongside. They had seen it – Lidya had shown them, in her urgency! They had heard them speak of it.

"The stone…?" he began nonchalantly.

"It was glowing, Prince Gamel – I have never seen such a thing! Does the Heartland engage in magic?"

"Magic?" Gamel laughed. "Only in games…"

Koram's hand was outstretched, now, to Lidya. "Where is it?"

She stared at the hand, at the face, and grimaced. "It is safe."

"Safe?" Taierre exclaimed. "Is it some kind of weapon?"

"It is no weapon," Gamel said. "It is a pendant: a family heirloom."

"A pendant of the King of the Heartland?" Koram asked, and Gamel met his gaze.

"A symbol of the Throne," he replied. "But we have much more to consider than a mere pendant, Koram. Tell me of the North – there is a Resistance? Is the Northern Kingship failing?"

Koram hesitated to answer, his eyes moving between Gamel and Lidya. Then he replied.

"There has always been some degree of resistance, Gamel," he said. "The King maintains authority – his Throne is not yet truly threatened."

"And how does he maintain authority?"

Koram held his eyes. He glanced at Taierre. And then he reached into his tunic pocket.

In his hand was a stone.

# CHAPTER ELEVEN: Exploration

Gamel froze. Koram had a stone too? And now Lidya moved alongside, pulling out the Stone of Soutar. The stone of the north was smaller, though still made of black stone – the shape of a lizard, with tiny greenstone eyes.

"How long...?" Gamel breathed.

"Since the Time of Hemin," Koram replied.

"What does it do? Why do you carry it for him?" Gamel lifted his eyes again to him, suddenly struck again with insight. "Why are you here with me, Koram of the North? You are no mere scout."

Koram's face shifted into a mysterious smile. "You are right, son of Maki – I am no mere scout."

"You are here on an errand for your King!"

"Yes."

"And you, Taierre?"

The Southerner's face was rigid – but Koram's raised eyebrows stirred him on.

"I do not trust him, Koram!" Taierre said.

"Yet that is not your decision to make."

"My King seeks an alliance..."

"We already have an alliance," Gamel interjected.

"An alliance of a different kind."

Silenced, Gamel looked at him. Taierre shifted, in obvious reluctance – and then he also reached into his pocket and withdrew a stone.

It was shaped as a locust: small, as that of Koram, with tiny eyes – of sapphire.

Gamel looked between the lizard, the locust, and the serpent, in between.

"This doesn't look good."

"What, Prince Gamel?" Koram asked. "What does it mean?"

"What does this stone mean to you, Koram?" Gamel quickly replied. "Why did your King give it to you to carry?"

Koram's face darkened slightly. "I entrust this information to you, Prince Gamel. My King is not well."

"Not well?" Gamel was drawn to his eyes.

"Many have risen against him in the past – he has overcome with a power he dare not speak of. He gave me this stone, though he did not say why: even to me, his most trusted guide. He told me to do away with it: to find a way to destroy it."

Gamel stared at him, tears pricking his eyes. "Really?" he breathed. There was another! Another who understood – another who was acting likewise!

And now he looked to Taierre.

The Southerner shifted, shaking his head. "Myth!" he muttered. "Legend!"

"A legend of today?" Koram replied a little gruffly. "Come, Taierre, my King speaks of his own experience – a power he has known: a power he considers the greatest threat."

Gamel stared at him, almost in disbelief, while Taierre responded.

"My King also seeks to destroy the stone. It wields too much power over the hearts and minds of men."

"How so?"

"They fear it, and so they fear the King."

Gamel studied his face. "The Southerners obey out of fear of the Stone?"

"Yes."

"And the King seeks to remove this fear?"

"Yes, Prince of the Heartland."

"Then why does he not destroy it himself, in front of his people? Why does he himself not remove the fear?"

Taierre paused – and then continued. "He has found no way to destroy it."

Gamel's eyebrows rose. "No way? To destroy a simple stone?"

"Apparently there is more to this stone than black rock. It will not be destroyed. My King seeks to remove it, and to forge a new alliance."

"What kind of new alliance?"

"A new form of rule, no longer bound by the conditions set by our forefathers: no longer bound by the stone."

Taierre's words filled Gamel's heart with sudden unexpected joy.

"Yes," Gamel said, "A new alliance! A new form of rule."

"And yet have you forgotten?" Koram interrupted, "The reason why this form of rule was taken up, five hundred years ago? It was war, Taierre. To remove the Throne's authority, in all of our lands, is to unleash anarchy."

Gamel looked at the stones set out before them. The rule of Hemin had been established by the Stone of Soutar. No-one had spoken of Soutar directly: did they not know of him? Did they not believe in his existence, separate from fear? Taierre's King, of the South, was dismissing the Stone – seeking a way to fully discard it, away from the South: probably away from all. Koram's King, on the other hand, feared the power of the stone, even while he still battled to maintain rule.

"How do you propose we discard of the stones?"

"You too are seeking to discard Hemin's stone?"

Gamel swallowed, and replied to Koram. "Yes: I too am seeing to dispose of our stone."

All three had declared their intentions.

Gamel looked between Koram and Taierre, and then looked at Lidya. She was quiet, her face fixed. Gamel knew she had much to say, yet she remained silent.

Taierre spoke first.

"We must remove the stones from Altenhine."

"Remove them?" Gamel asked, with fascination.

"Take them far away from any who would be influenced by them: away from any who would use them or be intimidated by them. They must be removed from any who have heard rumours of their power."

"Where would you have them taken?" Koram asked, "East? Into the heart of the Navigar Continent?"

"It would be too easy for them to return," Taierre replied, "With the merchants. No, west. I suggest we cast them into the Sea of Yerim."

"Cast them into the Sea?" Koram spluttered. "This is your plan? They would float back ashore with the next high tide!"

"Or float somewhere else," Gamel added.

"Too reckless!" Koram said.

"They are but stones!" Taierre sighed heavily. "And stones rest well at the bottom of the Ocean."

Lidya prodded Gamel, but he shook his head to her.

"What would you say, Sir Koram," he asked. "How should we discard of the stones?"

Koram frowned, staring at the black stone lizard. "Does such a thing wield power, Prince Gamel?" he began, "I don't know. If so, it would be unwise to cast such a thing into the Sea – even if the power is only believed. But if the thing does have real power, apart from our belief or lack of belief, how much more so should we not randomly toss it aside. Woe to us if we should unleash it on another unsuspecting people."

"Then what should we do?" Gamel asked.

"I don't know."

"You have no plan for your stone of the North?"

"As of yet I have no plan."

"Take them across the Sea."

It was Lidya's voice. Gamel looked at her. She was grasping the Stone of Soutar, now, in her palm – fixing her gaze intently upon him.

"You know what you must do, Gamel."

*Travel across the Sea, to the land of Yerim? Why? For what purpose?*

Taierre scoffed. "She is chasing fairy tales."

"She knows some truth," Gamel defended.

"'Across the Sea,'" Taierre continued, "Whispers, in the Heartland, of a sorcerer. We entertain no such illusions in the South."

"And yet your people fear the stone so greatly your King sends it away with you."

Taierre grunted, and was silenced. And Koram smiled slightly.

"Take the stones across the Sea? To the nation of Yerim?"

"Yes," Lidya said.

"Why do you suggest such a thing, Princess of the Heartland?"

Lidya's eyes held those of Koram. She hesitated, and Gamel held his breath – then she spoke.

"Because Soutar fears it."

Koram's eyes widened, staring at her. Taierre choked. Gamel shifted on his feet, suddenly very awkward. But Lidya remained steadfast.

"Take the stones across the Sea."

No one spoke. Lidya's words remained hanging. The stones were silent, the late night air chilled. Somehow there seemed nothing more to say – somehow it seemed the conversation was over.

63

Taierre was the first to leave, with the stone of the South – he wandered back to the tents. Koram watched Lidya for several minutes, silent, studying her face – and then he seemed to pull himself away, with his stone, to attend to his dead countryman.

Gamel was left alone with Lidya – and now he grasped her arm tightly.

"What are you doing?" He whispered. How could she reveal the Stone? Even reveal Soutar? But Lidya shoved him.

"No, Gamel," she retorted, "What are *you* doing?" And angry tears filled her eyes.

Astonished, Gamel watched her. "What do you mean?"

"This is no game!"

"I know that!"

"Consorting with our neighbours as though you know nothing?"

Gamel hushed her. "We can't tell them about Soutar!"

"That is his whole tactic, Gamel: don't you see?"

"Tactic?"

"Unseen, though feared: unspoken of, though secretly known. Speak his name, Gamel! Speak his name, and do away with him!"

Gamel stared at her boldness. Speak his name? He dared not! Dared not invite him – dared not invite more testing.

"Where is your courage?" she asked – but then, even as the words left her lips, something changed.

Her face clouded over – somehow turned a sickly shade of grey. She swayed, on her feet, and fell. The Stone was in her hand, clutched – Gamel grasped it, again, away from her: again to the ground between them.

"Koram!" he cried, and the Northerner was quickly by his side. Lidya was vomiting on the ground. Taierre passed her a cup of water – she received it, and sipped cautiously.

The Stone lay on the ground.

Swallowing, Gamel looked at it.

"Please, Koram," he whispered to the Northerner behind his back. "We must get moving."

"Yes," Koram's low voice replied gently, "Let's move immediately. We will pack up camp."

"To the peak of the Highland Elevation?"

"Yes, before sunrise."

"And then?"

"One phase at a time, Gamel – we all have much to consider."

*Much to consider*…Koram now followed Taierre to the camp, and Gamel stared after him. He longed to run, to move – but to where? To what? And to what end? There were no answers, only more questions – except for Lidya's certainty.

She was still, now, on her knees: the stone alongside her.

"Take them over the sea," Lidya whispered again – and Gamel swallowed.

"If I do this, we will be safe?"

Tears filled her eyes, as she stared at the ground. "I don't know, Gamel: our safety is not the point! This threat is much bigger than our lives."

He gazed at her for a moment, trying to comprehend her words. Then he quickly scooped the stone back into his right trouser pocket, and lifted Lidya to her feet.

"Time to go," he said, and she nodded.

"Time to go."

# CHAPTER TWELVE: Declaration

The sun was beginning to rise, behind their backs, as the four ascended the Highland Elevation.

Gamel had been dozing a little on Brena – Lidya, resting against his back, had sometimes jerked him awake, and sometimes succumbed herself against him. Gamel was amazed at Brena's perseverance at night, and his ability to weave between the trees, in the dark and cold.

Ahead again was Koram, on Tenith, and behind Taierre, on Stiar.

Gamel looked beyond Koram, up the slope ahead, between the trees. Surely they would reach the opening soon? Surely they would soon reach the top.

The ground was becoming more difficult. Gamel noticed the incline steepening – the snow laden brush giving way to rock. Brena slowed a little – Gamel called out to Koram, who glanced over his shoulder and then slowed Tenith in turn.

Pink hues from behind, scattered by leaves, illuminated their path as they proceeded – and then, quite suddenly, the ground swept up before them into jagged rock, too steep for snow to settle upon and yet coated with ice.

Koram gestured to Taierre, who went forward.

"An opportunity for Stiar to show her talent, Taierre."

"Indeed."

Taierre shook Stiar's reins slightly, and Stiar stepped tentatively onto the slope – then progressively ascending the precipitous incline. She reached the top, and Gamel watched Taierre dismount – then Gamel met Koram's expectant gaze.

"You next," Koram said, his face breaking into a warm smile.

"Us?" Gamel said. "Brena has never done such a thing."

"Then now is his opportunity to try something new."

Gamel reached to pat Brena, rubbing his face. And then he gently shook Brena's reins.

Brena moved forward. Gamel felt his own body tensing, and tried to relax his legs over Brena's back as he moved: one step at a time, slightly sliding but still progressing, up, up the incline. Lidya's breath, against Gamel's neck, was short – but then they had reached the top.

Gamel quickly dismounted from Brena, quickly pressed his head to the horse in gratitude – helped Lidya down. And then, standing a few steps apart, Gamel took a deep breath and looked out to the Valley.

The sun, in all its magnificence, had risen over the Eastern Ridge. Gamel could see the Blue Lake, in the far distance: glistening in the early morning light. He remembered how he had felt, ascending Raven Hill – but now the full breadth and depth of the land before him utterly transcended his earlier joy.

The valley itself was much lower, much further away – beyond the Highland Forest, spread out at his feet. And now, to his left and right, felt in the icy wind, were the mountains of the North and South: their peaks almost within reach! Snow lit with yellow sun, clean, pure – unadulterated.

He longed to climb the highest peak: to grasp the snow in both hands, to throw it into the air – to roll freely amidst it. Childhood! Childhood…And yet he could not. Instead his journey was forcing him down a different path.

With a heavy sigh, in great reluctance, he turned his back on the valley, and the mountains, and now looked west.

This land he had never seen. The Sea captivated him first: he gasped in surprise. It was so vast! Still very distant, near the horizon: a thin blue strip, but stretching as far as he could see – no end to its reach. And between Gamel, and the Sea, was this new land: the dropping away of the Highland Ridge back into soil, a pine forest close by, beyond this barren rock, and then a final forest curving down into the western plains.

The greater part of their journey was still before them.

Gamel fixed his eyes on the Sea – and now Lidya was alongside him.

"So far…" he whispered, and felt her touch to his shoulder.

"Keep going, Gamel."

The Stone was beginning to burn again. *You will never make it.*

Lidya's grip tightened on him. "Look how far we have come."

He glanced again behind his back, to the home he was about to fully leave. And then, setting his jaw, he stepped forward – and stumbled.

"Gamel!"

The rock suddenly gave way, to fissures and caverns beneath. And now he was tumbling toward a massive drop.

"Lidi!" he cried, desperately trying to stop himself – her outstretched hand missed him. He rolled, tipped over the cavernous opening, dangled precariously between death and life – and then felt two strong hands lifting him again to safety.

It was Koram. Gamel sank heavily against the rock, scrambling for breath.

"How did you…?"

"I know this rock well, young Prince: I am certain of my step."

"Thank you!" Gamel gasped. "Thank you."

Koram tipped his head with a gentle smile, and Gamel smiled sadly back at him – but then, lying sprawled on the rock, he was seized.

*Your life is in my hands, Gamel: how often must I remind you?*

Chilled, Gamel clenched his teeth. The Northern warrior attack! And now this.

*My life does not belong to you!*

*Then to who?*

"To me!" Gamel cried out loud. "To me."

Koram was watching – a frown darkening his gaze, though with compassion.

"Gamel?"

Gamel choked – but again he turned his direction within.

*To you?* Soutar laughed, *A Heartland Prince? No, Gamel – your life belongs to me, and I will have it! I will have it.*

Shuddering, Gamel fleetingly hid his face in his arms. Then he thrust himself back onto his feet.

"Let's keep moving," he said to Koram. "Keep moving."

And Koram, studying his face, nodded his agreement.

"Only to the forest, and then we all must rest."

"Very well," Gamel whispered, "To the forest."

The horses now trekked downhill – toward the forest. Gamel frowned, on Brena. His body was sweating – his face flushing, despite the cold. He felt ill, and leaned forward into Brena's neck as they rode on.

"Gamel?" Lidya's voice was faint behind him, her touch soft on his back – as if from a distance. He could not reply – only grasped onto Brena.

Time passed – he did not know how long. Trees were around him, now, cloaking them all in shade, and yet they continued.

Sleep lulled him, but he dared not sleep. He drifted, saw an image of blood, jerked awake – and then he fell.

"Gamel!" Lidya's scream was far away. He rolled onto his back on the ground, and suddenly he was being smothered by something: couldn't breathe! Couldn't see…

*Put on the Stone.*

"No!" he gasped. "Get off me!"

If he put on the Stone, he knew he would be giving Soutar full access to his heart and soul: surrendering to him! Obeying him.

Hands were on him, now – Koram's hands, lifting his body, Lidya's hands snatching the stone from his pocket.

His vision cleared. He sank against Koram for a moment – and then he sank back onto his knees.

The Stone was there on the ground, before him: before all.

Gamel swayed slightly on his knees. He glanced up at Taierre – his face was grim, his brow furrowed, but he remained silent. Gamel looked at Koram – he also was silent. And then Gamel looked at Lidya.

She was staring intently at the Stone: Gamel could almost see her thoughts.

"What do we do now?" He asked her quietly.

"I don't know," she muttered back.

"What just happened, Gamel?" Koram asked, and Gamel stiffened – then he rose to his feet.

"The Stone," he began, gesturing loosely to it. "It has some kind of power. I can't hold it for long."

Koram's gaze was fixed on him. "You were talking to it," he said.

"I…" Gamel lapsed into his own silence.

Koram wandered closer – to stand next to the Stone.

"I dare not sleep with it, Koram," Gamel whispered. "In sleep I will have no control."

"What do you fear, Gamel?"

"I fear…I fear…" His body shuddered as he struggled to respond. "I fear him."

"Who?"

"Soutar."

He had said it. Head hanging, he awaited Koram's chastisement – but it never came.

"Soutar?" The Northerner's low voice explored.

"Yes."

"I have heard of that name…"

Gamel looked up at him with hope. "You already know of him?"

Sadness filled Koram's face – a strange shift of expression. "Yes, Gamel: I know of him."

"How?"

Koram drew out the stone of the North, and turned the lizard over in his hand. On the back was carved, in fine and fading lines, a name.

"In our dialect, Prince Gamel, this name is 'Suta'; in your dialect, 'Soutar'."

Gamel stared at him. Koram called now to Taierre, who, with extreme reluctance, pulled out again the stone of the South. The locust was turned over – and there was another name, carved faintly.

"It is…?" Koram questioned.

"'Sutier,'" Taierre said. "In Heartland dialect, yes: 'Soutar'"

Gamel shivered. "Why the three? To control all the kings…"

"To control?" Koram asked.

"Yes, to bring submission: even worship. But why is it only the Heartland stone which is active?"

"Wait, Gamel: what are you saying? What is this 'Soutar'?"

Gamel held his gaze – and clenched his teeth.

"It is…this thing. I can't explain it! This creature. He plagues me! He presses in – but why me? Why not you? Why only our stone: why not yours?"

"Perhaps because our stones are not carried by the ones for whom they were made."

Astonished, Gamel searched Koram. "What do you mean?"

"The stones of North and South, Prince Gamel: they were made for the line of the Kings. The Kings have passed them on to us to destroy. Perhaps Soutar has no desire for us – we were not marked for him – but he does desire you."

"Me?" Gamel stuttered, staring at him.

"Yes: you."

Gamel writhed under his gaze – but now Taierre was shifting on his feet.

"Koram!" He said. "You are only feeding the boy's fears! What do you know of this Soutar, truly? All we have is a name on three stones: anything more is presumptive superstition."

His face was white and hard, his eyes green glass.

"Presumption?" Koram's voice replied. "Never, my friend – I am only exploring possibilities…"

"You are wasting time!"

"The Prince is faltering under the Stone."

"His mind is weak! He and his kind, in the Heartland – readily succumbing to the myth!"

"Now who is presuming?"

Taierre's face reddened – and then he stood straight. "Enough of this!" he said. "Someone must prove to you all that this thing is false: I will take the stone."

And, before Gamel could stop him, Taierre strode forward, stooped to the ground, and grasped the stone by its cord.

"Stop!" Lidya's voice cried – but Taierre ignored her. Looking straight at Gamel, jaw set, he lowered the cord around his neck and laid the serpent Stone of Soutar on his chest.

The garnet eyes suddenly lit up blood red. Taierre's eyes changed to horror. He gasped, and stiffened – then clutched the stone away from his chest and threw it to the ground.

Gamel stared as the strong Southern warrior's body swayed, as if in the breeze: sickening waves of rotation. Then he fell.

"Taierre!" Koram ran to him – and terror seized Gamel's heart.

"Oh no – it *is* true..." Somehow Taierre's strong voice of dismissal had comforted him – but no more.

Lidya was beside him – and the stone, once again, lay face up on the ground: garnet eyes glowing.

Taierre's body rocked on the forest floor, his head in his arms. Koram was bending over him, grasping his shoulders – trying to stir him.

The Stone lay amongst dead leaves on the ground.

Gamel looked into Lidya's wide blue eyes. "You know what this means."

"No, Gamel."

"What else can we do?"

"Don't you dare!"

"I have to carry it! There is no other way!"

Koram was now standing straight before Gamel, Taierre still turned away at his feet.

"Taierre believed you were weak," Koram said. "He was mistaken."

"No," Gamel quickly replied, "He was correct."

"It is not that you are weak, son of Maki: it is that Soutar is strong."

Gamel smiled sadly at him. Certainly it was too late for fatherly encouragement.

"Soutar is strong, Sir Koram," he said, "And so he makes us weak."

Koram grimaced. And then Taierre stirred – twisting himself around, searching with erratic eyes and then finding Gamel's gaze.

Gamel shivered under his desolate stare.

"Have you worn it yet, Gamel?" Taierre choked.

"No," Gamel whispered, lowering himself to his knees before him. "No, Taierre: I have not."

Taierre's fingers now gripped on Gamel's arm. "I didn't understand…" His nails were digging into Gamel's skin – but it was the agony in his green eyes that pricked Gamel's eyes with tears.

"I'm so sorry," Gamel whispered.

"Don't take it up, Gamel." Now Koram's voice penetrated his grief – but Gamel still could not tear his eyes from Taierre's face.

"How can I not?"

"This thing is more powerful than you are."

"More powerful than all."

"Our kings," Taierre choked. "I understand…"

"We have to get the stones away from here," Gamel said, "Far away!"

"But we are still many miles from the coast, Gamel!" Koram's brown gaze was direct in warning. "We still have the forest, the Barren Slope, the Western Forest, and then the plains – just to get to the Ocean! Then you must cross the Sea, Gamel – have you considered this?"

"We still must try!"

"Yes – but you must not succumb to Soutar, or we will have no hope."

"Bind my hands! Drug me! Keep me asleep – use my body as a weapon against him."

Koram frowned in silent consideration, while Taierre groaned. "I don't think it will work."

"He can't come unless I invite him," Gamel said, looking hopefully up at Lidya again – but Taierre was shaking his head at Gamel's knees.

"He rapes, Gamel," he whispered. "Take on the stone, and you give him an open door to your heart. Does a man have both spirit and soul? He will show you, Gamel! He will show you your spirit – even as he decimates it with himself…"

Taierre's body began to retch – and he turned himself away again into his own arms.

Gamel looked sadly at him. "To stand by and do nothing is to let others be raped by my legacy."

"Not your legacy," Koram said gently. "This was not your doing."

"No," Gamel said, closing his eyes. "Not my doing, in the beginning: but now, as the Stone falls to me, it becomes my legacy."

"It is a legacy that belongs to us all."

"Yet there is only one Prince of the Heartland: and I am the one he wants."

Chills went up his spine – and now Lidya was before his face.

"You must not wear this thing," she said. "Let me wear it."

Gamel was astounded at her offer. "Lidi – he rapes! Have you forgotten what he did to you?"

Her face clouded into grey. "I have not forgotten."

"I cannot inflict this upon you."

Lidya shook her head. "Do you not see?" she said. "He wants to rule all of Altenhine through you! The North and the South, and the Heartland: the kings are resisting! He is seeking new, young blood – a new body and spirit to dwell within: to rule within! Submit to him, and our downfall will quickly follow!"

Gamel swallowed. "Drug me!" he said.

"Drug you?" she replied. "In what state, Gamel? Locked within with Soutar? No control over body or mind?"

"That is the price I must pay to get rid of this thing!"

"It won't work!" Taierre cried. "He is too strong."

"It's too late: I must act." Gamel silenced all now with his words. "This is my decision: I will take on the Stone, now."

He looked down at the serpent at his feet. The eyes seemed to be watching him, still lit. Gamel swallowed – and then quickly stooped to lift the cord over his head, placing the Stone over his heart.

A gasp was torn from him. Suddenly a pulsating energy was upon him, surging through his body, throwing his head back – intoxicating him. He felt lifted from within – heat permeating through every part, stimulating: alive.

Gamel felt the presence of another: felt his substance, not physical, yet alive; unseen, yet known. He filled Gamel – he empowered him. He was the source.

For a moment, Gamel glanced outside of himself – and noticed his body was lifted above the ground. Then he was standing again – the energy within easing to a background throb.

Koram was staring at him. Gamel smiled. Taierre was sitting on the ground, watching – Gamel shrugged. He noticed his sister frowning at him – and felt strangely bored by her.

"Let's go," he said to Koram.

"Go?"

"Now! I will see you on the Barren Slope."

"Gamel – that is three hours ride…"

"We will do it in one."

"Gamel!" Lidya's hands were reaching for him, but he shoved her away.

"One hour, Koram – we will wait for you!"

And he seized the reins of Brena, thrust himself onto his back, and whisked him into a trot.

Trees flooded past Gamel, on both sides. Brena obeyed him – Gamel laid a hand on his neck, and whispered to him: he sped faster and faster. The energy within poured out through Gamel's hand into the beast, urging him on: empowering him also.

Gamel lifted his face into the breeze: invigorated. What more could he do? What more? He drew Brena to a halt, slipped off his back – and went to a tree. Here he could climb! Easily, without much thought, he ascended the tree – reaching near the top, before the trunk divided, looking out across the tops of the pines surrounding him, seeing colour as he had never seen it before: vibrant green, fine textured pine leaves, yellow and green pigeons startled at his presence, wings flapping – the beat of their movement crisp to his ears, low tones, vibrating resonance…

Swiftly he left the tree, seized Brena, trotted on and on, free, alive – his thoughts, his senses, his body, all fast, all growing, all excelling.

Gamel emerged from the cover of the forest onto the Barren Slope.

Here, his vision was unconstrained. Still on Brena, still trotting now over bare rock, digging his heels in, he stretched out his arms and lifted his face to the sky.

"Yes!"

The breadth of the land was his, as far as the eye could see: the forest behind, the stretch of the rock to right and left, and falling down away toward the Western Forest below: his!

*You are the King of Altenhine.*

The thought stole his breath away. He was the King! Now, here, at last: he was the King.

But there was also someone else. Gamel saw in the distance a figure, familiar, perhaps a hundred feet away – and then, suddenly, only ten feet: bringing Brena up short on his hind legs, with a protesting neigh.

It was Michel.

Gamel stared at his Heartland hair, and at his Heartland clothes. He clenched his teeth.

"Get out of my way."

Brena stood now, shifting on his four legs, disgruntled but unwilling to proceed.

"No." Michel said.

Gamel kicked Brena's side, but he would not move – and so Gamel dismounted to stand before Michel.

"This is my land."

Michel shook his head. "You are mistaken."

"I am the Prince of the Heartland."

"That you are."

"With Soutar I become King!"

Now Michel's expression changed – Gamel saw, with heightened awareness, every detail: the wrinkles at the corner of his downturned mouth, the darkening shade of his blue eyes – he saw all, but he could not comprehend the sorrow.

"A human kingship," Michel said, "Even in partnership with Soutar, does not bring you true ownership, Gamel son of Maki."

Gamel resisted his words. "This is my ancestral right!"

"No, Gamel: have you forgotten? This is your ancestral curse."

"Leave me!" Gamel cried. "I don't want you!"

"I will leave at the right time."

"The right time is now!"

He stared into Michel's eyes – but Michel's gaze did not falter. Neither did his body move.

"Will you force me aside, son of Maki?"

Gamel frowned.

*Move him.*

*No.*

*Move him now!*

A sudden urge took Gamel to hit Michel across the face – to shove him out of the way. He fought the urge.

"No!"

Something in Michel's face softened – a new light in his eyes. Gamel was suddenly taken by the purity of the blue: with his new vision, he could see – there was no blemish in the colour, as Gamel's blue had variation, rather, Michel's blue was perfect, like the colour of the eyes of a baby.

"Who are you?" Gamel breathed, and Michel smiled sadly.

"I am only a guide."

"A guide? From who? To where?"

"To choice, Gamel: to freedom."

Perplexed, Gamel searched him. "I have never felt as free as I do right now."

Again, Michel smiled sadly. "I know, Gamel, but beware. Do not so easily forget the lessons learnt by your father and brother."

There was a movement from behind him. Gamel turned to see Koram and Taierre emerging from the forest onto the Barren Slope, on Tenith and Stiar. And Lidya was there, sitting behind Koram, peering from behind his back to search for Gamel. He had left her behind, in his haste!

"The right time has come."

Astonished, Gamel turned back in response to Michel's voice – but now he was gone. And now, instead, Lidya was before him.

"What do you think you are doing?" Lidya said, quickly dismounting from Tenith. "Riding off like that, leaving me behind!"

"I..." Gamel spluttered. "I..."

Koram also dismounted, standing behind Lidya – smiling a little while Lidya poked her finger. But Taierre remained seated on Stiar, watching Gamel steadily: his green eyes dim, his voice silent.

Lidya slapped his arm, drawing back his attention. "Well?"

Gamel cast his eyes over her face. "Sorry, mother."

She scowled, and he grinned. "I felt like a ride."

"Indeed," Koram said. "And how was it?"

"It was great!" He stretched out his arms, and then reached out a hand to stroke Brena.

"So fast! He was wonderful!"

"He?"

"Brena! And...and the land."

Gamel cast his eyes now again over the barren slope – brown rock, up and down, a few tufts of grass in cracks, and across to either side the foothills of North and South: the Highland Elevation Forest above, the Western Forest below. Soutar was within him: he felt him – felt his power, and his presence; his ownership of Altenhine.

"What about the land?" Taierre asked, his gaze penetrating him – and Gamel shrugged.

"It is no concern of yours. You must be tired."

Taierre's jaw clenched before him. "I will not sleep."

"We have ridden through night and morning," Koram said. "We must rest."

"I'm not tired," Gamel said. "But you, Koram, and Lidi, can sleep."

Koram now looked across the slope. "There is an enclosure this way," he said, gesturing a little south. "Come." And he led them across the rock, to a crevice – into which the three horses could descend. "This will provide cover."

"Very well," Gamel said. "You hide in there with Lidya and Taierre – I'll keep guard out here on the slope."

"I will also keep watch on the slope," Taierre added – and Gamel raised his eyebrows.

"No need," he said. "I can guard us all."

"Nonetheless..."

"I don't need your services anymore."

Taierre was staring at him – but now Koram stood between.

"Let Taierre guard with you," he said quietly. "He will not sleep now, but later."

"Very well," Gamel shrugged. "Let him watch, if he wishes – it is no concern of mine."

Koram's brown eyes studied him – he frowned slightly. And then he nodded his respect, and moved away. Lidya's blue eyes also were on him – he shook his head curtly, and she grimaced and moved after Koram.

Gamel was now alone with Taierre, on the Barren Slope.

Gamel lounged back on the rock, hands behind his head, gazing up at the sky. Small white clouds were above him, converging – and, further west, grey clouds were forming.

"Might be tricky if it rains, Taierre," he said, ignoring formality. "How would our horses fare on a slippery Barren Slope?"

"Stiar is familiar with riding in rain."

"I don't know about Brena, though," Gamel said. "He might get scared. Do you think I should stop the rain from falling?"

Gamel looked at Taierre, now – still mounted on Stiar. His white face was stone – his jaw rigid in silence. Gamel pushed himself to his feet, and now circled around Stiar – around Taierre.

"What happened to you, Taierre?" he began. "You suddenly changed. One moment you boasted you could wear the stone – the next moment you were grovelling on the ground. I thought you said Soutar didn't exist?"

Anger flowed through his body, now: potent, and enticing. Was it his own? Was it Soutar? Perhaps it was both, together – escalating toward a kind of culmination. Taierre's body was rigid now, on Stiar – the horse also was beginning to shift in discomfort. Gamel enjoyed their responses, and sought more gratification again.

"You must feel a fool."

"I was wrong," Taierre muttered.

"You know his power."

"Yes."

"Then know this, Taierre of the South, first hand to the King: I am no mere boy!"

Gamel seized him now – dragging him with both fists off Stiar and onto the ground. Taierre's body was shaking as Gamel knelt over him.

"You do not fear death, Southern warrior."

"I do not," Taierre whispered – his green eyes fixed on Gamel's eyes.

"There are some things worse than death."

"Yes."

"Do you believe the Heartland is weak now?"

Taierre's body was stiff, his face contorting as he struggled to reply.

"I did not understand."

"Did you believe King Hemin was weak?" Gamel hissed, grasping Taierre's blonde plaits and tugging, forcing tears into the Southerner's eyes. "Do you see now the source of his strength to rule?"

"I see it," Taierre whispered.

"Do you see now, Southern fool, that I am his true heir?"

Fire filled Gamel, at that moment – fire flashing out of his eyes, and through his mouth: fire pouring forth through his pores. Taierre writhed beneath him now, as if in real pain – but not a physical pain: some other kind – a pain, a suffering, from within.

"Stop," he pleaded – but Gamel could not.

"Do you think I want a new kind of alliance, Southern messenger?" he cried. "I do not – and I will not! I desire the alliance of old: stronger, richer – I desire to own! I will be King!"

And now Gamel grasped Taierre's head, and bore down on him.

"You belong to me!"

Taierre's head fell back, and Gamel felt something shift from within him into Taierre. The man screamed beneath him – and the sound jolted Gamel. For a moment he floundered – and then he jerked himself away from Taierre, stumbling, and falling.

Gamel's body tumbled down the slope, further and further, and then came to a stop. Grasping the stone on his chest, now he curled himself up into a tight ball: staring out ahead of himself.

Koram was there, sword drawn, behind his back. Gamel did not see him, but he knew.

"Kill me," he whispered. "Destroy him."

But Koram moved in front of him, re-sheathing his sword.

"Take off the stone," he replied: his voice deep, gentle – father-like.

Gamel closed his eyes tightly shut. He tried to lift the stone from his chest: it was fixed over his heart.

"I cannot," he breathed. "It has become too much a part of me."

"What would happen if it was removed?"

"I don't know! Agony! Can't do it…"

"Must we?"

"I'm sure I would die – but you must."

"No, not yet: for someone must carry it."

Lidya was there, now, again. Her eyes were wet – red. She lay down in front on him, on the rock, as a child: her face before his.

"I'm here," she said – and he cried.

"The Stone!"

"I know, Gamel! I've always known."

"I can't control it!"

"I know."

"I can't control him…"

Gamel shuddered. Friedrich had succumbed – had been consumed by Soutar! Maki had somehow co-existed: somehow appeased him. But he himself, Gamel? What was his fate to be with the stone?

"If something happens to me," he said, "this horrible thing will fall to you!"

Her face was controlled in compassion. "I know."

"I can't let that happen: I must live! I must continue!"

He thrust himself back up onto his feet – onto the rock – and swayed a little. Koram stood to his right, his hand on the shaft of his sword: ready, but waiting. Lidya also rose to her feet. And Taierre…

Taierre lay motionless on the rock.

Gamel went to him: sank to his knees before him.

"Do not touch me, son of Hemin," Taierre said – staring through Gamel's body. Gamel closed his eyes.

"I am sorry," he whispered.

"That is no concern of mine."

"If the choice only influenced my own fate, I would accept your judgment."

This drew Taierre's gaze – slight surprise softening his rigid frown for a moment.

"So you would." The frown returned, and the distant stare. "And I would carry out your execution, Prince Gamel, if I believed that would truly liberate our lands."

Gamel trembled before him. "You don't believe it?"

"I do not: Soutar would merely choose another."

"Then what?"

"There is no hope."

Gamel stared at his expressionless face. No hope? Could it be that there was, in fact, no real solution to Soutar?

"I cannot believe that," he breathed – and now Soutar, within, responded.

Gamel was down, the rock cold on his back – and darkness smothered him. Soutar pressed in, stealing all light from his sight, filling his smell with foul waste, and his hearing with his own voice.

"Do not betray me, son of Maki," Soutar said, "Or I will make you suffer a thousand deaths."

And now the pain came. Gamel's body was burning, as if lit – his heart consumed by Soutar's hatred. His spirit was tormented: life, hope, and deepest love, overridden, raped by Soutar's own malice.

"You are mine!"

Gamel's body jerked, wholly out of his own control – wholly controlled by another. And then, after what seemed like an eternity, it was over.

Gamel lay on his back, on the hard rock. He stared up at the sky: the grey clouds had gathered, and now heavy cold drops were falling out of the sky onto his face. Koram and Lidya's face peered over him – both drawn with concern.

Gamel stared at them – and then he fainted.

CHAPTER FIFTEEN: Vulnerability

Gamel jerked awake, to find himself leaning over Koram's back – riding.

"What are you doing?" he cried, shuddering, "Stop!"

Tenith jerked, and then suddenly rose up on back legs – tumbling Gamel off onto leaves on the forest floor.

Gamel gasped, desperately looking around himself. It was dark! He was surrounded by trees – pine, maple: crimson dead leaves, barely lit by starlight and moonlight.

"Where are we?"

He felt naked – exposed, as a child. Someone had again draped a blanket over him, and he clung to it as Koram settled Tenith and dismounted.

"Lidya," Gamel pleaded, and Koram laid a hand on his shoulder.

"She is safe."

"Soutar isn't here!"

"Then where?"

"I don't know!" Gamel said, "But he'll be back soon!"

He lifted his arms over his face – and felt Koram's hands directing him up against a tree.

"Speak to me, Gamel of the Heartland," the Northerner said gently. "Tell me everything I must know."

"Soutar," Gamel whispered, "He wants to rule us all."

"Has he not already done so for five hundred years since Hemin?"

"No," Gamel said. "It's much more than that now."

"What?"

"I mean complete domination. Keep Lidi away!"

"What do you mean?"

"Keep her away! Keep her away!"

Desperately Gamel thrust himself to his feet, longing to run – longing to continue, but feeling confused.

"Where am I?"

"In the Western Forest."

"Oh, no!"

"What?"

"He has an army!"

"What?"

"An army, like him! An army of spirits, following him – he's gone, to gather them! They are here."

And now, suddenly, Soutar was back. Gamel found himself thrown down, smothered again as screams were torn from his throat.

"Stop it!" he cried.

*Obey me!*

"I can't!"

*Then suffer!*

Pain filled him, drowning him – but then it was gone, and, again, so was Soutar.

79

Gamel tried to lift himself up – his arms collapsed under his weight. But now Koram was lifting him again onto Tenith.

"Follow me," he murmured – and Gamel clutched on his back, closing his eyes as Koram rode.

*Help me!* Gamel pleaded silently within. *Help me, help me, help me...*

"Hold on," Koram said – and they rode, through dark shadows of trees, on and on, though Gamel felt a growing sense of inevitable doom.

Time passed. Gamel dozed on Koram's back, and then jerked awake. Trees flooded past – nauseating in their speed. Gamel's vision blurred. The Stone still rested on his chest, fixed to his skin – still Soutar's access, though Gamel no longer offered himself freely.

"How can he rule, without my choice?" he said, inadvertently aloud.

"He cannot," Koram said, turning his voice toward Gamel in the wind. "Or so the writings say."

"The writings? You have read them?"

"I have read the writings of the North."

"What else do you know? Do they speak of the Army?"

"They speak of a coming Age of Soutar."

Gamel shifted in fear on Tenith's back. "Please tell me, Koram."

"Slavery, Gamel," Koram said grimly. "He hates Mankind – so the writings say."

"Why?"

"The writings do not explain – but...there are other legends, Gamel, from much longer ago."

"You don't mean the whispers..."

"Whispers?"

"In the Heartland: something 'big'. The common folk whisper of such things."

"Sometimes 'common' folk are closer to the truth than the wisest of the wise."

Hana's face was before him.

*"They whisper of something bigger than a king."*

*"Do you wish for such a thing?"*

*"I feel no such need."*

No such need...and now here he was, Prince of the Heartland, next in line to be King – fleeing through forest, lying on the back of a Northerner, wholly at the whim of Soutar.

"What do your legends say, Koram?"

Koram threw back a smile to him. "They are legends, my friend: I cannot vouch for their accuracy. There are similar legends from the South."

"Please tell me."

"They speak of spirits: of powers. And of a higher power – a higher Spirit."

"A higher Spirit?"

"More powerful than the rest."

"The spirits in the legends: they are like Soutar?"

"Perhaps."

"And the more powerful Spirit?"

Koram paused. "They say he has frightening power: so great one cannot stand before him and live."

Gamel shivered. "There is no hope there, Koram: he sounds worse than Soutar."

"And yet..." Again Koram paused then continued. "I don't know, Gamel. There is much fear of him in the legends – and yet, also, something else."

"Something else?"

"Love."

Nausea filled Gamel's stomach at the thought: love? Love for a spirit?

"The 'Unseen One'," Koram continued. "He is spoken of quite often. He was perceived, somehow, beyond sight, by some. Who can say whether this is truth or fantasy?"

"Yes," Gamel said. "Who can say?"

They rode on in silence, for a time – and Gamel rested his head again on Koram's back. He longed for sleep – yet he could not dare succumb. Tenith sped forth, under moonlight and starlight – Gamel could not fathom how. Yet he somehow trusted him – and also, strangely, fully, in that moment, trusted Koram.

"Why are you helping me?" he muttered, half to himself, "I am your ultimate threat: I could take over your Land."

Koram again threw him a smile: this time tinged with sadness. "You forget, Gamel: I too am human."

"Human?"

"Human first, and a Northerner second."

The words filled Gamel's eyes with tears. "You are risking a lot, Koram, riding anywhere with me."

"You cannot proceed without my help."

"I cannot." The admission pained him. "But I don't understand: why do you not fear me as Taierre fears me?"

Koram was silent – and then he replied. "Do you wish me to fear you?"

"No," Gamel said. "I do not."

"Then what do you want from me, son of Maki?"

Koram's words went straight to Gamel's heart – straight to his pain.

"What do you mean?" he whispered, troubled.

"We both know what I mean," Koram gently replied. "I am human first, Gamel."

Gamel stared into the darkness: the shadows of the trees blurring in cold wind across his wet eyes, as Koram spoke.

"Your father..."

"Do not speak of him!"

"King Maki..."

"...had his duties."

"But there is one duty he clearly neglected, perhaps to the peril of us all."

Gamel bowed his head, closing his eyes. One duty…one responsibility, discarded: fatherhood. But was Gamel a fool to desire something more than mere duty from a parent: to dare to long for something so great and unreachable as love?

"It is a strange thing" Gamel said into the wind, "That the fate of us all could rest on a simple act of human compassion: a stranger riding with a friend in the night."

"And yet," Koram replied, "If not human compassion, on what else should our fate rest?"

Gamel frowned, straining to see ahead. Was there a clearing? Had they almost overcome the threat of the Forest, to thrust out onto the Western Plains? No – there were still more trees beyond.

Human compassion – for now Gamel leaned on Koram, and his compassion: for now he was carried by human friendship. But what was Koram next to the power of Soutar? Under the domination of spirit, how could there be any reprieve?

"Ride on," Gamel whispered – and silently Koram, and Tenith, obeyed.

CHAPTER SIXTEEN: Choice

Gamel awoke – to find light penetrating through leaves above his face. The sun had lifted, but not yet fully overhead – and the sky above was grey. It seemed a strange mixture of bright and dull, with cool moisture as during a sun shower.

Branches dug into his back. He shifted, and then searched – Koram was there, lying on the ground opposite, under another tree, asleep. Gamel rose to his feet, flicking off dead leaves from his trousers, and then looked into the shadow between the trees. They were still in the Western Forest? Gamel shuddered. Which direction was the right one? The ground now had flattened – they were not far from the sea.

Without Koram, now, Gamel knew he would be lost. And yet the man was sleeping – exposed, unable even to erect a tent: as if blissfully accepting of his own fate.

Gamel could not share in his sentiment.

He peered between the trees again, reaching out to touch the rough bark of a pine. What was it he feared? Soutar: Soutar, and all of his followers. He knew they were there, unseen: his skin pricked with cold. And who else hid in this Forest? What other exiles from North, and South, and from the Heartland, might have made their home there?

A heavy darkness resided there, amongst the trees – Koram did not know it, but Gamel, himself, knew it. They were waiting, the spirits: waiting to take their prize.

A branch snapped. Gamel spun on his foot, instinctively grasping the stone on his chest – and there, before him, stood Taierre.

Gamel's heart raced – yet the Southerner's face brought enormous relief. He breathed, while Taierre watched him – and now he saw the warrior's face become calm.

"I see you have returned," Taierre said.

"Returned?"

"You are your normal self again."

Gamel laughed, suddenly – nervously. "Normal?" he said. "I don't even know what that means anymore."

Taierre nodded silently, and Gamel looked at him. There was so much to say! And yet he struggled to get one word out.

"Taierre…"

"We need not speak of it."

"I should not have taken up the stone."

"You had no choice."

"No – but I am still sorry."

The green eyes softened. For a moment Gamel saw beyond the hardened and hidden Southern way – saw feeling in the warrior.

"I know," Taierre said.

"What should I do?" Gamel quickly asked.

"You must resist him."

"I will try."

"But that will not be enough." It was Lidya's voice.

Gamel looked to see her emerging between the trees, leading Brena by the rein. Lidya! Her hair was messy around her neck, her blue eyes wide, in seeing him – her face breaking into a joyous smile.

Gamel grasped her hand, and then drew her into his embrace.

"Where were you?"

"I rode!" she said, "On Brena! With Taierre and Stiar."

"You did it – well done!"

"And you, Gamel?" She drew back to search his gaze. "Tell me everything."

Tears filled his eyes. He trembled, exposed before her – but she grasped his arms, and he continued.

"It was horrible," he whispered. "He is horrible. You know, Lidya! You know…"

Sorrow filled her gaze. "Yes, Gamel – I know."

"He…" Gamel choked. "He wants to take over."

"I know."

"He has an army."

"An army?" It was Taierre. Gamel saw fear now undisguised in his eyes.

"Yes, Taierre," Gamel replied. "He wants to take over all of our lands."

"And so we will still proceed to the Coast." It was Koram – now joining them from the side.

Taierre shifted in discomfort, looking at his colleague.

"Koram…"

"Do not fear, Taierre."

"How can I not be afraid?"

Gamel watched Koram, longing for a response – longing for a reason for the trust he seemed to have gained in their quest. But no reason came.

Koram was silent – and then Lidya spoke.

"The One across the Sea."

"I don't know him," Gamel shrugged. "How can I know he will help?"

"Soutar knows him."

"Lidi…" Gamel whispered. "He might hear you!"

Now Lidya shrugged – the one who had once feared. "He already knows what we are trying to do, Gamel," she said. "My words make no difference to him. But they might make a difference for you."

"How?"

"Listen to me, Gamel, not to Soutar! Listen to me! This One, across the Sea – he is our hope."

Gamel trembled before her. Hope? Dare he trust in it? Dare he try for it? Her face was before him, waiting: expectant.

"Understand," Lidya said, "Soutar will not simply stand aside and let you leave! You must know, Gamel – in all of your being, you must know what you truly want if we are ever to escape him."

84

Gamel swallowed. What did he want? Freedom, yes – freedom from pain, freedom from domination: freedom for his friends. But at what cost? This Magician across the sea – what might his price be, to secure this freedom?

They mounted the horses: all four people of Altenhine now as one. Gamel on Brena, with Lidya behind, looked across to Koram and Taierre – the warriors instinctively took up their positions as before, Koram and Tenith in front, and Taierre and Stiar behind.

"Lead us," Gamel asked Koram – and the Northerner nodded, turned, and broke Tenith into a trot.

Gamel followed him, on Brena – feeling Lidya against his back. It couldn't be much longer, surely, he reasoned: on the flat, darting between the pine trees.

Hours past – Gamel could not say how many – and then they broke free from the forest onto the Western Plains.

Gamel took in a deep breath. Now Brena rode freely, across grass. Ahead, not so far away, Gamel saw the ocean: wonderful, vast, almost within reach. The sun was lowering in the sky, toward the flat horizon of water – yellow warmth reflected back, yet soon to disappear.

"Hurry," Gamel whispered to Brena, "Hurry."

A small dark silhouette was in the distance, bobbing up and down on the water – a ship! Gamel could just make out the shape of a sail, getting larger and larger as they sped toward the coast: a wooden craft, large hull, and a huge sail of linen.

"Who are they?" Gamel cried out to Koram, over the riding wind.

"Sailors from Yerim!" Koram called back.

"Why are they here?"

"I am never clear as to their purpose."

"They are no threat?"

"They never venture far onto the land."

"Why?"

Gamel glanced back – to the edge of the Western Forest. It still seemed dark, and foreboding.

"Could it be they feel the spirits too?"

Taierre was there, riding behind: closest to the Forest. Gamel glanced quickly at his stern face, and then turned back toward the Coast. The Plain, somehow, seemed safe – a neutral territory, owned by no one nation: a transition from land to sea.

And now the grassland surrendered to sand, on a vast white beach.

With delight, Gamel drew Brena to a halt and dismounted. He rushed to the sand, scooping it in his hands – fine grains, almost like dust, fell through his hands: shells were caught amongst his fingers – white, smooth, oval, others like snail shells, purple, or grey.

He laughed. And then he looked up.

Soutar was before him.

Heart pounding, Gamel stared at him. The spirit stood now as a man - tall, muscular, blonde curls: a strange light emanating through his Heartland white shirt and black trousers. The representation of his home adulterated with eerie spiritual power struck terror into Gamel's heart.

"Join me," Soutar said, smiling – and Gamel choked.

"I cannot."

Soutar's eyes were dark – almost black, as though without colour.

"Join me, or I will conquer you."

Gamel felt his throat constricting, robbing him of speech. "If you conquer," he gasped, "you will never truly rule."

Soutar stepped closer to him. Behind Soutar, the sun was beginning to set – blood red filling the sky, reflected in the ocean below.

Soutar breathed over Gamel – and he swayed, intoxicated. The stone became fire on his chest – Soutar was within him again, drawing him, enticing him.

*I will make you strong – I will give you life.*

Invigoration swept through his veins, and into his heart – power pulsating through his being. Gamel gasped with pleasure – but still he resisted.

"I don't want this…"

*Not this?* Soutar chided. *Then perhaps this.*

Now pleasure was transcended by pain: burning, through veins, into his heart, pulsating to every part – escalating to agony. Yet as soon as it was given, it was gone.

Gamel was now on his knees, before Soutar.

"Give yourself to me."

"Can't…"

"How long do you think you can fight me, Gamel?"

Gamel closed his eyes tightly – but cold long fingers lifted his chin.

"Look at me."

He looked – and saw, behind Soutar, a vast sea of faces: no bodies, white, angry eyes, with the fading light of the sun through and behind.

"We are ready."

"Ready for what?" Gamel asked, trembling.

"Ready for you – and for all."

And now Soutar pressed in to Gamel – now his father's face was before him: scowling, laughing.

*Fool!*

Gamel writhed, but Soutar pressed closer. *I will give you the power to overcome him.*

"Stop it," Gamel pleaded – but Soutar would not stop. Now another memory was upon him: beating pain, his father whipping his childhood back – tears squeezed from his eyes.

"I hate him!" Gamel cried.

*Hate him with me.*

"I…can't see…"

Light was disappearing – darkness was descending.

"He killed your brother."

"He killed Friedrich!"

"Together we will overcome him."

"I hate him! I hate him!"

Gamel clenched his teeth together, now – grinding them in his fury.

"Take my hand." Soutar's hand was outstretched to him: a human form, but blatantly not human. "Reject him, receive me, and you will destroy his influence over you forever."

"Father…"

A sudden flash of insight came to him – a sudden realization, on the verge of surrender: a different kind of voice.

*Who will be your Father?*

*Choice!* He screamed from within to Michel. *You said you would give me the choice!*

He felt himself slipping beyond control, reaching, in agony, for Soutar's hand…but then, suddenly, a different kind of agony took him.

Burning pain drowned him, tearing another scream from his lips, as the Stone of Soutar was ripped from his heart and chest.

Lidya also was a descendant of Hemin: the only one able to remove the Stone.

Shocked, Gamel fell to the ground – but now he could see: Lidya was standing between him and Soutar! She was taking the Stone to her own chest – not in submission, but in defiance! Gamel saw Soutar's face – his rigidity, his fury: his malicious intent. He smothered her, with his access – he raped her. But his invasion distracted him from Gamel – and now Gamel noticed another, standing on the deck of a ship, only twenty feet away: a figure lit, in the darkness – human, brown curls, and Heartland clothes.

*Now is your choice.*

Instinctively, Gamel moved. Grasping Lidya in his arms, the Stone of Soutar burning into her chest, he ran for the ship.

The vessel's anchor had been lifted – Gamel saw it, and ran harder.

"Wait!" he cried. "Wait!"

Faces looked out to him, from the deck: black skinned faces, framed by black crimped curls – frightened faces. They had seen the spirits too!

Koram's voice called out from behind him, in a different tongue – and somehow, in that moment, Gamel understood it.

"Wait!" Koram cried. "This is the one we spoke of – the one your sages spoke of!"

"How can this be the one?" A young voice replied, his dialect strange and beautiful.

"He is the King of Altenhine," Taierre's voice now added. "He alone can grant you access to our lands."

Astonished, Gamel reached the ship – and desperately reached out to the hands on the deck.

"Please!" he cried, trying to lift Lidya up over the wooden rail. "He speaks the truth."

Black skinned hands received her – even as deep dark eyes stared at him, and then over his head.

"You must come!" An older voice insisted to Koram and Taierre. "Or we cannot trust this boy."

"We cannot come!" Taierre protested.

The man was frowning, shaking his head – and then Koram's voice spoke.

"I will come."

Lidya was on deck, and Koram beside her. The ship was pulling away, and Gamel, clinging still on the outside, glanced back to Taierre. He stood, rooted to the ground, feet in seawater – white face pale now in twilight. Behind him, Soutar stood – and the sea of faces.

"Go," Taierre whispered – but Gamel shook his head.

"No," he said. "You must also come."

"I will distract him."

"No, Taierre – you still carry the Stone of the South! Your king has given you this mission."

Taierre's jaw set – and then he ran, and caught the railing, and easily dragged himself up.

Gamel was the last, draped still over the hull of the ship. Wind caught in the massive sail above him – an evening breeze taking a hold, and sweeping the ship backwards away from the shore. Gamel glanced over his shoulder, to see Soutar standing on the beach, with his army – staring, in fury, at Gamel. Was there some unseen law that stopped Soutar's pursuit? Surely a spirit could not fear water: but was there some other boundary that even the spirits must obey?

Wind blew through water in Gamel's saturated clothes. The Stone was off his chest – in that moment he breathed easy, invigorated with health and life from a natural means: the cool of the Ocean. But his hands were beginning to stiffen with the cold, in his grip on the railing.

Taierre's hands gripped his arms, and lifted him over – for a moment Gamel lay on the damp deck, struggling to believe that he could be on a ship leaving Altenhine. How had they succeeded? How had they escaped?

He glanced up to the bow of the ship – and there he saw the figure again, seemingly unseen by the others: brown curls lit now in starlight.

"Michel…" he whispered.

*Yes,* came the silent reply.

"You saved us."

*Not I.*

Now Michel smiled, and tilted his head. Then he was gone – and in his place stood the captain of the ship.

"To Yerim!" the older voice cried, and cheers joined his voice from the crew.

"To Yerim," Gamel whispered – and he closed his eyes, and finally succumbed to sleep.

# PART THREE

## YERIM

### CHAPTER SEVENTEEN: To Yerim

Lidya lay still.

The deck of the ship was dark. Night had descended – the same cool wind filling their sails, sweeping them to the unknown land, also blowing through her wet shirt and trousers, making her shiver hard.

In front of her, not one arm's length away, was Gamel. He was sleeping deeply – his face, young, handsome, was somehow more at peace: his sleep no longer disturbed by Soutar.

The grubby white shirt was soaking a little with blood from his chest – from the wound she had created, tearing the stone away. But he was at rest – and, for this, Lidya felt relief.

Yet now she carried the Stone.

The serpent gazed up at her, from her hand: blood red garnet eyes. Lidya swallowed – closed her eyes, and shuddered. *Soutar.* For a moment, again, he had taken her – she had been overcome. Horror! Smothering malice – choking control. And yet this time it had been different, somehow. Somehow, somehow, she had overcome him! Somehow, even the midst of his oppression, she had won.

Not by her own doing! She would never deceive herself into believing this – she was lost, she knew, in the grip of that place of utter torment: suffering forever – the Kings of the Heartland had written of it! The Pit of Death – the Death of the spirit: Soutar would have held her there.

And yet, something had happened. Out of her act, something had happened: she was in her brother's arms, and he was running! He had regained his sight – he had regained his true self, and now was propelling her forward to...to Yerim...

With tears, Lydia now stared down at the Stone. "You fear the One," she whispered to Soutar. "You are not pursuing us, because of Him."

In this hope she dwelt – curling herself up in a ball, wrapping her arms around her legs.

Koram now lowered himself before her – she gazed up into his warm face, lit by starlight. He was carrying a blanket, surely from the ship – and now laid it over her.

"Princess," he murmured, and Lidya smiled sadly at him.

"No," she said. "Not a Princess."

"A princess of heart, my lady: I saw what you did."

His words pained her, somehow – though she could not explain why. Princess? Why did she no longer feel this?

"He steals, Sir Koram," she whispered. "You do not understand."

Koram's face now reflected her own sadness. "I do understand, Lidya," he said, "But I still see beauty."

She gasped. "You see too much."

"Forgive me: I speak my mind."

"As do I."

"Your brother…" Koram paused, and Lidya frowned, shifting with discomfort. "He is your twin?"

"Yes."

"Both, then…" He seemed now to speak to himself.

"Both?"

Koram smiled sadly, and reached to touch her face – she struggled to push the familiar pain away, but could not fully disguise it.

"Both," Koram said again. "Both suffer the same ailment, but in different ways – brother and sister."

"Do you enjoy your study of us, Sir Koram?" Lidya suddenly asked curtly. "Perhaps you have the luxury of observation, while my brother and I fight for our very lives."

Koram now grasped her hand, and lifted her from her curled up position – to stand on her feet on the deck.

"There," Koram said, his face warm and smiling. "That's the spirit."

Lidya laughed in surprise, and then searched him. "You are a good man, Sir Koram."

"Insofar as any man can be good, young lady: I too have flaws."

Lidya looked at his rugged brown face, with a few wrinkles – his dark brown curls. He felt almost the same age as…as…

"Your father," Koram said.

Lidya flinched. "Father?"

"Does he know you are here?"

Now Lidya stared at him, caught. Then she shook her head, to try to jerk herself back to reality. What had she been thinking?

"Father?" she stuttered. "Yes, he knows. And yet would he really believe this, Koram: that Gamel and I are actually travelling across the Sea of Yerim? That I can't say."

"He underestimates you both."

Lidya smiled sadly. "He underestimates Gamel," she said quietly. "As for me, there has never been any estimation."

Koram's expression then made Lidya suddenly want to cry. What was it? A wry smile, a knowing gaze – worse still, even admiration?

"It seems King Maki has been blind to many things."

"Yes," Lidya quickly replied. "But I cannot blame him."

"No?" Koram said in surprise. "Your brother certainly does."

"I know, Koram, but that is my brother's undoing."

Koram tilted his head slightly in thought, searching her. "You understand a great deal, Lidya – a surprising amount for your age."

"Perhaps."

"And yet, you remain vulnerable."

Lidya clenched her teeth. Koram opened his mouth – and then closed it again. Lidya watched his thoughts, in his gaze – watched his consideration.

"Why do you not blame him, daughter of Maki, for his absence?"

Lidya held his eyes. "You forget, Sir Koram: I know what Soutar can do."

"Your brother also knows this, but you...you still love Maki."

She turned from him, to look at Gamel – to frown, watching his breathing: seeing the blood on his chest.

"Why should it surprise you, Koram, that I still love my father?" she murmured.

"It doesn't surprise me," Koram replied from behind her. "Not from what I know of you. But it does put you at risk."

"At risk?"

"To know, without being known: to love, without being loved – this is a risk."

Lidya swallowed, and looked down at the serpent in her hand.

"What would Soutar's hold be on you?" Koram's voice asked.

"I...don't know."

"Your brother was attacked in his hatred – in his rejection: in his desire for power, and strength. What must you be ready for, Lidya – daughter of Maki?"

She closed her eyes. "He's gone!" she insisted. "He's gone."

"We don't know that."

"I am trusting in it, Koram: I must."

Koram's voice was silenced – and now Lidya cast her eyes further across the deck. Taierre was sitting against the hull, a few feet away from Gamel. His Southern clothes were unusually dishevelled – his tunic half undone. Taierre's eyes were on Gamel – Lidya sensed somehow a kind of protectiveness in the Southerner, though this was entirely foreign to his previous inclination. Was it a common suffering? A common awareness? Lidya was not sure – but she was glad for what she saw, before Taierre noticed her gaze and quickly hid his thoughts.

Lidya turned, and looked forward past Koram. The ship had a large wooden cabin in front of them, and from the centre of the deck, within the cabin, rose the mast – high up into the sky, bearing the huge linen sail. Lidya gazed up at it, captivated. The power of the wind drove the ship – the deck dipping gently beneath her feet as they swept over waves. Who was steering? She searched, and found the man – a captain, raised up a few steps, in a wooden booth behind the cabin. He was looking forward across the cabin's roof, his hands on a large wooden wheel, tipping it first one way and then the other.

"Beautiful," Lidya breathed.

"What is?" Koram gently asked.

"The ship! Such grace! Such power, but controlled, and moving."

She searched now for the crew. One man was at the port of the bow, looking over the hull to the water below. Within the cabin lanterns were lit – Lidya could make out the shadows of a few men seated at tables: could just hear their voices, speaking a strange language – sometimes laughing. Where were the ones who had pulled them aboard? She looked behind, back to the stern beyond Gamel and Taierre, and now saw two men sitting within the shadow of the hull, one on each side. One was grasping a rope attached to the boom of the sail.

Their dark eyes watched her – and she wandered up to them, grasping the blanket around her shoulders as she knelt down on the deck. Both seemed quite young – the man on her right, grasping the rope, was tall and slim: he smiled at her. The man on her left, shorter and more muscular, looked intrigued.

"Greetings," she said, extending a hand out. They looked at her hand, and at her face, and laughed.

Lidya blushed – but now Koram was beside her again, as she rose to her feet.

"I suspect in Yerim a woman does not extend a hand," he said.

"No?" Lidya enquired, feeling a little foolish.

"No need for shame, young lady – they laugh because they are confused. They have never seen a white woman before."

Amazed, Lidya gazed at them – black skin, hidden in the night. "No," she pondered, "Of course. But they have seen you?"

"Yes, Princess Lidya: I am a scout."

"You are familiar with the Coast."

"Yes."

"Koram…" Now she began to remember something she had heard, as she had been dragged onto the ship. "They spoke with you!"

"Yes."

"In their language!"

"Yes, Lidya."

"And – I understood it! Gamel, too – he understood the words!"

Koram was quiet now, and Lidya looked at his face – to see his concern.

"I can't explain that, Lidi."

"What do you mean?"

"Taierre and I spent time learning Yeri with these explorers – we also taught them something of Altenhanse. I befriended them – Taierre showed more caution. We…learned some things from them."

"Take care, Koram," Taierre's voice now interjected. Lidya glanced at him – he was gathering himself, straightening his tunic and rising to his feet, even as Gamel still slept.

"She will learn it sooner or later," Koram said.

"Prince Gamel…"

"The legacy belongs to them both."

Lidya stared at Koram. "What do you mean?" she insisted.

"You are the ones."

It was the Yeri voice she had heard speak before – belonging to the slim man to her right: the one who smiled. The sound was lyrical, again: like music – the different language, and yet she understood it.

He rose to his feet, and the man on the left took the rope from him as he stepped forward.

"I am Echari," he said, reaching out his hand. She gratefully took it.

"Very pleased to meet you: I am Lidya."

"You are the Princess of the Heartland."

"Yes!" she said, surprised at his knowledge.

He bowed his head to her – and she hurriedly shook her own head.

"No!" she said. "Please – don't bow."

"It is right for him to grant you respect," Taierre said. "Your position affords you power, Princess Lidya."

Lidya shifted awkwardly on her feet.

"Though you would not wish it," Koram said quietly to her, out of earshot of the others, "Your position has saved you, Lidya."

"Gamel's position," Lidya hastily corrected.

"Not only that of Gamel: listen to what Echari has to say."

Perplexed, Lidya looked again to the Yeri face.

"Why do I understand you, Echari?" she asked.

"It is written."

"What is written?" she asked, astonished.

"Our sages predicted you and your brother would come."

Now Lidya suddenly sat down as Echari began to recite.

"'*Out of a land far away, the two will come.*
*White as snow, youth unknown:*
*Brother and sister will fight death to find life,*
*And salvation will spread through their lingering strife.*'"

Lidya stared up at Echari's face. "What does it mean?"

"Your understanding of me is the sign," Echari said, "You are the ones. Prince and Princess of the Heartland – your journey will make our nations One."

"One?"

"Free access to Altenhine – free access to Yerim."

"Yes, but for what purpose, Echari?"

"You do not know?" Now Echari laughed gently – kindly. "For the same purpose you came to our ship, Lidya of the Heartland: for the same purpose we all struggle on. To find the true source of life! Real life."

Lidya gazed at him – and Echari bowed his head again to her.

"Very pleased to meet you, Princess Lidya of the Heartland." And, having used her own greeting, he sat back down on the deck – and Lidya watched him.

"Koram," she murmured under her breath. "How do I understand him?"

"I fear it may have something to do with Soutar."

"Soutar?"

"Supernatural power, Lidi – you and Gamel both have touched Soutar."

"You may be right…"

And yet, as Lidya watched the young Yeri man, as he focused again on the rope and his task, she began to wonder: a true source of life? Real life? The words pulled on her heart strongly. Could it be true? Could there be much more than she and Gamel had realized?

Echari sat, in utter faith, in his task. Lidya longed to be as him – but she was not yet in the same place. Could she dare seek out a better life? Could she dare hope to be rescued?

She sat, a few feet apart, and pondered – and then night-time took her, and she slept.

CHAPTER EIGHTEEN: Sailing

Gamel stirred.

He was lying on the deck of the ship of Yeri. His clothes were wet, under the blanket.

Astonished, Gamel jerked himself to his feet. It was day time! A wind blew through his curls as he quickly cast his eyes over the ship: the cabin, mast and massive sail above, and the captain at a wheel.

Lidya was sleeping on the deck across from him, also with a blanket – Koram dozing next to her, against the hull. Taierre was sitting behind him, watching him – his face tired.

"How long...?" Gamel gasped, and looked back beyond two young men of Yeri grasping ropes, to the Ocean and the yellow sun lifting into a pale sky.

"We left Altenhine at sundown," Taierre said. "The sun rises in the east, as you see."

"The east," Gamel whispered – thrusting himself to the stern of the ship. Home! Could he still see land? He strained his eyes to see – looking to the horizon. A vague grey haze was there, above the blue water: he could not convince himself of any solid form. The Heartland was gone! For a moment fear gripped him – here he was, in the middle of the sea, surrounded by people not of his home: the ship sailing quickly away from the very place he wanted to be. And yet as quickly at the fear took a hold, so then purpose had its way.

Gamel now strode up past the cabin to the bow of the ship, and looked forward. Could he see land, looking west? Could he see their destination? Could he see Yerim? He strained, longing for some certain goal – feeling the ship tipping up and down with each random wave – but there also, on the horizon, was only white haze.

"What on Earth am I doing?" Gamel breathed – and Taierre's voice, behind his back, responded.

"Well might you ask."

"I had to act!" Gamel defended. "I had to save her!"

Yet he knew, in his depths, that something more had urged him on. Michel's form was before him again, in his mind's eye: standing on the very spot Gamel now stood, lit in starlight.

*Now is your choice.*

Choice. Something had grasped him, within – a hunger, a desire: a pursuit after something more than domination under Soutar.

"There was something else," Gamel said, "It wasn't just Lidya."

"Something else?"

"Something, or someone. I don't know."

"Not just a flight, Gamel? A flight from something too terrible to sustain?"

Gamel turned now, to look at Taierre. The green eyes were intense, but not attacking: challenging, but also, in this moment, strangely, and privately, very empathetic.

"You…" Gamel hesitated and then continued. "You are an intriguing man, Taierre."

"'Intriguing'?" Taierre smirked.

"Yes, curious. Somehow we are speaking exactly the same language, and yet we are worlds apart."

"Explain." The gaze softened.

"We both know the threat of Soutar." Gamel watched Taierre swallow. "But as to what that threat means, and what to do about it? There we seem to differ."

"Soutar is evil, Prince Gamel – to run is a feasible option."

"But only if there is a place to permanently hide."

Taierre frowned, and Gamel instinctively felt for his right trouser pocket – but the Stone was no longer there. He felt pain from his chest, and glanced down to see his blood stained white shirt, and the flesh wound beneath.

"Oh," he gasped – and then he remembered, "Lidya!"

He strode down the starboard side of the deck, to find Koram stirring, next to his sleeping sister.

"Prince Gamel," Koram nodded.

"Sir Koram."

Gamel searched Lidya's sleeping form. Where was the Stone of Soutar? She was not wearing it around her neck. Her right hand, beneath the blanket, might have been clutching it within her own trouser pocket – or was he just imagining it?

"The stone is safe," Koram said.

"Where?"

"She has it, Gamel: do not be afraid."

Gamel looked into his calm brown eyes. "She should not keep it."

"Why not, Gamel?"

"He will harm her."

"We are approaching Yerim: let her keep it for now."

"It was intended for me." He began to reach out to Lidya's form – but now Koram's hand was on his shoulder.

"Let her carry it for a while."

Gamel frowned down at his sister's form; felt Koram's warning. Taierre now was standing before him – his expression confirmation of Koram's advice.

"What will Soutar do, now we have left Altenhine?"

Lidya stirred, now, as if in answer – looking up into his eyes. She smiled – and his heart was set at ease.

"Very well," he murmured to Koram and Taierre. "Let things remain as they are for now."

And he reached down, grasping Lidya's hand and pulling her to her feet.

It was time to meet the captain.

Awkwardly Gamel shifted in his clothes – knowing, with blood and salt water, that he was a mess. How long had it been since he had bathed? Yet it seemed not to matter to the man now before him.

"Welcome to my ship, Prince Gamel of the Heartland," the Captain said – maintaining one hand on the wheel as he bowed his head and tipped his body forward to Gamel.

"Greetings," Gamel replied, returning the bow instinctively. The man's voice was low and lyrical – one of the voices Gamel had heard as the ship had pulled away from the Coast.

"This is Captain Nehu," Koram said. "We owe him our thanks."

"Yes," Gamel quickly agreed. "Thank you, Sir, for allowing us on your vessel."

Nehu glanced to Koram and then looked back to Gamel. "You are younger than I expected."

"Than you expected?"

"For a king."

Gamel shifted awkwardly under his gaze. "Does my age change my fate?" he asked. "My legacy is what it is: I am next in line for the Throne of the Heartland."

"Then let it be as Atua wishes," Nehu said. "We will bear you to Yerim."

"Is Atua your king?"

Nehu smiled. "He is indeed."

"He sent you to our land?"

"Yes."

"For what purpose, Captain Nehu? Why are we all here?"

Lidya shifted behind him – but Gamel kept his eyes set on the Yeri man. His eyebrows rose in surprise – and then settled. He looked again across the water toward Yerim, tipping the wheel a little to the right, and then returned to Gamel's gaze.

"Why are you here, Prince Gamel?"

"To search for a new allegiance."

"What kind of allegiance?"

"A political allegiance."

The eyebrows rose again – this time Nehu could not contain his surprise. "A political allegiance?" he said, "Then perhaps you have chosen the wrong land."

Gamel frowned. "How so?"

"Did Koram not tell you? Politically our land is in unrest, Prince Gamel. Altenhine has sustained a peace elusive to us for hundreds of years."

Gamel stared at him, his throat constricting. Had he made a huge mistake? Soutar had given his own land an advantage over the land of Yerim?

"We are not seeking political peace," Lidya's voice said – and Gamel jabbed her behind his back. Even so, Lidya appeared to his right – and Nehu looked at her, with some astonishment.

"Good day to you, Princess Lidya."

"And to you," Lidya said, bowing her head.

"The future King of Altenhine says he is seeking a political allegiance, but you say otherwise?"

Gamel glared at Lidya, blushing – but she did not look straight at him, though he knew she felt his stare.

"I do not say otherwise," she said, "Rather, I say that political peace is not what we are seeking: Altenhine has found political peace already."

"This is why we came to your shores, Princess: to find the secret of your peace."

His eyes returned to Gamel. Gamel's fingers sought out the Stone of Soutar, in his right trouser pocket – but he could not find it. Instead, he found the keys in his left trouser pocket – one to the cabinet of the history of the Kings of the Heartland, in the Throne Room, and the other to the altar of sacrifice to Soutar. These were the 'secret' to their 'peace'.

"There is no secret," Gamel lied, "Only a Throne, in the Heartland, to mediate the delivery of fertilizer to the North and South, that all may live."

"We in Yerim also battle over food," Nehu said. "And water. Many have died fighting for water."

Gamel sadly considered him. "Our land has plenty of water."

"You are blessed."

"'Blessed'?"

"Atua has smiled upon you."

"'Atua'?" Now Gamel began to understand, as he searched the Yeri man. "You said Atua was your king..."

Nehu shook his head slightly, as if in amazement. "You have not heard of Atua?"

"Should I have?"

"He is the One, from whom all things come!"

Now Gamel glanced sideways, to his left, at Koram – at his calm and knowing smile. He might have warned him! Then Gamel looked up at Taierre, standing behind the captain. The Southerner was grimacing – his white face drawn in camouflaged disdain. Gamel watched his efforts, and wanted to laugh, but knew he must not.

It was Lidya who spoke. "Some in our land speak of such a One."

"Some in our land, also," Koram said.

"A Great One, powerful and frightening," Lidya said. "Too frightening to state a name, though many have whispered of his presence."

"They fear him?" Nehu asked.

"We in Altenhine do not know him," Koram replied. "Our ancestors wrote of Him, though: most powerful of the spirits."

"Certainly."

"And some wrote of Love." Gamel was surprised at himself: that he had let these words escape from his lips – these words which had taken such deep root from Koram, on their race to the Coast.

Nehu paused. His face suddenly took on a glow, somehow: an aura Gamel could not explain. Then it passed.

"Yes," Nehu said gently. "They were right to write of love."

"We do not know of this Love," Lidya said – and Gamel blushed again. He knew she did not intend to reveal their personal quest – rather, she was revealing the experience of their people – but, at the same time, he felt uncomfortably exposed.

"I ask you again," Captain Nehu said to Gamel. "Why have you come? What is it you are seeking?"

Gamel searched his dark face. He was an older man – his black hair, crimped and short, had several strands of silver softening its impact.

"If you seek an audience with our political leaders, Prince Gamel, I cannot help you. Our land has no unifying political king: each tribe fights for its own survival. But Atua works, even amidst such disarray."

"Atua?"

"He is our King."

"How so?"

"Some battles are physical, Prince Gamel; some are spiritual. With all due respect, it was not a physical army you fled as you leapt onto our ship."

Now Gamel flushed openly before the Captain. "Did you see what I saw?" he whispered, and Nehu grimaced.

"I saw spirits, Prince Gamel, poised to take you."

Gamel stared at him. Another had seen them? He shot a glance at Taierre, who was frowning.

"Why did they not follow us, Nehu?" Gamel asked. "Why did they not flood your ship?"

"Because of Atua!" Nehu said, smiling. "Do you not understand?"

"The most powerful of the spirits..." Koram murmured, his expression thoughtful.

"If you seek a political allegiance, we cannot help you," Nehu said. "But a human allegiance will not overcome powers stronger than humanity."

Silently Gamel considered his words – and now Lidya stepped forward.

"What help can you offer to us, if not a political allegiance?"

Nehu's eyes passed over her face – and then he smiled.

"What I have I offer to you, Prince and Princess of the Heartland: a spiritual allegiance, in the place of a political one."

"A spiritual allegiance?" Gamel asked.

"There is someone I would like you to meet: someone whom I think could help you."

"Who?"

"A leader; a guide. His name is Yeshua – he will answer your questions better than I."

Perplexed, Gamel looked at him. "Who is he?" he asked, and Nehu shrugged slightly.

"You will see."

"How can I trust you?"

Now Nehu smirked – irony in his eyes. "Look around you, Prince Gamel: we sail in the middle of the Ocean of Yerim, and I am at the wheel. Would you like to set our direction instead? Your choice to trust has already been made."

He spoke the truth – at least for now. Gamel nodded his assent, and stepped back away from the captain – allowing him to attend again to his navigation. But how could he understand this plan? A land in disarray: was this not the very thing Gamel was fleeing? And yet strangely not: it was order Gamel was fleeing

– order, and control, but under the wrong kind of power; under the wrong kind of authority.

What could this Yeshua possibly offer into this kind of battle? His own kind had clearly not yet found the solution.

A fight for water…The Blue Lake! The Dandes River. Water in abundance! Life-giving sustenance. Surely the Heartland was a paradise, next to this land which he now approached: a land thirsting for the simplicity of water. And yet was the Heartland truly Paradise? Water, yes, food, yes – houses, yes. But was there more to life than this? More needed to live than this?

He could not say – and certainly could not answer the sudden multitude of questions rising up in his mind. But when he looked at Lidya, he saw a strange kind of trust. It was contrasted starkly, in her white face, with the florid distrust in the white face of Taierre. Gamel found himself somehow between them – sceptical, as Taierre, and yet also needing the same hope of Lidya: needing to continue.

Now Gamel felt Koram's hand on his shoulder.

"You might have told me," Gamel muttered, and he knew Koram was smiling.

"I thought I would let you discover it for yourself."

"Atua is the one the legends speak of."

"I believe so. Our ancestors shared the same kind of faith."

"But does that make it real, Koram? That they believed in the same thing?"

Koram was silent for a moment. Then he replied.

"I don't know, Gamel," he said. "But it does make me want to know more."

Surprised, Gamel looked at him. Koram was usually so non-committal! Not this time – there was curiosity in his eyes.

"And so we stumble on," Gamel muttered. "One step at a time, shoved one way and then the next, tossed with each wave of another person's choice."

"Tossed?" Koram replied. "No, Gamel – not tossed. Perhaps directed?"

The word sent chills up Gamel's neck. Directed? That meant someone else was in control. The thought felt too much like Soutar for his liking – he suspended it. And then he moved back to the bow of the ship, looking ahead: seeing, now, the faintest outline of land.

What would he find there, in Yerim? Soon the vague hints would materialize into some kind of reality, and he feared that reality. Would he find what he was looking for? Would he not? And which outcome would be the most terrifying?

He could not tell – but, for now, he surrendered to his imminent fate.

## CHAPTER NINETEEN: Yerim

Land was before them.

Heart pounding, Gamel stared at the flat stretch of land ahead. A cheer went up amongst the Yeri crew – Gamel could not help but catch their infectious enthusiasm. But, at the same time, fear gripped him.

Lidya was behind him – now alongside, on his right, gazing also ahead.

"There it is," she whispered.

"Yes."

"What might we find?"

"I don't know." Her hand moved, to her right trouser pocket: Gamel knew why.

"Is it safe?" he asked.

"I think so...So far as I know."

"No...no effect on you?"

She met his eyes. "I can't feel him."

"Has he actually gone?" Hope whispered to him.

"He was afraid to come: will that fear keep him away? I don't know, Gamel."

He swallowed – and then looked back ahead.

The land was near now. Gamel could see black rocks, white sand, and a wharf built far out into the sea.

"We are here," he whispered, almost in disbelief.

Echari now was at the starboard side of the yacht, at the bow, gripping a thick rope. The sail was being dropped on Nehu's command, the ship lifting on the waves – and now Echari threw out the rope, over a wooden pillar, and the ship was drawn to the wharf. Another crewman threw out a second rope, from the stern, and they were still.

"Welcome to Yerim!" Captain Nehu said with a smile – and Gamel bowed his head to him.

"Thank you."

Echari was on the wharf now, securing the yacht more tightly – and now he extended his hand to Lydia, who was standing closest to the wharf.

"Welcome, Princess of the Heartland."

She took his hand, and stepped over the hull onto the wharf. Gamel quickly climbed over, followed by Taierre and Koram – and Captain Nehu gestured them on.

"Echari will show you the way."

"Thank you for all your help!" Gamel said.

"Have a good day, Prince Gamel."

Echari, young and slim, led them down the wharf and onto the beach. Gamel looked at the sand – it seemed so similar to the Western Coast! But there were more rocks, and the sand, in some parts, was pushed up into small dunes.

Echari was smiling widely, obviously very happy to have returned to his home. Lidya smiled at him, and he reached again to take her hand.

"Steady on!" Gamel said, in Altenhanse – and Lidya jerked her hand away, casting a scowl back toward Gamel. He grinned at her – and all moved forward.

The beach gave way to slightly raised land, with wild yellow plants Gamel had never seen before. They pushed between them, and reached a dirt road – but the soil, unlike the Heartland, was a rich orange-brown.

"Is your soil fertile?" Taierre asked Echari in Altenhanse, and he smiled widely at him.

"Yes, Sir Taierre," he said in simple Altenhanse back again. "Water – water is our main need. Food, from water and soil."

"Yes."

Gamel followed Echari along the road, inland away from the coast – and they saw workers scattered, along the way, working in fields of crops of corn. The men carried large knives, and cut at the stems – as Echari walked past they greeted him and then stared at Gamel, and especially at Lidya. Women also looked up – from gathering corn into baskets. Lidya waved to them – they naturally waved back, looking astonished. And then, suddenly, children were running toward them – dark, wearing little, laughing and jumping around Lidya, and then around Gamel.

Gamel stared at them. One little boy grabbed his hand, and started to dance – Gamel laughed, and spun him around. Then he looked up, to see Taierre watching him with a stern face.

"What?"

"Playing with the children, young prince?"

Gamel flushed – his father's face was again before him: *What use for a second prince, but to play like a child?*

"Children are important, Sir Taierre," he replied. "The heart of a child can change the world."

Taierre's eyebrows shot up – and Gamel grinned at him. Then he continued forward, holding the boy's hand – as Lidya, ahead of him, also held onto the hands of a little boy and girl.

It was hot. Gamel only now began to notice the wet heat – his white shirt, still blood stained, began to cling to his chest: the wound over his heart began to sting. No wonder the people of Yeri wore little – the men often had bare chests, and the woman short shirts and loose long skirts. Gamel wished for shorts – but noticed the men always wore three-quarter length baggy trousers.

"Where are you taking us?" Gamel asked Echari.

"To my village."

"Your village?"

"The place of my birth, Prince Gamel   and still my home, when I am in Yerim."

They walked on, perhaps for one or two hours. Gamel struggled forward, sweat dripping from his face – thirst taking a hold. The sun was still low in the sky – how would it be if they were to continue to walk, even in the full heat of the day? The workers continued, around them: how could they sustain the effort?

They passed a man herding sheep – a kind Gamel had never seen before, thin and with scant hair – but then Echari turned off the main dirt road to the left.

Between olive green bushes and tall yellow grass they pressed, and emerged into a clearing.

There was Echari's village. Gamel gazed at it, and smiled. Five small dwellings were gathered together – walls of stick, a floor of polished mud, and each one round, not square, with roofs of bound straw.

The simplicity struck Gamel. Where was their toilet? Outside the village, surely: bathing in streams, and drinking from the same. Gamel glanced to Taierre. His face was neutral – what were his thoughts, from the south? And Koram? Gamel looked to him – to see the gentle smile. There was some commonality there – perhaps the Northerners also lived a simple life on the land.

Lidya looked captivated. Surprised, Gamel watched her response. Surely Lidi would need the comforts of home: the comforts of a palatial life? Soft beds, cushions, a bath and fancy food – she had made it this far, true, but for this to be their final destination? Yet, no: her face broke into a wide smile.

A woman emerged from one of the huts – and grasped Lidya's hands between her own, with a beaming smile.

"This is my mother, Berui!" Echari said, in lilting Yeri. "This is Princess Lidya, of the Heartland of Altenhine."

"Welcome, Princess Lidya!" Berui said. "We have been expecting you, and now, finally, the right time is upon us!"

Her dark brown eyes settled upon Gamel, also – and she bowed her head politely to him. Astonished, Gamel reached out his hand – and she gladly took this also.

"Expecting us, Madam?" Gamel asked – and her face beamed.

"The sages, Sir!" she said. "Did not Echari say?"

"'Out of a land far away, the two will come,'" Lidya said. "Yes, Echari told me.

'White as snow, youth unknown:
Brother and sister will fight death to find life,
And salvation will spread through their lingering strife.'"

Gamel stared at Lidya, and at Echari, and then again at Berui.

"Excuse me, Madam: I do not understand."

"We have been waiting here for you!" Berui said, eyes sparkling. "Near the coast – awaiting the white ones: the royal brother and sister. When the white ones come – this will also be the time of our own peace. Our sages, of Atua, spoke of this hundreds of years ago."

"Hundreds of years ago?"

"A curse was laid down, in a land far away in the east – but out of this curse would come two white ones, in a time to come: and when they come, we will know the time is almost upon us."

"What 'time'?"

"The time of peace."

102

Confused, Gamel searched her face – and Lidya voiced his thoughts.

"What kind of peace?"

Berui beamed at her, again reaching to grasp her hands. "Ah, dear girl – you even know my language! It is a sign: the time is upon us! The One is here."

"The One?"

"The One foreseen – the One yearned for: the One who can bring peace to all the Earth."

"What one is he?" Gamel asked – and she reached again for his hand, still holding onto Lidya.

"Come," she said. "We will take you to him."

"Now?" Gamel exclaimed, heart pounding again. "We have only just arrived! I'm..." he stuttered, now, a little embarrassed. "I'm thirsty and sore...and...I need to bathe."

Her eyes, brown, warm, saw him. She stroked his head, and he suddenly, foolishly, felt like crying. A mother! She felt like a mother.

"I am sorry," she said, "I am so excited to see you! I forgot to allow you time to refresh yourselves. Come – we will give you fresh clothes: you can bathe in the creek which passes close by, and drink! We have water here: Atua has been kind."

Wordlessly Gamel followed her, with Lidya – past the huts, and down a little pathway between the trees, to a little stream.

"There," Berui said. "You men can bathe here – I will leave clothes behind this bush. And, Princess Lidya, I will show you where we women bathe."

She hurried Lidya away – and Gamel looked at Taierre and Koram. Koram was smiling – grinning, even. Taierre looked somewhat more reserved.

"Don't be shy," Koram said. "We have seen it all before."

"It's just..." Gamel spluttered. "In the Palace..."

"We know."

"Privacy."

"Not in our lands, Prince Gamel: we are communal. But if you would feel more comfortable..."

Koram looked away, but Taierre still was watching. "You come to a new land, and will not adapt?" he said. "How then will you proceed?"

Gamel held his gaze, and swallowed. Then he nodded. "Very well," he said. "I will adapt."

He stripped off his clothes, in front of Taierre, and lowered himself into the stream. The cool water was a great relief to him – he was finally able to clean off Altenhine mud and salt from the Sea of Yerim, and, at the same time, clean the wound of his chest.

"Here," Taierre's voice said – and Gamel glanced back to see Yeri clothes laid out for him at the edge of the stream.

"Thank you," he said – and rose, out of the water, as Taierre and Koram began to bathe.

His skin dried quickly, and his hair. He drew on the Yeri clothes – underpants, baggy trousers, three quarter length, and a short sleeved shirt: all bright yellow and a bit too large for him. He laughed – and, as he wandered back to the village, reached down to roll up the waist of the trousers.

"I don't think that colour suits you," Lidya's voice said – and he looked up to see her, now dressed in a Yeri short sleeved red shirt, and orange loose long skirt. Her long black curls were now plaited down her back.

"No?" he chimed, reaching now to tighten the brown leather sandals. "And does red and orange suit you, do you think?"

"I…don't know." She reached to straighten out the skirt, looking thoughtful: but now fear seized him.

"Where is the Stone?"

No pockets! Where were her Heartland clothes? But she reached between the folds of the skirt – there was some kind of pocket there, concealed.

"Don't worry," she said, "It's still safe."

"As if anywhere is really 'safe.'"

"She said we could meet him now, Gamel! Meet the 'One'!" Her enthusiasm was overflowing – and he frowned at her.

"I don't know, Lidi," he said. "How do we know he is 'the One'? How do we know anything? How do we know there even is a 'One'?"

"The sages said…"

"I really don't know what to make of that…"

"They've been waiting for us!"

"I know! But…how could that be?"

He longed to toss the Stone of Soutar in his hand, at that moment, to think – to search for answers – but he resisted. And Lidya watched him.

"I understand why you might doubt all this, Gamel," she said, to his astonishment. "But we came for this very opportunity."

"I know."

"We still need to see it through."

"I know!"

"It all comes down to now."

Gamel swallowed, looking at her. "Aren't you afraid?"

She frowned. "No," she said quietly. "I'm not."

"Why not?"

"I don't know…I just get the feeling this is all how it was meant to be."

Gamel studied her face, and her eyes – and, in that moment, felt envy. Trust! She trusted in this One – even perhaps trusted in this 'Atua,' though she really knew nothing of him. Someone else seemed in control – she trusted in this control, while he could not.

"It's time," she said, and he swallowed again, and nodded.

"Very well," he said. "Let's go and meet this 'One across the Sea,' and see if he holds any true answers for us."

He glanced back, to see Taierre and Koram, dressed in Yeri clothes and waiting – and gestured them forward, toward the village, back to Echari and Berui.

104

CHAPTER TWENTY: Yeshua

The sun beat heavily down upon Gamel: it was now high in the sky.

He was sweating – again. So much for the wash, he thought to himself. The leather sandals, unfamiliar, were wearing into his feet, causing blisters as he continued to follow Echari and Berui, ahead of them, toward the promised One.

They had been walking for hours – down dirt roads, and sometimes cutting through yellow turf. Once or twice they had passed through larger settlements – what Gamel might have called 'towns,' but of the same kind of simple dwellings, sometimes with larger meeting houses in the centre. The children had waved, and some of the women – the men had stared. White faces! How many had thought of the words of their sages? How many had wondered what this all could mean?

Gamel continued – and often glanced at Lidya, to his left, as they travelled. Her white face was flushed, her feet even beginning to bleed in the sandals. Often Gamel wanted to call a halt – but then she shook her head, and so they continued.

Koram walked at Gamel's right side. Gamel often relied upon his presence, in his growing weariness – this quiet man from the North, strong, easily able to continue, despite the very different climate of his home land. And, to Koram's right, continued Taierre. He also was quiet and surprisingly dignified in the heat – though Gamel sensed in him a growing frustration.

They persevered until Gamel felt the sun beginning to burn him, on face and arms. Then, as his sight began to blur, they came to a halt.

Berui, wet faced but no less joyous, stood before Gamel, and bowed her head.

"We have arrived, Prince Gamel."

Gamel panted slightly, with the heat. "Thank you," he croaked.

The land looked rather similar to all they had seen up to this point, and Gamel could see no other people. But Echari now gestured to the right, through some bush.

"He is through there."

"He is?" Gamel almost laughed, but stopped himself. His reaction was not lost on Echari.

"You will see," the young man said, smiling, "When you meet him."

Gamel politely nodded. He drew himself up straight, straightened his oversized clothes as best he could, and walked through the bush.

A clearing opened up before Gamel – and there was a camp. Surprised, Gamel glanced across the entire breadth of the land before him: extending far, to his right and left. A number of animal hide tents had been erected on poles, not too different from those of Taierre and Koram. In the centre of the camp was a well – Gamel longed for water, seeing it. And all around were many men, women and children – some deep black, others lighter shades of brown, some even more olive in skin toning.

"Why such differences?" Gamel asked, intrigued.

105

"They have come from many parts; from many tribes."

"Really?"

"Some from other nations, also – like you."

Gamel glanced down at his white skin – and then looked up at the others. Suddenly he felt less out of place: comforted by the diversity.

Women worked around the tents, sometimes with open fires – cooking. Gamel swayed slightly on his feet – Berui gestured him to the well, and then drew out some water and poured this into a clay cup.

"Drink, Prince Gamel."

Hastily he drank – and then he remembered Lidya, and passed the cup quickly to her. All drank – and then Gamel looked expectantly to Echari.

"Come," he said, beaming – and he took his hand, and led him between tents to a greater clearing.

There a man stood: a little taller than Gamel, head of dark brown crimped hair, brown eyes, and medium brown skin. He wore clothes of Yeri – a short sleeved bright green shirt, and baggy green trousers. There was nothing special about his appearance – Gamel felt immediate disappointment, looking at him. What had he expected? He did not know: something of the aura of Michel, perhaps? Some kind of light in the persona – to show that this one was not merely human. This he did not find. And yet in front of this man many were seated – stretching out far before him, poised, it seemed, on every word that came from his mouth.

Gamel swayed again – on the verge of collapse. This was the one? This? A mere average looking human being – this the one he and Lidya had pursued to save their lives, and all of Altenhine with them?

Gamel turned on his heel – his vision swam before him. He felt himself falling – and then found himself caught.

The man's face was over him.

"Sorry," Gamel gasped. "I have made a mistake."

"No, Gamel of the Heartland," the man said, "you are exactly where you should be."

Shocked, Gamel stared up at him. His vision swam again – now the man was offering him more water. Thirstily Gamel drank and drank, until his stomach was bloated.

The man supported him. Gamel closed his eyes fleetingly – then shook himself, and staggered to his feet.

"Please," he whispered. "Don't let me interrupt you."

"Rest, Gamel – and then we may talk."

Gamel was taken by his manner – a kind of gentle charm: a strange unseen knowledge, but without intimidation.

He felt wholly inclined to obey. Berui led him to a tent, and Gamel immediately lowered himself to the ground on a mat, curled up, closed his eyes, and rested.

When he awoke, he was still in the tent. Astonished, he jerked his body upright – and quickly moved outside.

The sun was dropping in the sky – it was late afternoon.

The man was there. He was sitting on the ground, with Echari and Berui. Koram and Taierre were sitting a little further away, and Lidya was lying on the ground, with her eyes closed.

Gamel moved to the gathering, and lowered himself between Koram and Taierre. The man's eyes came to rest on him.

"Greetings, Prince Gamel of the Heartland. I am Yeshua."

He was speaking in Altenhanse. Heart pounding, Gamel grasped the offered hand.

"Greetings, Sir Yeshua."

How could he know his home tongue? Not only Altenhanse, but the Heartland dialect? He must have trained, somehow: must have learned from the sailors to their land. Gamel knew this explanation could not be true, but he had no alternative.

He released the hand, and Yeshua nodded to him.

"You have come a long way, young man."

Young? How old was this man: perhaps thirty-five?

"I have," Gamel agreed.

"And how can I help you?"

Gamel swallowed, looking at him. Somehow there, in that moment, he could not speak: could not divulge the true concerns of his heart.

Now Lidya stirred – and sat up from her sleep. She set eyes on Yeshua – and something passed between them. Perplexed, Gamel watched as their dialogue unfolded.

"Welcome, Princess Lidya."

"Thank you, Sir Yeshua."

"You too have travelled far."

"Yes."

"You carry a burden too heavy to bear alone."

Lidya's mouth opened – she was ready to respond. Gamel shifted in warning, she glanced at him, and then closed her mouth. Finally she spoke.

"Yes, Sir," she said, and Gamel wanted to hit her again. "I do carry a burden."

Yeshua's eyes remained on her for a moment. They shifted to Gamel, fleetingly, and then to Taierre, finally resting on Koram.

"And you, Koram of the North," Yeshua said. "Why have you come to our Land?"

Koram looked surprised to be addressed – but he bowed his head in respect.

"I have come to escort Prince Gamel."

"Excellent. But do you come with any other purpose in mind?"

Koram paused, holding Yeshua's gaze – and then he continued.

"There is another purpose, Sir, but I am not yet ready to determine my course of action."

"Understandable," Yeshua replied. "I hope in time your choice might become clear."

Yeshua looked now again at Taierre. With great interest Gamel watched as Yeshua studied the Southerner. Taierre's face was stone, as Gamel fully expected. Yeshua was silent for a moment – and then he spoke.

"Taierre, of the South," he said. "Might I be able to help your people?"

Taierre's jaw was tight. "No thank you, Sir," he replied.

"What of your King?"

"What of him?"

Yeshua smiled very slightly – Gamel knew he knew Taierre was testing him.

"King Faier has carried a burden something like the burden of Princess Lidya, has he not?" he said. "The curse of Soutar has extended across all your lands: North, South and Heartland…"

Now, suddenly, Taierre was on his feet – drawing his sword. Shocked, Gamel scampered to his own feet.

"Taierre!" he cried – but Yeshua was extending out his hand toward the sword.

"You mistake me," he said quietly. "I mean you no harm."

"No harm?" Taierre cried. "You have the knowledge of Soutar!"

"You are mistaken," Yeshua replied. "It is not Soutar's knowledge I bear. Peace, Taierre – be at peace."

Gamel watched as the Southerner stared at Yeshua, frowned, and then replaced his sword.

Koram was on his feet – he gestured Taierre away from Yeshua, and spoke with him. And now Gamel was standing before Yeshua.

Gamel looked at him. He was gentle! Kind, even. Gamel trembled before him – and Yeshua reached to touch his shoulder.

"Your burden," he murmured, "Is the greatest of all."

Tears filled Gamel's eyes, against his will – he blinked them away.

"I don't know what you mean."

"You do know, Gamel, what I mean – but you hide it. You run, you hide – even more than your sister. You see yourself in her – you hate seeing it. But what you see is potential strength, Gamel, not weakness. Do not despise that deepest part of yourself: the heart of a child can change the World."

Stunned, Gamel stared at him. Yeshua smiled, bowed his head, and backed away. Gamel found his gaze following after him. And then he looked at Lidya.

She was captivated: her eyes fixed on Yeshua.

"What do you see?" Gamel asked, and she smiled widely.

"What do you see, Gamel?"

"I don't know," he said, "Someone intriguing! Someone insightful."

"Yes, all of these things," she said. "But I also see hope, Gamel. I see hope."

"Hope, yes: but do you see salvation, Lidya? Do you see a way for Altenhine?"

Lidya frowned, looking after the man.

"Salvation?" she said. "I don't know, Gamel. But I see understanding – and I need to see more! I need to see more."

CHAPTER TWENTY-ONE: An Encounter with Yeshua

Lidya sat alone.

It was night-time. A short distance away from her, outside the tent, Gamel sat next to a small fire, with Koram and Taierre. Echari sat with them also – Lidya could hear his voice, in high Yeri, joking.

Gamel was laughing readily at Echari's jokes – he was actually laughing! Lidya was glad to hear the sound so familiar to her from the Heartland, from years earlier. But Taierre was silent, next to her brother – even more so than usual. His pale, rigid face hid frustration – arms folded, fingers tapping the hilt of his sword.

Koram's face, in the flames, showed his familiar warmth – a kind of open, gentle love of friendship: as surprising to her, under their circumstances, as it was consistent.

They seemed to be becoming almost a family – joined by a common goal: a common need for resolution. Yet this family, in itself, was not the resolution they all sought.

Fear struck Lidya's heart. The Stone of Soutar sat in her pocket, concealed amongst folds of her orange Yeri skirt – she gripped her fingers around it, and drew it out. The darkness shielded her from the eyes of others as she looked down to the garnet eyes of the serpent.

*Come home...*

His voice was returning. Throat tightening, Lidya trembled. What hold did Soutar have on her? Koram had asked the question – she had not answered. But she knew what kind of hold: she knew what kind of vulnerability.

Nausea took her. She rose to her feet, and wandered around the edge of the camp site. Some of Yeshua's other followers were there – lying, sleeping, on the ground. No-one noticed her as she escaped the camp, between gum trees. There was a tiny hidden lake! She hurried down to its edge.

Stars reflected in the dark water – quiet ripples on the surface. The Stone was getting warmer in her hand.

"Stay away," she whispered. "Stay away."

*You cannot keep me away.*

"I don't want you."

*Then you will have no-one else.*

"That is not for you to decide!"

*I have ruined you! You are tarnished, and will never love again.*

Lidya gagged, staring in the water. A face was appearing in the reflection – the same face that had appeared before Gamel, on the shore of the West Coast: just before they had left for Yerim.

"Stay away!" she cried. "Stay away!"

*Put on the Stone.*

"No!"

*Put on the Stone.*

"No!"

*Put on the Stone! Put on the Stone! Put on the Stone!*

If she put on the Stone, she would be his! Not only she, but all of Altenhine! Desperately she fought his impulse – yet the Stone now was heating in her hand. She glanced at it, to find the eyes lit up – bright and staring at her, bent on conquest.

"Atua..."

*You belong to me!* Soutar's intent burnt into her spirit – but now there was a different voice.

"Give me the stone."

Startled, Lidya shook her head – and then turned from the reflection to the voice.

It was Yeshua.

Throat constricting again, Lidya stared at him. He was speaking in Yeri – voice gentle, and melodic. His eyes, brown, were upon her – seeing her, in the darkness: making her blush.

"Sir," she whispered. "I can't be here."

"Then use this."

He was wearing a brown cloak, over his green shirt: now he removed this and handed it to her – rather as Gamel might have done, on a cold night in Raventown, ten years earlier.

Astonished, Lidya received the cloak – and quickly hid herself inside of it. Yeshua stood still, before her, as if waiting – she noticed him shivering a little with the cold. Then he extended his hand.

"Give me the stone."

Lidya stared at him – at the eyes, fixed on her: at the hand, extended.

"I cannot," she whispered. "It is not mine to give."

"Is it not?" he replied. "Are you not the Princess of the Heartland?"

His words now struck terror into her heart. Perhaps Taierre had been right!

"How do you know me?" she cried. "How do you know me?"

What was the true source of his power?

"I saw you," Yeshua said, "In the greystone Palace: hiding away from your father – hiding away from Soutar."

*Put on the Stone!* Soutar insisted.

"What else have you seen, Magician?" Lidya asked, searching the compassion in his eyes – hiding in the cloak.

"I am not a Magician."

"Then what are you?" Lidya enquired, "Who are you? By what power do you know me? Taierre's right: you might well be a servant of Soutar!"

"You know who I am, daughter of Tali."

Lidya trembled before him. "I do not know you."

"Do you not? You sought me for such a time as this."

Lidya clenched her teeth as he continued.

"'The One over the Sea.'"

In his eyes now was Love: a profound kind of love – all consuming, all demanding, all offering, inviting and requiring.

Soutar was pressing in hard, now: spirit to spirit – known, smothering her heart.

110

*You dare not trust him: you dare not surrender.*

*Leave me!* She cried. *Leave me!*

*He will take everything you have! Put on the Stone, now, or He will have you!*

Soutar feared Yeshua – Lidya knew it to be true! But now, at the final moment, clutching the Stone in her hand, she also feared Him! She also feared the very One she had sought. Surely it was better to live with Soutar – to live with the one she already knew, rather than be conquered: to submit to the demon already known rather than to dare the stranger unknown.

Her hands were moving, to place the Stone over her chest – to repel the terrifying offer of the Stranger – but then, suddenly, Gamel's voice screamed out.

"Lidya!"

With tears, she jerked her hand instinctively away from her chest – and Yeshua's face was before her, his hand outstretched.

"Give the stone to me," he said firmly. "You and Gamel were two from birth, not one, Lidya of the Heartland: brother and sister, from birth, to survive – but now the time for mere survival is over. Give the curse to me, young woman: face death with me, and live."

Tears filled Lidya's eyes, staring at him. Face death? Face death, with him? Death of the heart; death of the spirit – face this, and live?

She glanced over at Gamel – to see his white face, his terror, his confusion: but in this moment, strangely, Lidya felt no confusion. A sudden sense of destiny was upon her – a sudden strange and certain peace.

She lifted the Stone – and placed it into Yeshua's hand.

Now Soutar pressed in, in fury – and again raped her spirit. She screamed, sinking to her knees – but now a hand was firmly pressing down on her head, a voice strong in authority ringing over her.

"Leave her now!"

Soutar was torn from her. She screamed again – her voice strange to her ears, her cry a strangled mix of her own agony and an agony of Soutar: but then, remarkably, he was gone. As suddenly as he had taken her, he was gone. It was over.

Lidya looked up. She was on her knees, in the dirt – Yeshua was standing over her, his hand still on her head. His cloak was still around her – she clung to it, and began to cry. Soutar was gone! But now there was nothing! Nothing – a strange emptiness of spirit and soul.

The Stone lay in Yeshua's palm. Lidya stared at it, wanting to take it back – she resisted. And now Yeshua's hand was on her shoulder.

"You must not remain as an empty house."

"An empty house?" she whispered, reminded of the Heartland.

"Every home is built to be dwelt within," he said. And now, again, his hand was on her head: he murmured a few words, and she gasped.

Spirit. Astonished, she gazed at him: at the gentleness of his face, at the complexity of his eyes – a sudden ancient feel to his gaze.

The spirit flooded through her, as water to the parched desert of her soul – the Spirit of Atua. Darkness was overcome by light, evil undone by goodness. It hurt! At first it hurt, the cure to begin with as potent as the disease – but quickly the pain faded, to be replaced by a gentle presence, a secure peace and purpose.

Love. In wonder, Lidya held his eyes. Love: this was the entire purpose. This was the true Life.

She found herself flat, on the ground: prostrate. But then she was lifted to her feet. The cloak she returned to Yeshua. Then she watched as Yeshua laid the Stone of Soutar on the ground.

"You are not going to destroy it?" Lidya asked.

"Now is not the right time."

"But if we leave it here…"

And now Gamel walked up to the Stone, and lifted it.

"Oh, no…"

Lidya shook her head, meeting his eyes. "Don't wear it!" she pleaded, and he sadly touched her face.

"You have changed, Lidya."

"I am safe!"

"So it seems."

"What about you?"

Gamel's blue eyes looked a little wet. He glanced to Yeshua, who stood silently alongside, and then looked back to Lidya.

"I don't know," he said. "I'll keep it. I'll protect others from it."

"Gamel…"

"I don't know, Lidi! Don't push me!"

Lidya reached out to draw her fingers down his face. This was her brother! But now, suddenly, there was a huge chasm between them!

"Give the Stone to Yeshua," she said – and he shook his head curtly, and backed away from her a step.

"Don't you understand?" Lidya cried. "Soutar will come for you! Don't you see that?"

"Of course I see it!" he said. "Don't you think I know that? I have no choice!"

"You do have a choice! Choose Yeshua!"

"Don't be a fool!" Gamel cried. "Soutar I know – but this man? We've only just met him, Lidya! The first one who offers you kindness and you run to him with open arms? How could you entrust him with the Stone, Lidi? I thought you knew better!"

Flushing, Lidya stared at him. Yeshua stood quietly, not speaking – not moving. Gamel glanced at him briefly, seeming conflicted – and then he turned to walk again over to Koram, and Taierre.

Lidya stared after him, shocked. And then she felt the hand of Yeshua to her shoulder.

"Do not be afraid," he murmured.

"Afraid?" she whispered.

"For your brother. The One who is dwelling within you now is stronger, Lidya, than the one who still has power over him."

"But how can we save him?"

Yeshua paused for a moment – and then spoke.

"Not all people wish to be saved, Lidya: do you know this? Some cling to their illness, like you clung to my cloak – some cling to Soutar, though he abuses them and oppresses them. They, like you did, fear the alternative more: they fear a whole new life."

"But how can we change their minds?"

Yeshua smiled sadly. "Their minds have been given to them, Lidya – and so has their choice been given."

Lidya tilted her head, studying him. "Even if their choice should lead to suffering and death?"

A shadow passed over Yeshua's face – and then it was gone.

"Yes, Lidi: that has been our choice – to give them choice, even if it should lead to suffering and death."

Lidya frowned slightly. "But that means..."

"Yes."

"All of Altenhine lies in the balance."

"Even in the midst of great evil, goodness can be found. Sometimes the greatest goodness can be found at the depths of the greatest evil."

His expression intrigued Lidya now – he was hinting at something, she was sure of it: but then that moment also passed.

"What should I do?"

"Follow me," he said. "And keep following."

"And when all is done?"

"Keep following, Lidya: no matter what takes place. Never give up – never let me go."

Tears filled her eyes again – he was warning her! Something was going to happen – something difficult; perhaps many things.

"All right," she said, grasping his hand. "No matter what happens – I will never let you go."

He smiled: he grasped her hand in return.

"I know," he said. "And neither will I let you go."

He held her gaze for a moment; and then he turned, and returned to his followers at the campsite.

# CHAPTER TWENTY-TWO: An Invitation

Gamel sat still.

Lidya was sitting across the other side of the camp, with the followers of Yeshua: listening to him speak.

Gamel watched her, from the distance – wary. Something enormous had happened to her the night before – something well beyond his reach. She had given the Stone to Yeshua: how could she have done that? How could she have trusted him? And...and yet Yeshua had cast Soutar off her.

Gamel trembled. Could it be true that this man, in a few moments, had actually achieved the very thing they had sought? So quickly, and without ceremony, dismissing Soutar? Gamel had seen her torment, and then her peace: he had also seen the love that had passed between them – the love that dwelt within Lidya even now. That love: it seemed to be keeping Soutar away! But...but Gamel could not follow her into such a deep place of trust.

He turned away: but the words of Yeshua, in Yeri, were soft on the wind behind him.

"What is he saying?" Koram asked him, digging up the charred branches from the camp fire the night before. "I can only catch the odd word from what Echari taught us of Yeri."

"I don't know," Gamel quickly answered, lying – but then he thought better of it, and began to translate for both Koram and Taierre in Altenhanse.

"'Love others,'" Gamel quoted Yeshua, "'and love will come to you.'"

Gamel shifted in discomfort, but continued. "'If someone from another tribe comes up to you and hits you, what should you do? Hit him back? Or if someone from a village through the trees steals from you, what should you do: steal back from him?'"

"You are very fluent in the translation," Taierre commented – and Gamel frowned.

"I can't explain that."

"Keep translating," Koram said, with interest, and for his sake Gamel continued.

"'It's easy to hit back when you are hit, but I say this: don't hit back – let the other man hit you, and don't fight him. And it's easy to steal from someone who has stolen from you, but I say, don't: rather give something extra to the person who has stolen from you.'"

"Interesting advice," Koram said, "To those who are, from what Captain Nehu said, doing a lot of fighting."

"Let your enemy defeat you?" Taierre said. "This man clearly knows nothing of war."

Gamel felt himself captured, however, by Yeshua's words – as much as he felt uncomfortable. He turned back to look at him.

"Don't fight him..." he murmured, remembering the incident of the Northerner attack: his own dismay at Taierre's execution of the one who had almost murdered him. "He would not have killed him."

"Naïve," Taierre said, but Gamel shook his head.

114

"I don't believe that."

"My actions that night saved you, Prince Gamel."

Gamel looked at Taierre – saw the dignity in the man: a kind of nobility, even, in his actions, even as they had moved opposite to Yeshua's words.

"I know, Taierre," he said quietly. "I appreciate your defence on my behalf."

Taierre's face eased – and Gamel again strained to hear the words of Yeshua.

"'What does it achieve, to hit the one who hits you? Are you not committing the same crime? And what does it prove to steal from the one who steals from you? Are you not then also becoming a thief? No – I say give good things to the ones who do evil against you: undo their evil with your goodness. If someone hates you, don't pay them back hatred in return: rather, give them love.'"

At this, Gamel choked on the translation.

Taierre was silent, alongside. Koram also was silent. Gamel glanced back to see Taierre looking down into his hand, with a frown: fingering something. With a chill Gamel realized it was the stone of the South.

"Taierre...?"

"Undo evil with goodness?" Taierre said. "How? How does one overcome the evil of Soutar with good, future King of the Heartland?"

Challenged to his core, Gamel stared at him – and at his stone. Then he looked at Koram.

The Northerner now pulled out his stone of the North – and laid it quietly on the ground, for consideration.

"This stone," he began formally, "I would gladly give to you, Prince Gamel, if you had the power to overcome it with goodness. It is this kind of power I am seeking, on behalf of my king."

Gamel flushed before him. "I have no such power, Sir Koram," he said.

"Nonetheless, the task belongs to you," Taierre said. "Both of our kings recognise your authority."

Sweat poured down Gamel's face – and down his body. "I know what you are saying is true," he said, "but I don't know how I could be seen to have authority in this matter."

"Your authority is borne out of your bloodline," Taierre said. "You are the next in line for the Throne of the Heartland. Our kings continue to seek your allegiance. The one who wields the Heartland Stone has authority over the stones of the North and South also."

The Stone of Soutar was beginning to burn again in Gamel's pocket.

*You carry the greatest burden of all.* Yeshua's words returned.

"Please," Gamel whispered. "Don't do this..."

*Put on the Stone,* Soutar said, *and I will give you the strength you need.*

Gamel shuddered – and jerked the Stone away from himself, back onto the ground. He looked up, to see if anyone had seen – and found Lidya's eyes. She calmed him! Still, her presence comforted him. She knew, and did not judge, and did not command.

"Help me," he mouthed, only to her – but she gestured discreetly to Yeshua.

"'Love those who hate you, and do good to those who mistreat you.'"

*Love?* Soutar said from within. *Love him?*

115

And now the memory was upon him again – his father beating him!

*Worthless second prince! What good are you, but to play like a child!*

Gamel sank to the ground, wrapping his arms around his head – but then Yeshua was standing in front of him, casting a shadow from the heat of the sun.

"The heart of a child can change the World."

Gamel gazed up at him – at the face, slightly hidden in shadow.

"Who are you?" he pleaded – and Yeshua smiled sadly.

"I am not a Magician."

"I see that now. But – forgive me, Sir – I need to know who you are."

Yeshua knelt down before him now – a ripple of surprise passed through the crowd watching them. His face was serious as he held Gamel's eyes.

"I tell you the truth, young man," he murmured, barely loud enough for Gamel to hear, "My true identity is the key to life: my life and your life."

Puzzled, Gamel watched him. The Stone of Soutar was lying on the ground alongside them – Gamel began to panic as Yeshua bent to pick it up. But now he was returning it into Gamel's hand.

"This Stone," he said quietly, "Also is the key to life."

"What do you mean?" Gamel asked.

"The burden, the evil, the pain, Gamel – where can these be silenced? Where can these be put to rest? Your solution to the Stone is also your pathway into true life."

"Yes..." Gamel breathed. "And not just for me: for many after me."

"Yes, Gamel."

"But how does that fit with your identity?"

Yeshua smiled, and rose to his feet – lifting Gamel also before him. "Do you know, Prince Gamel of the Heartland?" he said. "It is the wonder of Atua to hide the things of most importance – the greatest treasures of all. But why does he do it? So that the truly noble man might declare himself in searching for them; so that the truly noble woman might reveal herself in finding them. Yet you must search with all your heart."

He had finished. Gamel tilted his head thoughtfully – and Yeshua bowed his head and then backed away.

"What did he say?" Koram asked – and Gamel gazed after Yeshua.

"Everything I longed to hear."

"Everything?" Koram sounded surprised, "In so few words?"

"It is the wonder of Atua to hide things..."

Yeshua led the crowd back over to the other side of the camp – Gamel watched, and caught Lidya's eye. She was enquiring – but found him to be settled. She smiled, and returned to her place in front of Yeshua, and Gamel released her to do so.

*...and the truly noble person will search for them and find them.*

He replaced the Stone back into his right trouser pocket – but the voice of Soutar had been silenced: at least for now.

CHAPTER TWENTY-THREE: Danger

Yeshua spoke to the people for a long time – it must have been many hours. Impressed, Gamel sat silently – listening to his voice, though from a distance.

Taierre often shifted impatiently, pacing a little outside of the tent. Sometimes, out of sight, he drew his sword, studying its edge – always ready: always the warrior. The Stone of the South was back in his trouser pocket – hidden in Yeri folds. Gamel understood his impatience – this was a man of action first, and of words second: a man who would readily die for the defence of his nation, and for his king. Gamel respected him: he had spoken the truth – his skills had saved Gamel's life that night. But had execution of the Northerner really been necessary? Gamel had wanted to show him mercy.

And here was Yeshua…a man of mercy.

"You feel drawn to him." It was Koram – watching Gamel.

"I do," Gamel said, his eyes still on Yeshua.

"What do you seen in him?"

"I see…" Gamel strained to find the answer. "I see love."

"Yes."

Now Gamel glanced at Koram: the older man. "And you?" he asked quietly. "What do you think of Yeshua?"

Koram frowned slightly, tilting his head as he studied the Yeri speaker.

"I think he is a man of real character," he said, "Unusual character. Certainly he is a leader…"

"Yes," Gamel quickly agreed.

"And…there is something else: I can't put my finger on it."

"No?"

"Something about him…some cost…"

Frowning, Gamel looked back at Yeshua – and then he started.

A group of men of medium brown skin, as that of Yeshua, and of Yeri clothes, had formed a standing circle around him.

"Gamel." Taierre was now standing behind Gamel's back. "Beware."

Koram also had risen to his feet alongside.

Gamel hastily searched for Lidya – and saw Echari discreetly drawing her, and Berui, to the back of the crowd. Gamel hesitated, feeling safer further apart – but then wandered over to the others.

The crowd was beginning to disperse – but some lingered. Gamel saw Lidya waiting, watching – Echari's warning hand on her shoulder.

"What is happening?" Gamel asked.

"It is the Beli Tribe," Echari replied. "These are their leaders."

"The Beli Tribe fights Yeshua's tribe?"

"The Beli Tribe *is* Yeshua's tribe."

Astonished, Gamel looked at Echari's face – his black skin.

"Not your tribe…"

"No: we are the Talu Tribe."

"Do the Talu fight the Beli?"

"No, Prince Gamel – we have not fought the Beli since Yeshua came. We have water, and have started to share freely with our neighbours the Talu: but now…"

Echari's face clouded. He glanced at his mother, who patted his arm.

"Do not fear," she murmured. "Atua will protect his own."

And she gestured to Yeshua.

A muscular man, older, stepped forward toward Yeshua – carrying a long, wide harvesting knife, speaking in Yeri.

"Send these people away!"

"That is the Beli chief," Echari whispered, "Teru."

"They are my guests," Yeshua said. "I received them to our land according to our customs."

"Our customs do not cater for thousands of foreigners, Beli Yeri," Teru said. "I sent you from our land, yet now you dwell with them amongst the Talu?"

"I go where I am welcome."

"You cover your own tribe in filth! You disrespect my wishes: I, your chief!"

Gamel watched as Yeshua held his angry stare. "I bring you no disrespect, my chief."

"Bow, then, Yeshua! Prove you still hold allegiance to me, and not to the Talu above me!"

Yeshua searched his eyes – and then promptly knelt before him.

Gamel watched, astonished, as the chief stepped back. The anger on his face eased – but then he lifted the harvesting knife to Yeshua's neck. Gamel held his breath – but then, suddenly, Teru lowered the knife to cut Yeshua on the right cheek.

Yeshua's eyes closed – but he did not move.

"It is a punishment," Echari whispered, "One slight for another. The chief has the right to draw blood."

Gamel swallowed – but now Yeshua looked up into his chief's eyes.

"I mean you no harm, my chief: I am not an enemy. I am amassing no force against you."

Teru seemed, in that moment, perplexed. Then another man stepped forward from the crowd: dark skinned, as Echari and Berui, clothed in richer thicker purple linen.

"Chief Teru," he said, bowing from the waist before him. "We welcome you to our land."

"It is our chief," Echari said, voice enthused, "Chief Dela."

"Receive water, and fish and corn," Dela said, "For you and your men. We still maintain our pledge: to share water with your land."

Teru bowed in return. "I thank you, Chief Dela, for your continued generosity."

"We," Dela said, "Unlike the Beli, are able to cater for the foreigners travelling to Yeri: we welcome all. We welcome Yeshua, also."

Intrigued, Gamel watched closely. Teru was frowning – yet he also seemed appeased.

"What interest have you in Yeshua?" he asked, and Dela smiled.

"We find his words, and his actions, intriguing."

"How so?"

"He speaks of peace, not war."

"Of peace?"

"Of patience; of generosity. We are happy to hear more."

Teru nodded, as if in acceptance – but then another man of the Beli Tribe stepped forward, dressed scantily, carrying a wooden staff.

"It is the witch doctor Kami," Echari whispered, "The spiritual advisor to Chief Teru."

Kami circled around the kneeling Yeshua – and then, suddenly, he hit him with the staff, across the cut cheek.

Yeshua gasped – and his jaw clenched tightly. He remained on his knees.

"Patience?" Kami spat over his head, "Patience, child of Atua? We will not bow to your spirit – our spirits are in command: taste their power – taste the wrath of Satine!"

Now the man was pressing some kind of plant into Yeshua's mouth: now he was forcing his hand against his head, speaking some other language – pressing in. Gamel stared, sweating – and then felt the Stone of Soutar burning hot in his pocket. He grasped it out, staring at the glowing red garnet eyes – his hand burning under it. Taierre and Koram were behind him – they also were drawing out the stones of South and North, staring at them: dropping them with a gasp.

Gamel heard Taierre draw his sword, heard Koram insist 'No' – but Gamel's eyes were fixed on Yeshua. His body was shaking, under the intensity of the attack – but then his eyes opened. He held the stare of the man – he spat out the plant.

"Atua is King of all the spirits," he said. And then he rose to his feet.

The Stone of Soutar went cold in Gamel's hand. Astounded, he stared at Yeshua.

"Who is he?" he whispered. "Who is he?"

Chief Teru glanced at his own advisor with some disdain – and then nodded to Chief Dela.

"We accept your hospitality," he said – and his party began to move after Dela. Kami glared at Yeshua, and Yeshua held his gaze – but then Kami was compelled to follow after his chief.

"What was that?" Koram asked, from behind Gamel, and Echari answered with excitement in his tone.

"Yeshua just defeated Kami!"

"What does that mean?" Lidya asked.

"He overcame Satine!" Berui said. "Satine is the most powerful of the evil spirits."

"The evil spirits?" Gamel asked.

"The witch doctors of Satine – they sacrifice to him! They appease him. He gives them power!"

Now chills went up Gamel's spine. Soutar! Sacrifice – and power...He glanced back to Taierre and Koram, to see their stern expressions of recognition – and then looked back to Yeshua.

"He just overcame Satine?"

"Satine is the leader of the evil spirits!"

"The leader?"

Now, gasping, Gamel stared down at the Stone of Soutar in his hand.

"But that means..."

"Yeshua has the power to overcome Soutar."

It was Lidya's voice.

Gamel looked at her – at the gentle beauty of her white face, amongst brown: at the love in her eyes.

"I know what you would have me do," he said – but then Echari's voice interrupted.

"What is this, Prince Gamel?"

He had seen the stone.

Heart pounding, Gamel stared at him. "I..." he stuttered. "I..."

Echari reached to touch it – but Gamel seized it away. "Don't!" he said.

"It looks like other stones I have seen."

"Others?"

"Chief Dela has one – though he does not wear it."

"No?"

"Chief Teru, too – I have seen him sometimes wearing one."

Gamel gazed at his inquisitive face. "What do you know of them, Echari?"

"They are stones used in black witchcraft."

Gamel swallowed, glanced at Koram and Taierre and looked back to Echari. "What are they used for?"

"To control, Prince Gamel."

"What do you mean, my friend?"

Echari glanced at his mother and then back at Gamel, looking sad.

"My father, Prince Gamel: he was involved in the craft. He was spiritual advisor to Chief Dela."

Lidya now shifted, next to Echari – and took his hand. "What happened to him?"

"He died."

Gamel stared at him – his throat constricting. Friedrich! Tears filled his eyes – he blinked them away.

"How did he die?"

"He began to follow Atua."

Now Lidya jerked her hand away. Gamel felt his hair standing on end. Lidya! Lidya was following Atua!

"But Yeshua..."

Now tears filled Echari's dark eyes. "He won, Prince Gamel – do you not see it? In the battle, spirit against spirit, he won!"

"Yes," Gamel choked, "Yeshua won, but what about Lidya?"

Lidya's face was pale. "I will go to him," she said.

"Go to him?" Echari asked.

"I need his strength."

"Do not be afraid." It was Berui – her motherly face warm and calming. "My husband was a priest of Satine: death was the price of his freedom."

"What do you mean?" Gamel whispered.

"He gave himself fully to Satine: his life was bound to him. He controlled others through Satine's power. But then, when Yeshua came, he turned and followed Atua instead: he led Chief Dela to do the same."

"He led your Chief to Yeshua?" Gamel was amazed.

"It cost him his life, Prince Gamel: betraying Satine. He chose Satine's enemy. But true life comes after death, young Prince."

"Life after death?"

"This life is not the end: only the beginning. It is a pathway into what will be: a birth into a fuller life beyond."

"What…?"

Gamel felt surreal, listening to her: transformed to another place. But now he blinked, shaking himself, and turned his attention back to Lidya.

"I will go to him," she said – and she gathered herself, and moved away.

## CHAPTER TWENTY-FOUR: A Revelation of Yeshua

Yeshua had moved away from the camp – to a place through the trees, next to the small lake.

Lidya stood at the edge of the clearing, watching him for a moment. Should she allow him privacy? What was he doing? He seemed lost in thought, staring down at the water – his lips moving, as if in conversation with an unseen companion.

She hesitated, almost turning to leave him in peace – but then decided to move forward, toward the lake.

He was sitting, now, on a rock at the waterside. Lidya wandered quietly up to him – and sat herself down on the ground, alongside the rock, looking into the water.

For a long moment he remained silent – and both sat, side by side. Then he spoke.

"What do you want from me, daughter of the Heartland?"

Lidya frowned, gazing at the ripples in the water. "I'm not sure, Sir," she said. "I think I need you."

"What is it you need from me?"

She hesitated – and then shook her head. "Only to be with you. My need now has gone."

"You are safe."

Happiness filled Lidya. Yes! With him, she was safe – with him she felt strong. She smiled at him – and then was shocked to find his eyes wet with tears.

"Sir!"

He was so human! Remarkable as he was – he was still thoroughly human. She frowned, searching him – trying to understand.

"Where is your family?" she asked gently – and he smiled sadly.

"Anyone who receives me is my family."

"You seem…" The answer struck her hard in its familiarity. Lonely! Or not so much lonely – rather wholly alone. Not lonely, because…there was another…

"Sir…"

"You may call me Yeshua, Lidya."

Moved, she gazed at him. "Yeshua."

Again he smiled sadly. His cheek was still bleeding. She reached to attend to it, but he grasped her hand.

"No."

"But why?"

"It is…" He sighed heavily. "It is necessary."

"What is necessary?"

"The pain."

Tears filled her eyes, now: she did not blink them away.

"Why?" she whispered.

"Because…" Again he sighed. "Such is the cost."

"The cost?"

"Of being human."

122

Lidya cast her eyes over his face – brown, dark crimped hair: his eyes, wide, brown. It really wasn't his appearance that drew her – it was something else: something more – someone more...

"You feel Atua..." she breathed, and he looked a little surprised.

"I do," he said.

"Atua is to you what Satine is to that witch doctor."

"Yes, but there is much more to it."

"Much more? Tell me."

"I cannot – it is not yet the right time."

"The right time for what?"

"For the truth to be made known."

She tilted her head, watching him. He rose to his feet, and wandered down to the water – crouched, and dipped his fingers in.

"You..." She was struggling to find the words for her impression, in that moment: struggling to understand. "You..."

He lifted his finger to his cheek, and then back down to the water – rose to his feet, and turned: and the wound on his cheek was gone.

Lidya stared.

"Tell no one," he said.

"But..." she whispered. "But..."

Again his eyes filled with tears. "My time is coming, but it is not yet here, Lidya! Soon you will see it: soon you will know. When you realize it, Lidya, say nothing! Tell no one what you have discovered..."

"The evil spirits..."

"Can evil love, Lidya? Can evil create goodness? Can evil bring life to those who are in darkness?"

Lidya began to weep. "Only you!" she sobbed, "Only you."

"Not only me," he said, grasping her arms. "Atua, Lidya! All life comes from Atua. Soon you will understand."

"Soutar kills!" she sobbed. "Satine kills! Even those who follow Atua, Satine kills!"

Now tears poured down her cheeks. Yeshua wiped the tears away with his hand.

"Grieve, Lidya," he said, "In this life, to grieve is to keep choosing to love. But soon the time for grieving will be over! Soon! Sometimes death is necessary for new life."

He smiled at her – a gentle smile of encouragement. "Go," he said gently. And she backed away from him, and turned to leave.

As she reached the edge of the camp site, she turned back – and saw him. He was on his knees, his arms over his hidden head, his body shaking hard in silent weeping. She sobbed, just once – then turned away, back to the crowd.

Gamel approached her – and she swayed slightly before him.

"What is it?"

Sorrow filled her – but she could not put words to it. "I don't know," she whispered.

123

Gamel's hand was on her shoulder – her brother! She was grateful for his touch. He embraced her, and she cried – he hid her in his arms. He asked no questions – somehow knew not to ask. And then there was a movement.

Lidya looked up – to see Yeshua emerging from between the trees.

His eyes were set with purpose. Perplexed, Lidya watched him – and Yeshua walked straight down to a group of children sitting on a mat next to the well.

One child, very dark, was reaching with his hands – he could not see. Yeshua reached to lay a hand over the boy's head, murmured a few words, and the child rose to his feet – jumping up and down, looking around at the other children, reaching to feel their faces.

"Gamel…" Lidya whispered, grasping his arm.

Yeshua now reached for another child – a young girl, lying on the ground with a twisted hip. He murmured over her, reached for her hands – pulled her up to her feet. And she was walking, jumping, skipping…

"Look!" Lidya cried. "Look!"

She pulled Gamel around to look – and another child was reaching for Yeshua, asking for help: he laid a hand over him, and his twisted hands were set free.

Now adults began to see – now adults began to move. A huge shout was raised in the air – men staggered, women hurried: scars disappeared, backs were straightened, the staggering were set straight on course – women wept, children laughed…

Lidya stared – and wondered.

"Recreated…" she whispered. "It's almost as if…"

"What?" Gamel breathed, behind her.

"Wait here."

Lidya moved now, away from the crowd, searching for Koram and Taierre – she found them again at the other side of the camp, inside the tent.

"Sir Koram!" she called out, and he emerged.

"Yes, Princess Lidya?" he said, tipping his head to her.

"The legends, Sir," she said. "What did the legends of the North say of the greater spirit – the one more powerful than the others?"

Koram frowned at her. "There was fear, and love."

"Yes – and what else?"

"Worship."

"Yes – anything else?"

Koram tilted his head thoughtfully – and then Lidya pointed to the activity across the camp. She watched Koram's eyebrows lift in astonishment – he called Taierre out also to look. And then he looked to Lidya.

"The beginning," he said. "They say he was the beginning, when there was no other."

*Can evil create goodness?*

"Spirit…" she whispered. "Not just 'a' spirit: '*the*' Spirit…"

*All life comes from Atua.*

The origin.

Astonished, Lidya turned to watch Yeshua recreating broken and diseased bodies before him. Who was he? He was so human, and yet he was with Atua – human, but one with Atua.

She felt, within herself, love – she felt, within, the Spirit: life, joy – but not as he. She felt, if she should pray, like he, the opportunity for Atua to move – for the Spirit to move. She felt, if she should submit, the opportunity for Atua to heal through her spirit – through her hands. She felt herself a vessel for him – a house for him. But not as he: not as Yeshua.

What, then, was the difference? Who was Yeshua?

'Child of Atua,' the witch doctor had said. 'Child.' 'Son.' One.

*At the beginning...*

Lidya gasped. At the beginning? But that meant...

She stared at him. The people were pressing him from all sides, now: presenting him with all kinds of disease. He persevered. He would surely work for hours. He was tired – they did not see. But they did talk. They rushed to each other – they shouted of their healings. And they began to leave the camp – to rush to tell others, and bring them also.

*Tell no-one.*

They were about to tell! They were about to tell the world!

*Tell no-one what you have discovered.*

Koram was behind her, also watching Yeshua: also staring. Taierre's teeth were gritted: his face a wall. Lidya turned back to the crowd – and then she saw Gamel, very close now to Yeshua, always watching him. He turned, now – Gamel looked straight into her eyes. And there, in him, she saw naked fear.

## CHAPTER TWENTY-FIVE: Exposure

Gamel was close to Yeshua.

Shuddering, he watched the on-going outpouring around him. People were pressing in from all sides, to get to Yeshua – calling out to him with their sicknesses, crying out for healing.

Gamel could see clearly, now, everything that was happening – a man was in front of him, old, both eyes scarred: Yeshua laid a hand over his eyes, murmured a few words, and Gamel saw the scars dissolve away. The man could see! He looked at Yeshua, grasped his face, jumped up and down – laughed.

Another woman was there, her foot turned in from birth – Yeshua spoke to her, reaching down to the foot, and it straightened.

A cheer went up, and more pressing took place – people were asking for rashes to be healed, pains, seeing strange lights…and then a man was before Yeshua, with a stone.

Gamel jerked back away. The stone was black, carved in the shape of a vulture. The man was on his knees, writhing before Yeshua – crying out, his voice strangled.

Yeshua laid a hand on his head, closed his eyes – spoke a few words, and the man screamed. Gamel closed his eyes tightly at the sound – but when he looked again the man was on his feet, looking relieved.

Yeshua took the stone, and placed it in a shirt pocket. Gamel watched and then froze – Yeshua was looking directly at him! Then the moment passed. Yeshua continued, and Gamel continued to watch – unable to move with the crowd pressing in.

At last Gamel freed himself – and returned to the tent. Lidya was away somewhere – still watching Yeshua, with the people. Koram also was gone. Gamel wanted to hide away – but Taierre was still there.

"What do you make of this charade, Prince Gamel?" Taierre said.

"Charade?" Gamel said.

"The people flock to him, after a few children mock healings. No doubt they were paid."

"You really don't respect him much, do you."

"I do not."

"But why not, Taierre? Why do you not allow him a chance for your respect?"

Taierre held his gaze, and his expression softened a little.

"There are many reasons why, Prince of the Heartland."

"Explain them to me."

"Firstly, I cannot respect a man who will not fight to defend his own."

Surprised, Gamel looked at him. "But he is fighting to defend them, Taierre: can't you see that?"

He gestured toward the crowd. "He is simply fighting in a different way to how you would fight."

"A sword is a sword, Gamel: and so is a staff a staff."

"And words are words, and actions are actions. There are many kinds of weapons, Taierre."

"Perhaps – but a teacher cannot pass on anything if he is dead."

Gamel swallowed – and then prodded him. "Why else do you block him?"

"He lures weaker men and women."

"'Weaker'?"

"Those who find no hope elsewhere."

"You mean like us?" Wryly Gamel considered him. "Next to Soutar, anyone would be weak, Taierre: you know this."

A shadow passed over Taierre's face. He swallowed – but continued.

"I value strength, not weakness, Prince Gamel."

"I know," Gamel replied. "But sometimes the greatest strength is found in the most profound weakness."

"What does that mean?"

Gamel searched him – and took a deep breath. "I would not wish it on you, Taierre – not again. I would not wish profound weakness on anyone. But it does teach us."

"It teaches us what?"

"What we can do and what we can't do."

"Indeed?"

"Where our limitations lie: where our true needs lie."

He paused for a moment – and then nodded to Taierre again.

"Tell me more of your reservations."

"I cannot accept another Leader."

"Another leader?"

"This man: he expects the listeners to follow. My allegiance is to my king."

"They need not conflict: the two allegiances. He knelt to his chief, though he also kneels to Atua."

"I think, Gamel – I do not simply blindly follow."

"Then do think, Taierre: think about what the man is saying! Don't just block him at every turn. Do you think I want to carry your stone?"

At this Taierre flushed. A little agitated, Gamel left him in the tent and stepped outside.

Now Koram was there. Gamel looked at him – and took a deep breath.

"What do you make of all of this?" he asked – and Koram's eyebrows rose.

"I don't know what to make of it, Gamel."

"He makes blind people see again."

"Perhaps...or perhaps their blindness was not so fixed after all."

"Really?" Gamel surmised. "Think they made it up?"

"Perhaps they convinced themselves."

"I saw scars disappear! They made it up? Surely there are better objections than this!"

Gamel began to pace, feeling Koram's eyes upon him.

"You are searching for better reasons to reject what you see, Prince Gamel?"

Gamel rubbed his arms. "I don't want to be here!" he said. "I don't want to be here."

127

The Stone was warming up again in his pocket.

Gamel slipped away, again, from the tent – from Taierre and Koram. The sun was lowering in the sky – darkness was beginning to settle, and the cool of evening. He shrank away from the camp – amongst trees on the furthest most side. Soutar began, his voice a whisper – the stone enticing. Gamel resisted – and sweated.

*You don't want him.*

"Go away!" Gamel cried. "Go away."

*He will make you weak! He will strip you, as Taierre fears! He will rule over you. I will empower you – I will strengthen your desires.*

The Heartland was before Gamel, now – he longed to be there: to be home! Ownership pulsated through his body.

*I will give it all to you to keep – no more struggles here! No more heat, and sweat – no more thirst.*

"Leave me," Gamel pleaded.

*I will never leave you – not until I have my reward.*

And now Soutar pressed in. *Put on the Stone.*

"Leave me."

*Put on the Stone!*

"Leave me!"

*Put on the Stone! Put on the Stone! Put on the Stone!"*

Desperately Gamel clawed in front of himself – but could not rid himself of the voice within.

"Let me heal you."

Sinking to his knees, Gamel stared helplessly as Yeshua came to stand over him. He looked tired. How had he escaped the crowd? Perhaps by the cover of night.

"What does healing even mean?" Gamel asked.

"You must forgive your father."

Gamel felt a stab to his heart. "Forgive my father?" he said, "That I could never do."

"Then Soutar will always control you, Prince Gamel: future King of the Heartland."

Gamel gazed up at him – into his tired eyes. "Why are you doing all of this for us?"

Yeshua smiled slightly. "You do not know?" he asked, "and you are to be a king?"

Humbled, Gamel held his eyes. "Help me," he pleaded. "I don't know how to be a king without Soutar."

"Give me your heart."

Gamel trembled hard before him. "I want to give you my heart," he whispered, "But I can't give you the stone, and I can't forgive."

"Understand," Yeshua said, "You cannot be healed unless you surrender the stone."

"I know," Gamel pleaded, with cold sweat.

"Don't you see, Gamel?" Yeshua said. "Your anger and your hatred corrupt you: they turn you into being a child of Soutar. They make you into a temple for his bidding – they block the Spirit of Atua."

"I can't forgive him!"

"Then why should I forgive you?"

Stunned, Gamel stared at him. "Forgive me?"

"Yes, Gamel: why should I help you?"

Gamel shook violently before him now.

*He will never forgive you!* Soutar hissed. *I have you in my grip! I have blackened you – what would he want with you, but to throw you away as a worthless and spiteful child?*

Gamel's back arched in agony. "I'm useless!" he cried. "I was useless to Daddy!"

"Give me the Stone!" Yeshua said.

Gamel screamed. "Useless! Useless! Useless!"

And now Soutar stirred the pain in his depths, channelling it into anger – channelling into darkness.

"I hate him!" Gamel gasped. "I hate him! I hate him, I hate him!"

"The Stone is your hatred, Gamel! The Stone is your pain! Give it to me, and live!"

"The hatred saves me!" Gamel insisted, feeling himself hardened: feeling himself girded. "The anger protects me!"

"Atua will save you!" Yeshua said. "Atua is Love. Give me the stone!"

Now Gamel laughed – bitterness flowing through his body.

"Atua will save me?" he cried. "Save me from a lifetime of King Maki? He will not save me, any more than he saved my Friedrich! Is Atua strongest of the spirits? Then where was he when Soutar destroyed my family? Where was he when Soutar killed my brother?

"He left him to die! He leaves me to die! I hate Atua! I hate him! I hate him! And I hate you!"

Now Gamel began to beat on Yeshua's chest. "How dare you?" he cried. "How dare you try to tell me that Atua is Love! How dare you? How dare you?"

Gamel beat on his chest, again and again and again. "I hate you! I hate you! I hate you!"

Soutar was gone, somehow: Gamel knew now his outpouring was his own – his hatred was his own.

He spent himself – and found himself sinking on the very chest he had beaten.

"Father...?" he pleaded, with tears. "Father...?"

Yeshua was weeping! Astounded, Gamel looked up to see Yeshua's wet face – he reached, again as a child, to touch the face: to try to understand...and then, suddenly, Yeshua was dragged away from him.

## CHAPTER TWENTY-SIX: Offering

Kami stood tall, in front of Yeshua – drawing his staff along Yeshua's right cheek. Three other men, of Chief Teru's group, were with him – holding Yeshua still.

Gamel cried out for help – he was struck across the face, and fell to the ground.

From the dirt, at Yeshua's feet, Gamel looked up. Kami was scowling at Yeshua – grinning, with crooked teeth. Yeshua was quiet – his face surprisingly calm.

"I see you also practise witchcraft, child of Atua!" Kami hissed. "Healings? Your cheek is whole."

"Witchcraft is not my practice," Yeshua said. "The power I wield belongs to Atua alone."

"You despise the practices of your ancestors! You despise the practices of your Chief!"

Now Gamel saw Chief Teru, standing in the distance – nodding his assent, commanding Kami's actions.

"I despise no one," Yeshua said. "My ancestors worshiped Atua. Our sages worshiped Atua."

Kami encircled him now – while Yeshua stared out ahead of himself.

"Your mother was a precious girl," Kami began, "Raped, at fifteen, to conceive you."

Yeshua's eyes closed. "She was not raped."

"No father, child of Atua! You have no father! I cannot believe such a fine girl offered herself as a whore..."

Yeshua swayed slightly on his feet. Gamel stared at him, and at Kami – and then felt hands pulling him up from the ground. Koram and Taierre were there! And Echari, and Berui – and Lidya...

Dismayed, Gamel looked at Lidya. Her face was white, staring at Yeshua: listening to the words.

"Certainly she does not act the whore now, Yeshua, in our captivity. But rape? Yes: this is more than feasible. It seems Atua does not protect her now – just as he did not protect her then, as your conception testifies."

Yeshua's hands clenched into fists at his sides. "The past rests in the testimony of my mother and of Atua," he said. "As for the present: you will stand before Atua with your crimes exposed."

"You call me a criminal?" Kami spat. "I say the true criminal is Atua himself! She worships him, she follows him – she loves him! She even endures rape for him. Yet he stands back and does nothing! Even you, now, knowing her torment, do nothing!"

Taierre shifted behind Gamel, his sword sounding in its sheath – yet again Koram moved to stop him.

"He is impotent!" Taierre whispered loudly.

"He is restrained!" Koram replied.

130

"If the man stands restrained at the rape of his own mother, what in the world would move him?" Taierre strode forward now, with his sword drawn – striding toward Kami.

Kami turned, and reached out a hand to Taierre – as if he had been expecting him. Now Gamel watched as Taierre was seized. He stiffened – and reached into his pocket. The Stone of the South! It was alight: glowing! Soutar was here!

"Bow to me, warrior of the South."

Taierre's sword fell from his hand – his body fell to his knees. Koram, now, moved – Gamel knew he was compelled to defend his colleague and friend. His sword was drawn – his body, also, was seized: his hand reaching, drawing out the stone – his solid form collapsing onto his knees.

Gamel stared at them. Yeshua was looking at him, frowning! And now the Stone of Soutar came to life.

He reached for it, from his pocket: the eyes were glowing – the whole stone, now, was glowing. *Now is my time.*

Gamel looked between Yeshua and Kami, and then to his friends, on their knees, before Kami. He stepped forward.

"The stones of the North and South belong to me," he said. "I am the King of the Heartland – I demand my inheritance."

He reached now, for the stones: took them, from the hands of Taierre and Koram. The warriors jerked back onto their feet, regaining their control – Taierre backed away, but Koram hesitated.

"Gamel…"

"Leave." Gamel was not looking at him – but he knew Koram also backed away.

Kami smiled at him, now: the crooked smile.

"If these stones are yours," he said, "then you belong to Soutar! And Soutar belongs to Satine. Your fate is in my hands now, boy."

His fingers stretched out toward Gamel's head – Gamel stared at them, shaking hard, falling to his destiny: falling again to conquest…but then Lidya's voice penetrated his defeat.

"The stones also belong to me: and I also demand my inheritance."

And she grasped the three stones from his hands.

Stunned, Gamel stared at her. She was standing alongside him – her face, in beauty, fixed in determination.

Kami grinned at her – and drew a finger along her face. "Pretty, and white," he said. "Even Atua's sages fall into our hands – the sign of the white brother and sister falls under our power!"

"You are mistaken," she whispered. "I do not belong to you."

Now Kami's face hardened into a scowl, as he laid a hand on her chest.

"Atua!" he hissed. "So one belongs to the enemy, and one loiters in distrust of both sides. So be it! You remind me of Yeshua's mother, but with fewer years – with less strength."

"I am his sister," Lidya said.

"Then your fate will be as hers! We will defeat you: you will bow to Soutar, before we are done. Both brother and sister must submit – and then Altenhine will be ours."

Gamel stared at him – and then at Lidya. She might be taken! Might be…

"Lidi!" he sobbed. "I can't let this happen! I can't let them do this to you!"

"Would you give them Altenhine to save Taierre and Koram?" she asked. "Would you give them Altenhine just to save me?"

Her eyes were earnest – and they struck him hard.

"You are the true monarch," he whispered, "Not I."

"You're wrong," Lidya responded. "I need you, and you need me! It's always been that way, Gamel! I need you now! I need you now, and all of Altenhine needs you too…"

Grief-stricken, Gamel watched her. Kami was pulling her to the men. The stones were in Gamel's hands: she had given them to him! They were in his hands…

Yeshua stood apart – the men were now encircling Lidya instead: physical strength added to the spiritual. Gamel found Yeshua's eyes, distraught.

"If I give these to you…"

"…you know what will happen."

Death! The stones brought death! Yet death was necessary, to neutralize them! To break their power!

Gamel shook before him. "Why should you die?" he pleaded. "Why should it not be me?"

Yeshua touched his shoulder. "Your death would not neutralize the stones: only mine. But with me it will end, Gamel: with me it will be finished."

"How do I let the Stone of Soutar go?"

"You also must die."

Gamel shivered before him. "Die?" he breathed.

"For you it is a death of the heart," Yeshua said. "You must face the pain of your father – no longer fight it, Gamel! You must face it – let it be. Let him hurt you – and forgive him for it."

Tears filled Gamel's eyes – childhood returning to his heart. "I was useless to him," he whispered – and now Yeshua touched his face.

"Atua has a purpose for everyone he has made."

The men had Lidya on the ground. Gamel looked to her – saw the nobility in her eyes, with the dread. He looked at Yeshua: saw the same nobility. And then he acted.

In one motion, Gamel laid the three stones upon Yeshua's chest – over his heart.

The Stone of the South. The Stone of the North. The Stone of Soutar.

All, suddenly, joined together as one: all lit up, blood red, as one.

Yeshua's head was thrown back, and he gasped. Gamel stared at him, distraught – what was happening? What was happening?

Kami let out a shriek. "What have you done, fool?" he cried. The men abandoned Lidya to rush back to Yeshua – but now others also were gathering.

Chief Dela stared, and Echari and Berui were behind him.

"Give him the stone!" Echari cried. "Undo the power of Satine!"

Dela strode forward, carrying his own stone by the cord. He hesitated, before Yeshua – and Yeshua grasped his hand.

"Give it to me!" he gasped.

Dela shifted on his feet – and then laid his stone over Yeshua's head, upon his chest. Again, the stone came to life – again it joined with the others, as one: again it shone blood red.

Yeshua's body shook. Tears pricked at Gamel's eyes, watching him – and now others were approaching him, bearing stones: dark brown, light brown, yellow and red – stones of white, black, yellow, green.

"Give them to me!" Yeshua cried. "Give them all to me! All the pain! All the evil! All the guilt – give it all to me!"

The stones were laid over Yeshua's heart – they lit up, they joined as one with the others, they shone blood red: they were forming a shape.

Lidya was beside Gamel now – he felt her hand take his own.

"The suffering of the nations," she whispered, "And the evil of all the nations."

Gamel moaned. "Yes."

"Different spirits, all upon him? How can he survive? The guilt of all humanity? How can he bear it?"

Gamel trembled, his eyes fixed on Yeshua's strained face.

And now Chief Teru stepped forward – and Kami followed.

Teru held up the stone of the Tribe of Beli in front of Yeshua's face.

"By the power of this stone, your mother was raped," he said, and Yeshua's eyes stayed on him.

"By the power of Atua my mother conceived," he whispered.

"Kill him!" Kami hissed, next to his chief. "Kill him now."

Teru frowned, looking between Yeshua and Kami.

"You say Atua will lay bare all of our crimes?"

"All of the crimes which are not surrendered to me," Yeshua gasped. "There will be a Judgment."

"You would carry my crimes, son of Teri? You would carry my order to rape your mother?"

Yeshua swayed before him – still holding his eyes. "If you turn away from Satine and submit your heart to Atua, I will carry your crimes."

Teru seemed stunned. He stood motionless.

"My forefathers…"

"You too can be free," Yeshua said. "Give me the stone."

Teru stared at him – and then, arms jerking, laid the stone on Yeshua's chest.

Yeshua's back arched in a kind of silent agony. Gamel's fists clenched at his sides – but now Kami shrieked out.

"It is finished!"

The stones were combining – the shape forming on Yeshua's chest. It was some kind of symbol! A letter Gamel had seen somewhere before…

"Who are you?" Kami cried. "Tell all of us, son of Teri – son of your mother, fatherless bastard! Who are you?"

133

Yeshua's face was pointing up now to the sky.

"It is finished," he whispered – and now the symbol took full form.

Gamel stared. An eerie quiet took the crowd. Kami pointed to the symbol, and laughed loud and hard.

"Look!" he proclaimed – and now Echari was alongside Gamel and Lidya, unfolding a parchment.

"Look!" he whispered, tears in his eyes. "The writings of the sages! Look!"

"What is it?" Gamel breathed.

"It is the symbol of Atua."

Stunned, Gamel stared at the blood red glowing symbol on Yeshua's chest. The stones had been transformed – their colours melting into one, their shapes lost to the one symbol.

Atua.

"Atua!" Kami screamed. "The man declares himself to be God! He shuns our ways – he shuns the ways of our ancestors! Kill him!"

"What...?" Gamel breathed.

"Kill him! Kill him! Kill him!"

The symbol was lit – and the stone drew evil to itself. Gamel felt Soutar drawn to Yeshua – felt his rage, felt his glee.

*Kill him!* Soutar said. *Kill him, kill him, kill him.*

Lidya's hand tightened on his own. He felt the compulsion, even now! Felt the urge to murder the flailing man before him. He closed his eyes tightly, submitting to Atua instead.

*Forgive me.*

*Forgive your father.*

*I...I forgive him.*

His father's rage, his rejecting scowl, was before his face – he reached out to touch him, to draw his fingers down his face, and wept.

*I'm sorry!* He sobbed within. *I'm so sorry, father! I'm sorry! I'm sorry...*

Grief filled him – love filled him. Love for his father! Love for Atua.

But, around him, people were moving.

Disturbed, Gamel looked around himself. People were reaching down – reaching to pick up rocks.

"Gamel..." Lidya gasped – and Gamel stared at them.

"What are they doing?"

"They hate him!"

"Why?" Gamel cried. "Why?"

"He wants them to change – he wants them to give up who they are."

Dismayed, Gamel searched out those he knew. Echari looked stunned – Berui, next to him, was shaking her head, crying. Koram! Where was Koram? Gamel found him – with relief he found sorrow: inaction. But Taierre...

Taierre was reaching to pick up a stone.

Gamel rushed to him. "What are you doing?" he cried.

"Step aside," Taierre said.

"He's trying to save us!"

"He is dangerous arrogance, Gamel! He should be wiped off the Earth."

Stunned, Gamel fell back a step. He turned, to look at Yeshua – to see the man beginning to stagger beneath the load. And then the stoning began.

Rocks hit Yeshua: hard rocks, large, against chest, against arms – against face...

"My God!" Gamel breathed, watching him. "Oh my God..."

Blood spilt from his chest, from his arms – from his face. He didn't run! He didn't turn. He faced the onslaught of hatred – he bore it.

"Oh my God..."

Gamel could not bear to watch – but he forced himself to do so. Yeshua's skin was broken! His body was breaking. Surely he could have fought! Surely he could have hurled the power of Atua! But he did nothing. Just stood – and received the stones.

Gamel searched again for Lidya, and found her. She was standing very still. Her face was drawn in dismayed grief. She closed her eyes – she began to shake. Gamel wrapped his arms around her – but he could not protect her from the dismay also overwhelming his own heart.

Yeshua staggered – and then he fell. Gamel longed for the assault to be over – to his horror, it intensified.

Kami stood near Yeshua, pointing his staff at him – rocks flooded in. Soon his body was no longer moving – still they pounded him.

"Enough!" Gamel cried. "Enough! He's dead!"

But the stoning was not enough for them.

Taierre now strode up to Yeshua, his sword drawn.

"Stop it!" Gamel screamed at him. "Stop it!"

But Taierre would not stop. He pierced Yeshua's chest – between the stones of Satine, within the symbol of Atua, he pierced him and penetrated his heart.

"It is over," Taierre announced to the crowd. "Yeshua is dead. Atua is dead. Return to your homes – return to your lives. Make the most of them: they are all that you have."

Shocked, Gamel stared at Taierre. Lidya squeezed his hand in warning.

"I hate him!" Gamel whispered. "I hate him, Lidi! I want to kill him!"

"I know," Lidya murmured next to him. "But if you give yourself to that hate, Yeshua will have died for no reason."

Gamel felt numb. The crowd began to disperse – they left Yeshua there. Kami stood over his body, gloating – Gamel wanted to kill him, too.

"Well done, Heartland boy," Kami said. "You killed him: it was you! You did my work for me."

A sword pierced Gamel's own heart: he? It was he? He had laid the first stones on Yeshua's chest – he had led the movement...

"Oh my God," he breathed – and, shaking hard, he fell to his knees next to Yeshua's body and covered his face with his hands.

135

## CHAPTER TWENTY-SEVEN: Grief

When Gamel lifted his head again, the crowd had left. Only a few remained.

Chief Teru stood a few steps away. He was frowning. Kami lingered – Teru pointed him away. And now Teru approached.

"How are we to understand this death?" he asked. "Did he not know his claim would be unacceptable?"

"He knew," Lidya whispered, tears silently pouring down her cheeks. "But it was Atua's time."

"Faith?" Teru said, looking at her. "You still have faith?"

"He offered to carry your punishment," Lidya said. "What did you think that punishment would be?"

"Death?" Teru exclaimed – and then he tilted his head in thought. "Death..."

Chief Dela also stood near at hand.

"We must bury him," he said to Teru. "I offer the burial site of my ancestors."

"Truly?" Teru said. "That is...an unusual offer."

"Yeshua was far from a usual man."

"His mother..." Now Teru swallowed, and Gamel saw the conflicted guilt in his face.

"She would have him decide."

"Bury him here," Lidya said.

"Why, white one?"

"To commemorate the nature of his death."

Teru's eyebrows went up – but then he nodded. "Very well," he said. "I consent. You may bury him amidst the Tribe of Talu."

Dela and Teru moved off, Kami staying away. Echari and Berui waited, a short distance away. Koram! Koram was there, hesitating: uncertain. But Taierre was gone.

Gamel looked down at the body of Yeshua. He was still. His face, covered in blood, swollen with the beating of rocks, also was at peace.

Lidya trembled, next to him.

"Why did he have to die, Lidi?" Gamel whispered, and she sighed heavily.

"It was necessary," she said.

"Necessary?" Gamel breathed. "Why?"

"To save us, Gamel," she said – surprisingly calm, "To save us."

And she drew off a cloak, from around her shoulders, and laid it over Yeshua's face and body.

For a time they both knelt with him – brother and sister, silent, unmoving. The darkness of night was deepening – a cold chill filling the air. There were no stars, though the full moon gave them light.

In time, Chief Dela returned with some men.

"I have prepared his grave," he said, and Gamel numbly looked up at him. Sorrow was in his eyes – but maturity, also, to handle the sorrow.

"Thank you," Gamel whispered – and now Lidya rose to her feet.

136

"I will go with him."

Gamel frowned, eying the men of Dela – but he had no energy to resist.

"So be it," he said – and now Dela's men bent and lifted Yeshua on their shoulders, to carry him away.

They left – and now only one other remained.

It was Koram.

Gamel could not move – and so Koram moved. He knelt alongside Gamel – he laid a hand on his shoulder. Gamel kept staring at the spot where Yeshua's body had lain just a few moments earlier. There was still blood on the dust – he reached out with his fingers to touch it: to try to comprehend it.

Gamel could barely feel Koram's touch on his shoulder. Taierre's actions were before his eyes: his driving of the sword into Yeshua's heart. Gamel's body felt cold – stiff.

"I am so sorry," Koram whispered – and Gamel shook his head.

"Don't be," he said stiffly. "It wasn't your fault."

"I...I have never seen such a thing, Gamel."

Gamel lifted his heavy gaze to look at him. The usually warm brown face now looked aghast. Gamel reached to touch his face – felt his own face contorting – and then Koram caught him.

Gamel's voice lifted into a scream. On and on he wailed, rocking backwards and forwards on Koram's chest – clinging to his shirt: clinging to some semblance of humanity.

"Atua!" he cried. "Atua! Atua! Atua!"

Koram's arms were strong around him – Gamel beat his chest, in utter agony, and Koram sustained him. How could this have happened? How could they have stoned him? How could Yeshua have died?

His anguish spent, Gamel now covered his face and wept. How could Yeshua be dead? How...how could he, Gamel, have laid the stones of Soutar upon him?

"I killed him!" Gamel gasped, lifting his face to again stare at the place where Yeshua had died. "I killed him! I killed him!"

"All killed him," Koram moaned. "I have never seen such a thing."

"They hated him!" Tears filled Gamel's eyes, now – blurring his vision. "They hated him..."

"I don't understand."

"Taierre understood!" Now Gamel's throat constricted. "Taierre hated him too!"

Koram's voice was silenced, alongside him. Gamel looked at him again – saw the frown, as he also stared at the place where Yeshua's body lay.

"Soutar..."

"I can't blame Soutar!" Gamel said. "It wasn't just Soutar, or Satine, or Kami..."

"I know, Gamel," Koram whispered, his gaze intense. "It was us too."

"You...?" Gamel breathed, desperately hoping otherwise.

"Some were spared. Some resisted. I...I saw something in him I could not attack, though I also felt the hatred: though I also despised the notion of a single human claiming to be God."

"What did you see?" Gamel breathed – and Koram's face contorted.

"I saw him wearing the Stone of the North."

Relieved, Gamel clung to him. "You saw it?" he sobbed. "You saw it?"

"I did not see Atua," Koram replied gently. "But I saw sacrifice, Gamel! I saw a man attempting to carry all the burdens of the World – willing to die to save us all."

Tears filled the Northerner's older eyes – and now Gamel wept freely with him, and Koram also wept.

Koram stayed with Gamel, for the rest of the night – sitting a little removed, behind him, while Gamel lay down on the ground near Yeshua's resting place.

Gamel stared out in front of himself, in the darkness, unable to sleep. What would he do now? The stones were gone! His purpose was complete. Taierre and Koram were free to leave! Free to report to their kings that the stones had been neutralized. They were still pressed into Yeshua's chest – buried with him, in the grave.

Buried with him...In dismay Gamel considered what Yeshua had done: the cost of relieving them from the Stones of Soutar. How could Yeshua have done it? How could he have died for them – to release them: to set them free?

Gamel could not comprehend it. Gamel was virtually a stranger to Yeshua – and yet, somehow, he had not been a stranger: somehow, strangely, he had been known. In such a short time, he had become known; in such a short time, he had become family.

Family...Gamel buried his face in his arms. Family. Surely Taierre and Koram longed to return to their homes – but did he, Gamel, long to return the Heartland now, after all this? Did he wish for home: to see Mother and Father, and the Palace again? Where even was his home, now, after everything that had taken place?

Gamel fell into a troubled sleep. Nightmares plagued him: stones, hitting Yeshua! He jerked awake. Was it Soutar? No – Soutar was gone. It was him! The beating of his own heart! The torment of his own soul.

He lapsed again into a doze – and the night began to lighten. Relieved, Gamel sensed the pink in the eastern sky of sunrise: at least the darkness was over, for now – at least this most terrible of nights was gone.

Gamel stirred, and sat up. Soon would come the heat, and the thirst – soon he would need to seek shelter, and face a return journey: face emptiness – a future with no stone, no Soutar, and no replacement.

Stretching, Gamel reached out again to touch the tiny spots of Yeshua's blood in the dust – but then noticed a shadow cast over him, and saw Lidya's feet.

He looked up – the sun was in his eyes, but he searched for her face. Her eyes were wide – Gamel was sure she had had no sleep.

"Gamel..."

The tone of her voice led him to stand up quickly. "What is it?"

"Something has happened."

Fear struck him. "What is it? Did they hurt you?"

"No!" Tears filled her eyes. "No, Gamel! I have to show you something."

And she dragged him after herself – across the land, for perhaps twenty minutes, to another clearing.

There were graves. Pain filled Gamel's chest – he swayed on his feet, staring at them. The Yeri dug deep holes in the ground, as did the Heartlanders – they covered the bodies in dust, clay, and then with stones.

"Which one?" Gamel whispered – and she led him between the different sites, to stop at a fresh grave site. At the foot of the grave was the name of Yeshua, carved in Yeri in a large rock. But something was wrong with the grave – the dust, and clay, and rocks seemed to have caved in.

"Don't do this to me," Gamel pleaded, "I can't see his body again."

"His body isn't there."

"What do you mean?"

Lidya's silence made him urgently look at her. "What do you mean, Lidi? What do you mean?"

Her eyes were wide – her face strange. "I can't say it, Gamel: you have to see it for yourself."

"See what?"

"Look, Gamel." She was gesturing behind him.

Fear took Gamel: all-consuming fear. The hairs were rising on the back of his neck. He stared at her face.

"What is behind me?"

She smiled gently at him. "Look for yourself."

"I can't, Lidi!" he pleaded. "Don't do this to me! Don't play these games!"

"Look at me."

The voice invited him, from behind: stirring terror within. It could not be! It could not be. Gamel dared not look, for if it was true, what would that mean? Everything he had ever known, everything he might ever know, would be overturned. Life would never be the same again.

"It is your choice," Lidya murmured gently to him, "Whether to look or whether to walk away."

139

Gamel stared at her. The stoning of Yeshua was before his eyes: his agony, his death – the crowd's hatred, the supremacy of Satine. A part of Gamel had died with him! A part had died. But now, if he turned, the rest of him would be demanded: the rest of him would be consumed, as surely as Soutar had sought to consume him.

"Look at me."

Gamel turned, and looked – and it was Yeshua, standing before him.

Heart pounding, Gamel stared at him. He looked young! He looked healthy. Gamel was shaking so hard he thought he might fall over.

"You..." he stuttered. "Taierre killed...we killed..."

Was he a spirit? Gamel swayed – but now Yeshua was grasping his hand, and directing it to his chest.

Taierre's stab wound – it was still there! Healing, but still there.

"I don't understand," Gamel pleaded. "Did you die?"

"Yes," Yeshua murmured. "I did die."

"What was it like?" Gamel exclaimed, "After death?"

Yeshua touched his face gently. "There is a place of suffering, Gamel: like the suffering of Soutar. And there is a place of joy. Atua is the Master of life and death."

"How do we reach joy, Sir?" Gamel breathed, with tears, and Yeshua smiled.

"Stay with me: forever stay with me and you will have joy."

"Atua..." Gamel reached now to finger the stones still on Yeshua's chest: the symbol of Atua, and the symbol of sacrifice.

"I have a different stone for you now to wear," Yeshua said – and he laid a new pendant in Gamel's hand. It looked to be made of the same greystone of the Palace! But now, instead of the serpent, it was carved in the shape of the symbol of Atua.

Gamel gazed into his face – and now easily sank down to his knees before him. Yeshua laid the new stone over his head and over his heart: he kissed his head. And then Yeshua closed his eyes and murmured over him.

A new spirit flooded into Gamel – the Spirit of life. He gasped, and submitted – and was filled, and was consumed.

"Love," Yeshua murmured over him. "Love others as you yourself are loved. Love is costly, Gamel: love is sacrifice. I command you to love – but always remain in our Love, that you might continue."

Gamel loved, and was loved. Yeshua lifted him to his feet, and backed away one step.

"What would you have me do, Master?" he said.

Yeshua smiled at him. "Submit to Atua," he said, "And act, Gamel. We give you the gift of choice: use it well! Use it with responsibility. Use it with our love – and we will be with you, always, until the very end."

"Use it well?"

"Give to the others what you yourself have already received. Pass on everything I have shown you, Gamel! Pass it on: do not keep great treasure only to yourself."

Gamel's heart filled with purpose. "I will!" he said with joy. "I will pass it on."

"You certainly will," Yeshua said, eyes shining.

"And then," Yeshua continued, "at the right time, after everyone has been given a chance to choose, I will return."

"Return?"

"To rule, Gamel."

Gamel gazed up at him in wonder as Yeshua explained. "The World needs her King! She struggles, without right leadership, and Atua is her King. But now is not the right time! Soon I will come – but not right now. Not until everything has taken place."

"You are the ruler..."

"Pass it on, Gamel! Pass it on."

And then, suddenly, he was gone.

Gamel rose to his feet, looking around himself in the space where Yeshua had been – astonished. He felt the Spirit of love within him: he felt wholly owned, and yet simultaneously wholly free. He laughed. And then he turned to Lidya.

Tears filled her eyes. He rushed to her, lifted her bodily in his arms, as he had done in childhood, spun her around – and she cried.

"I have waited for this day for a long, long time," she whispered, and he kissed her head. Then he took her by the hand and led her to stand next to the empty grave.

"His words burn in my heart, Lidi!" he said, and she squeezed his hand.

"They burn with passion," she said, and he nodded.

"Yes! With passion!"

"That passion can change things, Gamel! Love, for Atua, and Yeshua, and the Spirit of Atua: love, for humanity."

"It is...strangely childlike..." He swung her arm high, and she smiled.

"The heart of a child..."

"...can change the World!"

They laughed at each other – twins, once again, joined together. Gamel smiled at her – but then he looked down at the empty grave.

"He is alive," he whispered. "We will have to tell people, Lidi! We will have to tell them! But...who will believe it?"

Lidya held his gaze. "Echari," she said quickly, "And Berui."

"Yes."

"Chief Dela – I think he will believe it. The empty grave is right here, in his ancestral burial ground!"

"Yes...But what about Chief Teru?"

Lidya's face clouded. "That would be dangerous, Gamel."

"I still must tell him."

Lidya was silent. And then, suddenly, she grasped his arm. "What about Taierre?"

Gamel held her eyes. Taierre? The one who drove the sword into Yeshua's heart?

141

"I fear he may wish to kill me next," he said grimly, "And what would stop him? What would stop him?"

Lidya frowned – but then she smiled. "This is risky news," she said, "But I know our true calling is yet to come."

"Our true calling?"

"For the Heartland, Gamel: have you forgotten? We have our own people to release!"

Gamel gazed into her eyes, and his heart swelled with joy. The Heartland! Now he had a reason to return: now he had a true leadership to offer.

"Yes!" he cried out. Now, at last, he felt his calling! Now, at last, he found his purpose.

In time he would return, across the Sea, to his own precious homeland: in time, he would set his own people free.

## CHAPTER TWENTY-NINE: A Witness

The sun was rising higher in the sky when Gamel and Lidya started back toward the campground.

Lidya held tightly onto Gamel's hand. Her leather sandals still cut into her feet – she did not care. Her hair was falling out of its tie – she was indifferent. She gathered her Yeri skirt into her other fist, eager to return to tell the others: Yeshua was alive! He was alive...

Again and again her mind went over the events of the night: the terrible events that had led to the life-changing morning. He had died! Yeshua had died. She still could see, vividly, the stoning: still could feel the horror of the attack.

Taierre had pierced him! Lidya still felt the piercing, as though it had happened to herself – still felt the death within herself. The symbol of Atua was there, on his chest: pierced, but still intact, on his death. His identity! His identity had been revealed: his identity had killed him. But his identity also had saved them.

In that pit of darkness, Lidya had felt preserved. How? Because she had known. Somehow she had known, all along, what must take place: through all of his hinting, she had seen him – and had known the cost of the offering he would inevitably have to make. The Spirit of Atua had preserved her – holding her, in love and peace, even in that most evil of nights.

*Atua...*

They had taken Yeshua's body! And she had followed, into an unknown land – with unknown faces. She had watched him buried in the ground – she had sat, when they had left: she had wept.

And then...then...

At first, she had thought herself dreaming. The grief had been a haze – everything all around her a graveyard. Pain had filled her – and then had come his voice.

"Lidya."

She had not believed it! Not turned. But then his voice had come again, "Lidya."

The grave in front of her had been disrupted. She had been certain it was a dream, and had given herself to it: rising to her feet, willingly turning to greet him – but then his hands had grasped her arms firmly, shaking her slightly.

"Lidi!"

She had jerked out of her stupor – he had remained in front of her.

"Sir," she had gasped, reaching to touch his face – to poke at his face.

"It's finished, Lidi," he had said, tears in his eyes. "It's over."

"What's over?"

"My death."

Moved, she had gazed at him. "To carry the pain of the world," she had murmured, "To carry the guilt of the world."

"It is finished," he said. "Go and tell everyone. Go and tell your brother."

"He won't believe..."

"Show him, Lidi – and I will show him what he now must do."

143

He had gone – in a moment, suddenly left. She had stood there, stunned – had pinched herself. She had prodded reluctantly at the grave with a stick – it truly was empty. And then she had run – back to the campsite: back to the scene of death.

Gamel had been there: she had never seen him like that before. His face – wet, pale, drawn: like death, though he still lived. She had known not to tell him – to show. She had shown.

That moment, when he had pivoted on his decision whether or not to look at Yeshua: that moment Lidya would never forget. His eyes: the fear, the vulnerability – the boy she had always known and loved.

He had turned – and now he was safe with Yeshua.

Lidya cried now, as they hurried toward the camp – she squeezed his hand all the harder. Gamel was saved! Gamel was saved. Soutar had been defeated! Gamel would live.

She remembered the sight of Friedrich, in the Palace, tormented by Soutar: the knife, pointing inward – his death. She remembered! She would never forget. But now there was a stronger scene to remember – a stronger scene to live by. Yeshua had carried the Stone of Soutar – he had taken it into the grave! The stone was gone! And now, not defeated even by all the forces of evil, Yeshua lived! He lived – and now all could live.

It was news almost too good to be true! Who would believe it? And yet this good news was true. She had seen it: she had watched it all, with her own eyes.

The camp was near. Gamel cast a glance to her – with a slight warning in his eyes. She nodded – and they moved forward, between the trees, into the clearing.

Many people had left. Surprised, Lidya looked across the camp – at the many bare spaces where before many had lived.

"Is it too late?" she whispered, and Gamel shook his head.

"We have all our lives," he said – and promptly moved forward.

Women were scattering camp fires, and men were folding up tents. Children were quiet – staring silently at them, while their parents kept their backs firmly turned.

Lidya saw Gamel's puzzled frown. "Why are they leaving?" he asked.

"They stoned him!"

She watched Gamel swallow. "So they did."

But then Lidya saw Echari.

He saw her, from a distance – his black face broke into a wide smile, his eyes lit up.

"Princess Lidya!" he cried – and now he ran to her, and grasped her arms, and swung her in the air.

Astonished, Lidya gazed at him – and began to understand just as he spoke.

"We saw him!"

"What?" Lidya breathed.

Now Echari also turned to Gamel, who was fumbling at his arm.

"What are you saying?" Gamel asked, his eyes intent on Echari.

"We saw him, Prince Gamel!" Echari said. "We saw him alive!"

"What did he say?" Gamel gasped.

"He said to pass it on! Pass it on!"

And now Echari began to dance on the spot – a Yeri dance, his arms lifted, his voice lifting in worship.

Lidya watched him with tears of joy – and now Echari was grasping her into his arms, leading her in the dance: now Lidya also was lifting her arms, lifting her voice in worship of Atua.

Gamel was still beside them – but now Berui was there behind him.

"I saw him too, Prince Gamel!" she said, her wide face beaming, "Yeshua is more powerful than death: do you know what this means? My husband lives! All can choose to live. Dance! Let us show you how to worship in Yeri!"

The Yeri mother grasped Gamel in her large arms, and now Gamel also was laughing, tossed in the older woman's embrace – stamping his feet to her beat on the ground.

Lidya smiled at Echari and at Berui – she smiled at Gamel. But then she glanced outside of their Yeri circle of worship, to see hardened eyes watching them.

"Gamel," she whispered – and Gamel quickly stopped, looked, and broke away from Berui.

A smaller crowd was gathering before them.

"We're leaving!" One man called out – light brown skin, and foreign clothes.

"We're leaving too!" Another woman said: she of the medium brown of the Beli tribe.

"Don't leave," Gamel said – now standing up straight. "Stay here, with us."

"Stay?" It was Chief Dela – he had returned to the camp, and was standing just at the edge of the gathering. Lidya watched Gamel turn to him.

"Yes!" he said, "If you are willing, Chief Dela: everyone can still remain here, together."

Dela looked at Gamel, his expression puzzled. "Why should we stay?" he asked. "Isn't our leader dead? Hasn't our teacher gone?"

The crowd began to stir – Lidya looked across the faces. What were they feeling? Discomfort, yes, at what had taken place the night before – a longing, perhaps, to run from it and never think of it again. Might some be feeling remorse? Perhaps even guilt?

Gamel was pausing – Lidya felt his hesitation. And then he lifted his voice high above the crowd.

"There is something we must tell you!" he cried out. "Yeshua is not dead! We saw him this morning, next to his grave – he has come back! He is alive!"

Lidya's heart stirred with the words. But now the crowd began to move against them.

"Alive?" One woman shouted. "He is lying! Yeshua led us nowhere – and now why should we bother listening to this white foreigner? Yeshua is defeated! It's time to leave."

"We also saw him!" Echari called out. "He spoke to each of us."

"Why would he speak to you and not to us?" a man called out.

"We don't know!" Berui said, "But he did."

145

The crowd erupted into an argument – but now Chief Dela stepped closer.

"Silence!" he called out. "I want to hear what they have to say."

His authority settled the voices – for they were visitors on his land. And now Gamel spoke.

"We killed him," he said, his voice sounding a little tremulous to Lidya's ears. "We killed him! We stoned him, we hated him – we condemned him to death for his audacity to claim authority over us. But I tell you this now: we killed him, he died – but now he is alive again! Can any of us claim this kind of power?"

The crowd was silent as he continued.

"He died to carry our grief – to carry our pain. He took the stones onto himself! He took our evil onto himself. Do you think now, after we stoned him, that he did it to judge us? That he did it to condemn us?"

Now Lidya could see tears forming in Gamel's eyes. "He did it to forgive us! He did it to heal us."

Lidya trembled, her vision blurring. A woman near her began to weep. Lidya went to her – laid an arm around her shoulders. And now Dela moved alongside Gamel.

"People," he said to the crowd. "The grave of Yeshua is empty."

Voices lifted loud in the crowd – some protesting, some shouting for change.

"Are you telling me, now," Dela said to Gamel before all, "that the body was not stolen? Are you telling me that this man, this child of Atua, has truly come back to life?"

Lidya watched Gamel's face light up with joy.

"Yes, Chief Dela," he said. "We are witnesses of this fact! We saw him with our very own eyes! I thought he must be a spirit – but he reached out and pulled my hand to touch the sword wound in his chest. He is alive! And now he wants us all to follow after him: to follow Atua."

"Through the grave and out again to new life," Dela said. "He wants us to follow after him! I will follow after him."

And Dela clapped his hands, raised his arms, and began to offer a Yeri dance of worship to Atua.

Gamel was smiling at him – but then Lidya noticed another man step forward. It was Chief Teru – and Kami was standing beside him.

Kami's eyes were on fire. Lidya swallowed, and began to murmur to Atua under her breath to ask him for help as Gamel stepped forward.

"Insolent boy!" Kami hissed at him, lifting his staff. "Your leader is defeated, and you dare to spread rumours of his coming to life? I killed him, and I will kill you too!"

He swung the staff to hit Gamel across the head – but the staff was stopped. Lidya stared – the hand of Teru was blocking the blow!

"Surrender your staff, Kami!" Teru ordered. "It is not Yeshua who has been defeated, but you!"

Kami spluttered protestations – but Lidya knew he could not defy his own Chief. He handed over the staff – and Teru now bowed his head to Gamel, and handed the staff to him.

With tears, Lidya watched Gamel's face – his astonishment.

"I have no authority..." he stuttered, and Teru smiled.

"It is not your authority I am acknowledging, Prince Gamel," he said. "Rather, I am acknowledging the authority of the One you now represent."

Lidya watched Gamel's comprehension – watched his smile of joy. Chief Dela also stepped forward – and handed Gamel his staff, bowing his head. Gamel looked at the two staffs, once in each hand, closed his eyes fleetingly – and then, when his eyes opened again, his gaze shone with purpose.

He handed the staffs to Echari.

Echari gazed at Gamel in wonder. "Sir?" he said, and Gamel grinned.

"It is meant to be, Echari: don't you see it? Your father was spiritual advisor to Chief Dela – spiritual adviser to Satine. He changed, to follow Atua – he died. But you have seen Yeshua with your own eyes! You saw his death! You saw him alive after death. The staff now moves to you."

Lidya clapped her hands with joy as Gamel continued.

"These are your people, Echari – lead them, now! You know your sages, you know your writings – you know Satine's way, and you love Yeshua.

"Lead them! And I..." Now Gamel's eyes came to Lidya. "We must return to our own people."

The Chiefs turned to grasp Echari's young hands, Berui danced in worship behind, the crowd divided – some to press into Echari, others to leave. And Gamel stepped away, to join Lidya.

He grasped her hands – and she squeezed his back again.

"It is time to leave," Gamel said – and Lidya smiled with happiness.

"Yes, Gamel – it is time."

# CHAPTER THIRTY: Conflict

Gamel rummaged in the tent – dragging out rugs and blankets, moving to pull out the thick sticks and collapse the animal hide covering.

"What are you doing?" It was Koram's voice.

Happily Gamel turned to him. "It's time for us to go home."

"Home?" Koram said.

"Back to Altenhine!"

Gamel grinned at him – but Koram was frowning.

"What's wrong?" the warrior asked. "What happened?"

"What do you mean what's wrong?"

"You're smiling!

Perplexed, Gamel studied his face – and then began to understand.

"Oh!" he said. "You didn't hear..."

"I was waiting at the lake, Gamel, for you to return. I heard your voice, and came to check on you."

Gamel searched his eyes, and gently smiled. "It's all right, Koram," he said. "I am well."

"What?" Koram frowned intensely. "But how can that be?"

"I'm well because..." Gamel hesitated, yet compelled himself forward, "Because I've seen Yeshua."

Koram's face did not move – there was no hint of response. "What do you mean you've seen him?" he quietly asked.

"He's not dead!" Gamel chimed playfully. "He's not dead! He's alive."

Koram stared at him – and then suddenly grasped his arms. "Gamel," he said, "I hate to do this to you, but Yeshua is dead! We watched him die! The grief..."

Gamel's head hurt – but now he grasped Koram's arms in return.

"No, my friend," he said in all seriousness. "I am not losing my mind. This has become the most amazing day of my life."

"What are you saying?" Koram demanded. "How can anything about this nightmare be amazing?"

"Because I saw him, Koram!" Now tears filled Gamel's eyes as he sought to reach Koram. "I saw him, with my own eyes!"

Koram pushed him back slightly – and fell back a step from him.

"Gamel," he whispered. "You can't seriously be claiming such a thing."

Gamel's joy suddenly ebbed away looking at Koram's face.

"I am not claiming it, Sir Koram," he said quietly. "I am testifying that he is alive."

"How can that be possible?"

"I don't know how! I only know that it is true."

Koram frowned again. Gamel held his searching gaze – and knew his thoughts.

"The grief is tricking you," Koram began.

"It's not the grief!" Gamel insisted.

"How do you know that, Gamel? I know what his death did to you! I was there!"

Now sobs threatened to erupt from within Gamel, as the image was before him again: Yeshua being stoned, beaten, bleeding, a sword into his heart...

He stretched out a hand to stop him.

"I knew it was over, Koram!" he said. "I knew! Taierre made it final! Do you think I could make this up?"

"No!" Koram choked. "No."

"I knew he was dead!"

"Then..."

"Lidi took me to the grave! It's empty, Koram: see it for yourself!"

Koram held his eyes. "I can't see it, Gamel," he said quietly, "It is sacred land – belonging to the Chief."

Gamel held his gaze, and swallowed. "If you cannot see it yourself, can you not trust what I saw?"

Koram also swallowed – his eyes passing over Gamel's face. "I know you would not willingly lie to me, Gamel."

"Not lie..." Gamel choked.

"But could it not be that you were deluded? That you saw what you wanted to see?"

"What did you see, Koram? Yeshua willingly died for us!"

"I don't deny that! But does that give him the power to come back from death?"

Gamel searched his face. "What if it was so, Koram?" he asked. "What would it take for you to believe it?"

Koram frowned. "I don't know, Gamel: an appearance to me? Would I even trust that?"

"Lidya saw him first. The grave was empty. Echari saw him, and Berui."

"I don't know what to make of that."

"If it was true, what would you expect to hear?"

"Just what you say! But...I don't know if I can believe it."

Gamel shifted before him, suddenly impatient. He glanced back at Lidya, with Echari – at the two Chiefs. How quickly they had believed! And many of the crowd, though not all – not all.

Koram was before him, frowning – obviously perplexed. Gamel laid a hand on his shoulder.

"He was dead, and now he's alive," he said gently. "I was dead, and now I'm alive. You saw me before, you see me now. Could grief fool me this fully? I touched his side, Koram – I felt him and saw him, and the empty grave."

"I can't comprehend it."

"It won't go away, Koram! I won't suddenly wake up tomorrow and believe I did not see him. I will tell the World, and keep telling it – even if it kills me."

Koram now smiled sadly. "May it not kill you as it killed him."

Gamel smiled sadly back at him – but then, suddenly, he saw a movement behind Koram.

149

It was Taierre – his face fixed in fury. Fear took Gamel – but as Taierre stormed into the tent, his hand gripping around the hilt of his sword, Gamel was compelled to follow.

Taierre faced him – his sword drawn.

Heart pounding, Gamel stared at him. "What are you doing?" he whispered – and Taierre's gaze bore down upon him.

"What am I doing?" he spat at him. "What are you doing, Heartland Prince? You don't even belong here!"

Face flushing, Gamel met his gaze. "Yeshua will receive anyone who receives him."

"I do not want to hear it!"

Gamel clenched his teeth together as Taierre began to pace backwards and forwards in the tent.

"Destroy the stone, my King commanded," Taierre muttered, "Destroy the stone! Well the stone is destroyed, only to be replaced by an even greater threat!"

And now Taierre thrust the tip of his sword to Gamel's neck.

Gamel stood stiff and still, trembling – staring out ahead of himself to the back of the tent. Sweat began to drip down his face as Taierre circled around him.

"Yeshua has come back from death, you say," Taierre began, "And you are intending to tell the whole World? Well I do not want you taking this myth to the Southland! I do not want you taking this lie to my king!"

Gamel fleetingly closed his eyes and opened them again.

"I cannot remain silent," he whispered. "I saw what I saw."

"You did not see!" Taierre insisted. "You wished to believe! He died. He is dead! I will not have you spreading this deception across all of Altenhine."

Gamel swayed slightly. "That is not your choice to make," he said, and the tip began to cut his skin.

"Your king!" Gamel pleaded. "You must honour your king! I know your loyalty, Taierre."

Now there were tears in the Southern warrior's eyes: tears of conflict.

"Honour my king?" he cried, "By doing what? By replacing one stone of oppression with another faith in deception? How is that honouring him?"

"It must be his choice, Taierre!" Gamel said, now looking straight at him. "Just as it must be the choice of us all."

Taierre stared at him – and then began to shake.

"Do you know, Gamel of the Heartland, what stops me from killing you this instant?"

Tears filled Gamel's eyes – caught in tension: caught in Taierre's control.

"What?" he croaked.

"Not the right of my King to choose, not the death of Yeshua," Taierre said, "certainly no belief in his return from death, and no belief in Atua. None of these things, Gamel! It is this which torments me: that you took the Stone of the South from me! That you saved my life!"

Now Taierre drew back his sword, and fled from the tent.

150

Gamel swayed, and then fell to his knees. His body was shaking hard – he wrapped his arms around himself, and began to weep. Taierre had almost killed him! Because of Yeshua! Because of Yeshua...

Gamel struggled to gather his strength – but still felt dismayed. Why did Taierre carry such hatred? Why did he wield such a desire to kill?

"You threaten him," Koram murmured gently from behind his back.

Gamel closed his eyes tightly. "I do not mean to threaten him," he whispered.

"I know: and yet the threat remains. You represent everything he is against."

Gamel opened his eyes – and stared at the end of the tent, still remaining on his knees.

"I have no desire for war, Koram."

"That is a good trait in the future King of the Heartland."

"I would wish for conversation."

"So would I."

Tilting his head, Gamel suddenly realized: "Koram – you heard Taierre's threat, but did not come in!"

"I knew he would not kill you."

"How did you know?"

"You are his friend."

Now tears blurred Gamel's vision: but he rose to his feet, and turned to Koram – searching out his gaze.

"You say I am his friend?" Gamel said. "Does a friend put a sword to the neck?"

Koram smiled wryly. "Sometimes," he replied, "Even a brother may put a sword to the neck, if necessary – but he will never execute."

Gamel studied him. "He is a friend to me, but no friend to Yeshua."

"Correct."

"A sword..." Gamel turned, and paced a little down the tent. "A sword to the neck without execution..."

Gamel's hand went up to the position of the Stone of Soutar – but now the Stone of Yeshua, the Stone of Atua, was in its place. His thoughts were returning to the Heartland – returning to his father, on the Throne in the Palace.

"I see it now," he murmured to Atua. "I know now what I must do."

## PART FOUR

## THE RETURN TO ALTENHINE

CHAPTER THIRTY-ONE: Across the Sea of Yerim

Gamel and Lidya were travelling back to Altenhine.

With delight, Gamel now stood at the bow of Captain Nehu's ship – grasping the railing. Wind filled the vast sail above him – wind blew past his body and face, and through his hair. He was back in his Heartland clothes! Berui had kindly washed them for him: grey jacket, white linen shirt, grey trousers, socks, and leather shoes.

Yerim was disappearing behind them – Altenhine was a sliver of land ahead. The sun was high in a clear blue sky. Home! They were returning home, at last!

Lidya appeared beside him – her pretty face radiant, her long black curls blowing freely in the breeze.

"Beautiful!" she cried, stretching her arms out to enjoy the wind. "Just like the Spirit of Atua!"

Gamel grinned at her. Yes! The power, the refreshment – the joy, and love, returning home! Very much like the Spirit of Atua.

Lidya was also back in her Heartland clothes – the ones Hana had supplied: shirt and brown linen trousers. Gamel studied them, remembering her Palace silk dresses – wondering. Then he turned.

Captain Nehu was at the wheel of the ship. Gamel bowed his head to him. Echari was not travelling with them – though Berui and Echari had both walked them back to the wharf, and had embraced them with great joy and tears at their departure. Lidya had particularly cried, in leaving Echari – Gamel wondered what the future might hold between them. Would there be many trips between Altenhine and Yerim? He very much hoped so – though he knew Echari would be very busy in his role as leader of the Faith in Yerim.

Other crew, on the ship, worked diligently – grasping ropes, winching cables. Gamel watched them for a few moments – then he wandered to the back of the ship.

There Koram and Taierre sat on the deck: one to the right side, the other to the left – separate in their own individual thoughts.

For a moment Gamel considered them: one from the North, one from the South, and he himself from the Heartland. They were all so very different! And yet for a time they had been bound by the same need: to discard the stones.

In the minds of the warriors, that task was complete. They were free to report to their kings the success of their mission – they were free to leave. And yet so much more had taken place on this journey: there was, in truth, so much more to report.

Gamel wandered up to Koram first. The Northerner smiled at him, and rose to his feet.

"Greetings, Gamel."

"Greetings!"

"Are you glad to be returning home?"

"Very glad!"

"I am also glad – I have missed my family."

Astonished, Gamel considered him: he had never thought to ask of his family!

"You have children?"

Koram's face brightened. "A beautiful and patient wife, and two little ones."

He stretched his hand down to show their height, only two feet above the deck.

"I didn't realize!"

"Why would you?"

"I would like to meet them!"

Koram held his gaze. "I also would like you to meet them, Prince Gamel of the Heartland."

In wonder Gamel considered the moment. When had such a thing happened in all of the history of Altenhine? A Heartlander being invited to a Northerner's home: much less the royal family?

"Sir Koram," he now began. "I would be delighted to meet your family. But there is another matter I must raise with you."

"As you wish."

"I also request a hearing with your King."

Koram held his eyes – and bowed his head before him.

"Very well, Prince Gamel," he said. "I will arrange such a hearing."

"You carry no concern regarding the news you know I will bring?"

Koram's face softened before him.

"No, Gamel," he said. "I carry no such concern. I myself am perplexed by the news: but you will find no barrier to sharing it from me. I will open the way before you."

With deep gratitude, Gamel grasped his hand.

"Why, Koram?" he murmured, and Koram smiled again.

"Because you neutralized the Stone of the North!" he said.

"Not I!" Gamel protested quickly. "It was Yeshua…"

"I understand that, Gamel – but it was you who took it from me: and it was you who chose to give it to him. The North does not yet see Yeshua: only you. And your actions have opened the door to the North for sharing your news."

Humbled, Gamel gazed at him. Koram bowed his head again. And then Gamel turned to Taierre.

Taierre was sitting on the other side of the ship: his face pointed down to the deck, his gaze intense. His sword lay alongside him, sheathed. Gamel looked at it – and then wandered up to Taierre.

"May I join you?" he asked – and Taierre looked up at him.

"Do I have a choice?" he asked in return. "You are the future King of the Heartland."

Gamel frowned, looking at him. A choice?

"Friendship is always a choice," he said. "I come as both a king and a friend."

Taierre searched him. He glanced down at the Stone of Atua on his chest, and then again met his gaze.

"Friendship was impossible with a Kingship wielding the power of Soutar," Taierre said. "Is it possible with a Kingship of Atua?"

"Friendship is possible," Gamel replied, "At least in this age."

"In this age?"

"If Yeshua, in Atua, is the true King, he will reign directly in the end."

Taierre shifted in great discomfort at his words. "I find no pleasure in such a thought."

"I know," Gamel said. "But I myself am not that King. I do not seek such a direct rule."

"What then do you seek, Prince Gamel of the Heartland?"

Gamel smiled, and sat down next to Taierre. "I can't tell you," he said whimsically.

"Playing again?" Taierre said. "Like a child?"

"Perhaps," Gamel grinned. "A little fun can lift the soul. But also, it is not yet time to say."

Taierre was silent, though Gamel sensed him relaxing a little – and now Gamel also frowned, looking at the deck.

"There is a lot still to take place, Taierre," he said, "When I return to the Heartland."

"What do you mean?"

"I need to bring the news to my father: the news of what happened with the Stone."

Taierre's eyes were on him. "Why are you telling me this?"

Gamel shrugged. "Friendship, Taierre – explanation."

"Explanation for what?"

"For what must follow after I have told my father."

Now Gamel met his eyes. Taierre swallowed, and then looked away – his teeth grinding.

"I don't want to hear this."

"And yet you must hear it, because I am a king as well as a friend."

"Speak."

"After I have entered back into the Heartland, after I have told my father, after all is done, I will travel to the North and have an audience with the King – and I also seek an audience with your King, Taierre."

Taierre's eyes misted as he stared ahead of himself. "Now you have the sword at my throat," he said, and Gamel grimaced.

"I know," he said quietly, "But I do not want to draw blood."

Taierre took a deep breath, while Gamel fingered the healing wound of Taierre's sword on his own neck.

"Why must you do this?" Taierre asked. "Why must you spread this fable?"

"You know why," Gamel answered, "Because I know it to be true."

"Strange," Taierre said, "Because I know it to be false."

154

"Then we must allow time to reveal which one of us is correct."

"Perhaps."

"And we must uphold freedom: that each one might choose for themselves in what truth they will put their trust."

"Freedom?" Taierre said, looking at him. "You would not force this new 'truth' on your neighbours?"

"I would not, Taierre."

"Why not, if you know it to be true?"

Gamel smiled sadly at him – felt tears pricking at his eyes. "Do you not know why I would not, Taierre?" he whispered. "I felt the power of Soutar! I felt the enticement of him! I felt my rule over you – and I know it is wrong."

Now tears filled Taierre's eyes – he hastily blinked, looking away. For a long moment there was silence between them – and then Taierre returned to Gamel's gaze.

"Very well," he said. "When all is done in the Heartland, you will visit my King."

Gamel brightened before him. "Thank you, Taierre!"

"But don't make the mistake of assuming that we will change, Prince Gamel," Taierre quickly added. "With freedom of choice comes the ability to refuse!"

"I know," Gamel quickly replied. "I know, and I respect that."

"And don't think I will suddenly believe everything you are saying about Yeshua coming back from death."

"Hmmm."

"I do not believe it! But…I will arrange a hearing."

Gamel smiled at him – and suddenly wanted to hug him, but thought better of it.

"Very well!" he said, "A hearing with your king!"

"He will hear my arguments."

"Naturally!"

"I have ready access to his throne."

"Yes."

"But…you do have the benefit of having neutralized the Stone of great threat…"

"Yes."

"…and of being the future King of the Heartland."

"There is that."

Gamel grinned at him – and then rubbed his hands together in anticipation.

"Let the debate begin!"

"Let the debate begin," Taierre agreed – and Gamel rose to his feet and strode to the railing of the ship, leaning over the ocean: willing Altenhine, now a larger sliver, to quickly emerge before them.

Altenhine was approaching!

With excitement Lidya leaned over the railing of the ship. She could see the sand of the beach approaching, and the grassy plains behind – the West Coast.

"There she is!" she said to Gamel alongside, and he grasped her hand, his eyes shining.

"There she is."

"Prepare the anchor!" Captain Nehu called out – and one of his crew stood at the bow of the ship, ready.

"Drop the sail!"

Lidya looked up, to watch the massive sail released from above: dropping, crumpling to the mast. The ship still moved forward, carried at first by its own momentum and then by little waves which then broke on the beach.

"Drop anchor!"

The crewman released the anchor, by chain, and it dragged on the ocean floor – then suddenly jerking the ship to a halt.

They had arrived.

Lidya took in a deep breath of Altenhanse air, and rubbed her hands together. The sand was only a few feet away! She went to throw herself over the railing into the water, to rush to the land, when she felt Gamel's hand on her shoulder.

"Wait," he warned.

"The spirits!" Captain Nehu said behind them. "Where are they?"

Lidya cast her eyes over the sand, and the heaped shells – over the grassland behind. She could see the horses far away, grazing! Brena! And Tenith, and Stiar. Taierre whistled, from behind Lidya, and Stiar's ears perked up – she began to approach, and Tenith and Brena began to follow.

But where were the spirits? The angry faces they had seen on their departure?

Gamel was frowning. "Are they gone?"

"We have always felt them," Nehu said, "Whenever we have arrived."

"Could it be what Yeshua did?" Lidya asked, heart pounding in excitement. "Could it be that the Spirit of Atua now keeps them away?"

"You mean the Spirit of Atua in us?" Gamel asked.

"The Spirit is everywhere!" Lidya said. "Atua is everywhere! You saw what Yeshua did: Atua is stronger. Atua is the King of the spirits."

Gamel looked uncertain – but Lidya felt joy. She thrust herself off the deck into the water, gasped in delight with the cold, and ran onto the land.

Altenhine! With tears she spun around, lifting her arms into the air. She was back!

"Thank you!" she whispered to Atua, clapping her hands. "Thank you, thank you, thank you."

Now she bent to scoop the sand into her hands and threw it into the air, laughing.

Brena approached her, venturing onto the sand – Lidya reached out and rubbed his nose, and then wrapped her arms around his brown neck.

"Good to see you!" she said. "How have you been, boy?"

He neighed, and Lidya rubbed his mane – then turned to see Gamel reaching to do the same. He had tears in his eyes.

"We're here," he whispered.

"We're back."

"Last time we were here…" His eyes suddenly, for a moment, looked haunted. "Soutar, Lidi: this is where he had us."

Lidya grasped his hand. "He never had us, Gamel," she said.

"He would have!" Gamel said. "He did! I would have fallen…"

"Your hatred of father."

Gamel's eyes intensified. "The hatred is his way in."

"Do you still feel it?"

Again his eyes filled with tears, as he took a deep breath. "No, Lidi," he whispered. "I don't hate him anymore."

Lidya touched his face, with joy. "That's good!" she said. "That means you are ready."

"Ready?"

"To confront him."

Gamel shifted on his feet, looking at her. "But what will we find, Lidi?" he asked. "When we return?"

Lidya frowned slightly, watching him. "What do you fear?"

Gamel swallowed. "The spirits, Lidi – where are they? Where is Soutar?"

Lidya stepped back away from Brena, and turned to cast her eyes over the beach. Koram and Taierre were crossing the sand, swords on their hips – stepping up to the grassland, to greet Tenith and Stiar. The ship was moving away again: already back to Yerim. Captain Nehu was waving farewell: Lidya waved back to him. Gamel must have already shared their thanks.

Here, on the beach, Soutar had stood: in human form, though without a body. Here Lidya had watched him attack Gamel. Her brother had reached for him! Reached, in his agony, for the enemy…

She had torn the stone from his chest – she had taken into upon herself! And then…and then…

Lidya shuddered hard. Soutar had had her! For a moment he had been within her – raping her spirit, smothering her. She swayed on her feet, now, giddy with the memory – longing to vomit. But then she felt Gamel's hands on her arms.

"It's all right," he murmured, and she sobbed.

"He…"

"It's over now."

She reached to draw her fingers down Gamel's face – felt the pain of the past.

"He could have destroyed us."

"Yes," Gamel murmured gently. "But he did not."

"You…" Lidya whispered. "You carried me."

Gamel's brow creviced. "I had to save you."

"And I had to save you."

"It was meant to be this way."

157

"From the start."

"Two, not one, from birth."

"Yes, Gamel: two – male and female, from the start."

Silently they looked at each other – and then Gamel grasped her hand again.

"I want to talk to Atua," he said, and Lidya tilted her head.

"Talk?"

"Atua is stronger. We found him, Lidi! We found the One across the Sea! We found Yeshua."

"Yes!"

"We found what we were looking for – the One who could properly save us."

"Yes."

"So, now – I want to talk with him! He helped us before – we need his help now."

Lidya smiled at him – and then nodded. "All right," she said. "Talk with him."

Gamel reached to take both of her hands, and bowed his head – and Lidya closed her eyes.

"Help us, Atua," Gamel whispered, and Lidya agreed.

"Help us."

"We need you! Your strength, your love – your way to think, and act…"

"Have your way," Lidya whispered. "When the right time comes – instead of Soutar, let it be you in our spirits: let it be you reigning in our hearts."

She opened her eyes to find Gamel looking at her. "His way?" he asked. "His control?"

"Don't be afraid of him," Lidya said. "Atua is not Soutar."

Gamel smiled sadly. "Isn't a kingship what we have been running from?"

"To be wholly owned," Lidya said, "Is death in conquest, but paradise in love."

He tilted his head thoughtfully. "Choice…" he murmured to himself. "Choice is the difference between death and paradise."

*Stay with me: forever stay with me and you will have joy.*

"We will bring them the choice," Gamel said. "Let's do it, Lidi! Let's return to the Heartland, whatever we may find."

Lidya's heart lifted with happiness, as Gamel lifted her onto the back of Brena and then joined her in front. The Heartland! It was time to return home!

It was time.

Gamel sat on Brena, with Lidya behind. They had left the Coast, and were now riding through the Western Forest.

Wind blew through Gamel's curls, as Brena darted between the pine trees. Koram was ahead of him, on Tenith, and Taierre behind, on Stiar, as before.

"It's wonderful!" Lidya laughed into his ear, "Better than before!"

Gamel smiled to himself, with Lidya's freedom – and searched amongst the different trees. The heavy darkness he had felt riding to the Coast with Koram was no longer there. Why? Were the spirits gone? Was Soutar really gone?

"This forest," Gamel yelled to Lidya behind. "It actually looks beautiful!"

"It is beautiful!" Lidya yelled back. "The way it is supposed to be!"

Yellow sun scattered through leaves, from high in the sky, falling on their uplifted faces. Gamel grinned – and pulled gently on Brena's reigns, to move faster.

The flat of the forest floor lifted into a slope. Eagerly Gamel led Brena up, between trunks, knowing that this was the beginning of the Highland Elevation: the barrier between the coast and the Heartland Valley.

For hours they travelled – and then emerged onto the Barren Slope.

Here Gamel pulled Brena to a halt. He lowered himself down to the ground, and turned to look across the extensive spread of brown rock, the tufts of grass in cracks, and the foothills of grass and rock, leading to the mountains of the North and South.

"I'm coming!" he whispered up the slope toward his home. "It won't be long now!"

Koram stopped on Tenith, further up the slope; while Taierre lowered himself down from Stiar, alongside Gamel. Where was the enclosure, where they had stopped on their journey to the Coast? Gamel remembered, now, his state with the Stone of Soutar – his state with Soutar.

*"Do you think I want a new kind of alliance, Southern messenger?"* he had cried. Swallowing, Gamel now looked at Taierre – and saw in the green eyes his friend's reciprocal memory. *"I do not – and I will not! I desire the alliance of old: stronger, richer – I desire to own! I will be King!"*

Gamel drew his arms into his chest, and sat heavily down on the rock – staring back into the Western Forest. Had he really said it? Had he really wanted it?

*"Kill me,"* he had whispered to Koram. *"Destroy him."*

Now, shaking, Gamel closed his eyes – and saw, in his mind's eye, the image of Yeshua carrying the Stone of Soutar: Yeshua dying in his place.

"Forgive me," Gamel whispered. "The evil was mine."

*It is dealt with,* came the reply. *Now go and make things right.*

Gamel rose to his feet, and turned to Taierre.

*"You belong to me!"* he had said to him! Taierre had screamed beneath him, under Soutar's influence.

159

"I'm so sorry!" Gamel blurted out in his haste, reaching out a hand. Taierre smiled sadly, looking at the hand – and then he took it.

"I have forgotten it," he said quietly. "Just don't do it again,"

"Again?"

"We approach the Heartland, Prince Gamel. The source of your power is soon to be before you."

'Prince.' Fear seized him again: the same fear of old. The same power; the same Throne – offered to him! Offered…

*Submit to me.* It was Atua, now: not Soutar.

*Submit?*

*Submit.*

Gamel sank down to his knees, on the rock, and bowed his head. He reached to grasp the Stone of Atua lying on his chest.

"Have your way," he whispered. "Have your way, have your way, have your way…"

"Don't be afraid." Lidya was standing before him now – he looked up to her face, but there was an unusual expression about her eyes. "The Spirit within you is stronger than the spirit in him."

She was quoting Yeshua.

"What must I do?"

"Submit. Continue to submit."

"I am not the king!"

"No – you never were."

"Yeshua!" he said. "He is the King!"

"Yes. There is no other."

"But…conquest means death…"

"…while choice means paradise."

Gamel gazed up at her. "I understand," he said. And then he rose to his feet.

Koram now stood before him. His older eyes held their familiar warmth. Gamel studied him for a moment, and then reached to touch his shoulder.

"Thank you," he said quietly, and Koram smiled.

"For what?"

"For…" Gamel struggled to find the words, "For riding with me; for trying to protect me. For…for seeking to do all that a father would do."

Koram's brown eyes brightened. "You are welcome," he said quietly.

"Soon this part of our journey will be over."

"Perhaps."

"And yet…" Gamel tilted his head. "I think there will be more conversations ahead."

"Undoubtedly."

"I…" Now Gamel hesitated, searching Koram's eyes. "For a time, I…"

"You need not say it."

"I wished for something more."

"I know."

"But I could not receive it."

"I know that also."

"And now…" Gamel explored his own heart in Koram's presence. "Now it seems…"

"That this hidden wish of yours has gone."

Silently Gamel held his gaze. "Why should that be, my friend?"

"It is simple, is it not?" Koram said, smiling. "You have found a better father elsewhere."

Gamel laughed, before he could stop himself. "A better father?" he said.

"Difficult to compete with Atua himself," Koram said – and Gamel stared at him in astonishment.

"Atua…?" he breathed. And then he turned, to gaze across the barren rock: to a crevice like the one he had fallen dangling into, where he had almost died. Koram had rescued him! But now another father had rescued him: a salvation from within.

"Atua…" he breathed – and his eyes filled with tears, but now he did not blink them away.

They rode forward, up the Barren Slope for hours – and now they approached the Highland Forest. Gamel remembered his ride on Brena, willingly one with Soutar: his exuberance, his energy – the pulsation through his body. The speed; the strength! It had been wonderful – and yet, at the same time, he had played with fire. He remembered Soutar's torture! He remembered his control. Gamel had felt strong – but in truth he had been at Soutar's mercy: a child enticed – a child overridden.

In this place, the entrance to the Highland Forest, he had seen Michel.

Now Gamel pondered this one – this guide. He had come as a Heartlander! Come as Gamel's own kind. It had been a gift – a gift, as Michel had said, to offer him the choice: to offer him freedom.

"Not that having choice is easy!" Gamel muttered to himself.

*We never said it would be easy.*

Gamel smiled at the words – and then looked up. Koram had stopped, just before the forest. Gamel also stopped Brena, and stepped down again to the Barren Slope.

"Can't we ride to the top?" he asked enthusiastically. "We're almost there, Koram: almost within sight of the Heartland Valley!"

And yet the light was dimming. Gamel turned to look west, toward Yerim. The sun was dropping toward the horizon – red and pink filling the sky. The light was reflecting off Lidya's captive face.

"Rest," Koram said from behind his back. "You will need all your energy for tomorrow."

"Very well," Gamel agreed reluctantly. "Let us rest – and be ready for everything tomorrow will hold."

CHAPTER THIRTY-FOUR: Nearly Home

The sun had risen.

Excited, Gamel thrust himself out of a crevice in the rock to stand again on the Barren Slope. Today would be the day! Today he would set sight on the Heartland Valley.

The morning was young – the air cool. Gamel shivered a little more than usual, and was surprised at himself: could it be he had started to get used to the heat of Yerim? Surely not! He wandered over the Barren slope, and murmured a few words to Atua – he prayed, and trusted, and felt Atua's love within himself, and found himself at peace.

His voice lifted into natural song – and he began to notice birdsong from the Highland forest nearby. Soon he would see ravens! Soon he would ascend Raven Hill, and in open freedom: no longer in secrecy!

He rubbed his hands together in delight, strode up toward the forest, walked in between oak and pine, and suddenly gasped.

Bodies lay at his feet, scattered on the forest floor: bodies of Northern and Southern warriors, perhaps twenty in total.

"Taierre!" Gamel cried out. "Koram!"

Gamel stared at the men before him – knives in chests, blood dripping; sword wounds, white faces, stiff bodies…

Koram and Taierre were quickly around him, with Lidya – swords drawn. Each warrior walked slowly around the bodies, sometimes crouching to study something more closely. Taierre wandered through the trees and a few minutes later returned.

Northerner looked at Southerner – and then both looked at Gamel.

"This happened yesterday, Prince Gamel," Taierre said, and Koram nodded his agreement.

"Some, of course, moved on from the battle."

"Battle?" Gamel said. "You interpret this as war?"

Koram's eyes were fixed on Gamel. "It is the Resistance, Prince Gamel," he said quietly, "The Resistance in the North and the South."

Gamel looked at Lidya, whose face looked pale – her eyes serious – and then looked to Taierre.

"What does this mean?" he asked. "What do you expect to find in the Heartland?"

"I don't know, Prince Gamel," Taierre quietly answered. "Rumours spread quickly."

"Rumours?"

"The stones have gone, Gamel: the kings reside without their source of power."

Gamel swallowed, looking between Taierre and Koram.

"Soutar…?"

"He wanted to conquer," Lidya said.

"But how, without the Stone?" Gamel asked. "How, without all three stones?"

162

"He has no direct access," Lidya said, "But he still has influence, Gamel."

"What kind of influence?"

"Influence on a man's desires, without takeover – influence on a woman's fears."

Gamel frowned at her. "What will he try to do?"

Lidya grimaced. "He will use whatever he can."

"To achieve what?"

"Rule! Control. He takes pleasure in corruption – he takes pleasure in suffering."

"True evil..."

"He will take whatever he can get, Gamel – he will use whatever he can use to get more."

Gamel looked down at the bodies at his feet.

"Are we pawns?" he muttered to himself, "Pawns in someone else's battle? Why is he doing this?"

"He hates Atua," Lidya said. "He hates humanity."

"Why?"

"Atua loves humanity – Atua made humanity! He made us to be pure."

"Without corruption..."

"But Soutar – he doesn't want to follow Atua. He doesn't want to bow to a King."

"Why not?"

"He hates him."

"But why, Lidi? Why does Soutar hate?"

Lidya watched him. She hesitated and then she responded.

"Worship," she said. "He wants to be worshiped – not to give the worship. He wants to be served – not to serve."

Troubled, Gamel shifted on his feet. "He wants to be King."

Gamel wandered a little away from the scene of fighting – back onto the Barren Plain. Soutar's motives were so familiar! So...understandable. No wonder the enticement! No wonder the potential for partnership in the goal...

In this place, he had succumbed – for a moment he had succumbed. Gamel frowned, and looked out toward Yerim. The early morning light brightened the trees of the Western Forest behind him, though clouds were filling the sky to the west.

"I wish you were here," he whispered to Yeshua. "I wish you would rule now."

"He will not rule yet," a familiar voice said – and Gamel started slightly to find Michel standing next to him.

"Why?" Gamel murmured, "If he is the true King?"

"Consider it, Gamel," Michel said. "How would it be if Yeshua came and ruled before each one was given a chance to make a choice? Would you have handed the Stone to him before even leaving the Heartland Valley?"

Gamel swallowed. "No," he said. "Not unless he had forced me to."

"One day force may be required," Michel said sadly. "But until that day Yeshua prefers more peaceful methods."

"As do I," Gamel pondered.

"Yet more peaceful methods require more sacrifice, Gamel: do you understand?"

Gamel frowned, and looked at Michel. "I don't entirely understand…"

"To resist war is to risk being killed."

Gamel shifted on his feet. "Yes…"

"To be willing to take the first strike without retaliation."

"Yes."

"Do you understand, Gamel?"

Tears filled Gamel's eyes, though he could not explain the awareness that was beginning to stir in his heart.

"I understand," he whispered – and now Michel disappeared.

Slowly Gamel returned to the edge of the Highland Forest.

"What is it?" Lidya asked, and Gamel smiled sadly.

"I don't know: something big."

"What kind of 'big'?"

Gamel held her eyes quietly – and then turned to Koram.

"Can we leave now, Sir Koram?" he said. "Let's make for the top of the Ridge – let's look out across the Valley."

"Very well, Prince Gamel," Koram said. "Let us depart."

And they gathered together, with horses, and rode briskly through the Highland Forest.

Hours passed – Gamel could not say how many. The trees cloaked them, the sun blocked by leaves. Brena persevered uphill, behind Tenith – Lidya was silent behind Gamel on Brena's back. Up they continued – and then the trees fell away behind them.

Rock was before them – scattered fissures and caverns between. The tip of the ridge was only perhaps fifty feet further up.

Gamel gently nudged Brena's side with his heel – and Brena carefully walked between the fissures. Here Gamel had fallen! He held his breath, but Brena's steps were secure – Brena bore them up, closer and closer, and then they were near the top.

Carefully Gamel lowered himself to the ground, and ran up to the peak of the Highland Ridge.

The Heartland was before him.

With tears, Gamel stretched out his arms and took a deep breath. The sun was high in the blue sky – reflecting brightly off the pure white snow of the mountains of the North and South: the peaks were so close! So stunning!

The Highland Forest was near, below his feet – and beyond, in the greater distance, at the bottom of the Highland Elevation, began the Heartland Valley. Farmland was spread out before him, far away, with a hint of cottages beyond – and, further again, was the beauty of the Blue Lake bordered by the Eastern Ridge.

Lidya was by his side – the sun reflecting off her radiant face.

"Oh, Lidi," he whispered. "We are nearly home!"

She squeezed his hand – and he shook his head almost in disbelief. He had made it! He had survived! And now home was before him.

*Atua,* he breathed within. *You saved my life! You saved my life...*

Lidya's eyes also were full of tears – now she was crying. Gamel embraced her tightly, silently: words were unnecessary. Then he released her, and turned to Koram and Taierre.

Taierre was peering out across the valley – frowning. Troubled, Gamel approached him.

"What is it?"

"I'm not sure, Prince Gamel."

"What do you see?"

"A shadow, to the south – at the foothills, lining the valley."

Koram also was looking – and now also frowned. "Yes," he muttered, "A shadow also to the north, at the foothills."

"What kind of shadow?"

"I don't know, Gamel," Koram said, "It may be nothing – perhaps a trick of the sun and clouds."

Koram's eyes shifted to Taierre – silent thoughts were exchanged. Gamel grimaced.

"Speak your minds!" he said, and Koram met his eyes.

"The Resistance," he said. "It might be the Resistance."

Gamel stared at him, heart quickening.

"What do you mean?"

"North and South, Gamel! They are unchecked by the stones – Soutar has no direct access of control. The route of the fertilizer is the route of power."

Gamel turned again to stare out across the valley. Could he see them – the shadows to north and south? Perhaps a slight shadow – perhaps a slight movement.

"We have to get there," Gamel whispered – and now Koram's hand came to his shoulder.

"We can't complete the entire journey today."

"The Heartland!" Gamel said. "She might be under attack!"

"We must remain steady and on course."

Now Taierre was alongside Gamel. The Southerner was carrying a second sword, surely from the fallen warriors, and now offered it to Gamel.

Gamel met his green eyes, and shook his head. "We have already been through this, Taierre."

"Your land may be under threat," Taierre said.

"I know."

"You are the future King..."

"...of the Heartland! I know that! I need to think."

Gamel moved away, from both Taierre and Koram – on the rock of the ridge, looking out toward home.

*What should I do?* He whispered within.

*Proceed.*

*But then what?*

To this he received no answer.

Lidya approached him, a little unsteady on the rock – she stopped alongside him, to gaze out to the valley. She was silent – and then she spoke.

"The Heartland is so beautiful, Gamel."

"Yes," Gamel breathed. "She is beautiful. And yet I fear for her."

"You shouldn't fear."

"Why not?"

Lidya turned to him, her eyes shining. "Because she belongs to Atua."

In wonder Gamel stared at her – and then cast his eyes over the majestic mountains, sparkling lake, and fertile farmland.

"It is yours!" he suddenly cried out to Atua in realization. "Our land never belonged to us! It never belonged to Soutar. It all belongs to you!

Gamel now remembered Yeshua's words. *Don't hit back*, he said. *Don't commit the same crime. Don't give hatred for hatred: rather give love.*

"Love..."

Gamel looked over the mountains of the North, the mountains of the South and the Heartland. He looked at Lidya, and Koram and Taierre. Why should the land be divided? Why should the people be divided?

Koram met his eyes and smiled slightly in question. "Prince Gamel?"

Gamel smiled back, bowing his head slightly to him. "I am ready, Sir Koram."

"Ready?"

Gamel gestured down at his feet, to the steep and jagged slope sweeping quickly down to the Highland Forest.

"I am ready to proceed."

"Very well – let us proceed."

And Koram mounted Tenith, and slowly and carefully led the four on three horses down the precarious slope into the relative safety of the forest.

CHAPTER THIRTY-FIVE: Courage and Purpose

For a few hours the four rode down the slope of the Elevation, within the Highland Forest – but now the light was dimming through the trees.

Gamel peered between the trunks expectantly – and then the clearing opened up before them, leading to the Ice Lake.

Koram brought Tenith to a halt, and Taierre joined Koram alongside.

"We should set up camp here tonight, Gamel," Koram said.

"Is that wise?" Taierre questioned, and now Gamel remembered: here he had been attacked! Here the Northern warrior had thrown him down.

"The risk is no higher here than anywhere," Koram said. "Only one Northerner learned of our presence here, and you killed him."

Taierre grimaced at Koram. "It is against my advice to stay here," he said, "But so be it."

Gamel looked at Taierre. "You are still protecting me?" he asked. "Though the stones are now gone?"

Taierre looked surprised at the question – and still more surprised at the reality.

"Yes," he said. "I suppose that I am."

"Why?"

Taierre paused in thought and then answered. "Because you are a friend," he said, "And also because you are soon to be a king."

Gamel smiled widely at him, nodded, and then turned away.

Koram and Taierre set up tents, while Gamel wandered with Lidya around the Ice Lake. The temperature was dropping quickly now, as darkness began to settle. Gamel was grateful for Hana's packed clothes – still in the leather packs on Brena's back when they had returned from Yerim.

"You remember what happened here," Gamel said, as Lidya poked curiously at the hard surface of the lake with a stick.

"I remember."

"We all revealed the stones."

"Yes."

"I felt the pain – I fought Taierre, and almost…"

"You would not have killed him."

"I'm not so sure. And now…"

"…you're not sure what you might do."

Gamel looked at her: crouched by the edge of the lake. Then he reached instinctively into his right Heartland trouser pocket – for the Stone of Soutar.

The stone was gone – and in its place he found a handkerchief. It was Lidya's gift! His name was written in red – and two lanterns were embroidered underneath, with the day of their birth.

"Lidi!" he said. "Look!"

Now she was reaching – to pull out the gold circle pendant from its hiding place under her shirt: the pendant Taierre had sold to him, and that Lidya had worn around her neck all this time.

"Loyalty!" Gamel said. "That could not have been truer."

Lidya smiled at him. "Two from birth."

Gamel smiled back – but then, in sudden memory, he reached into his left trouser pocket. There were the keys of the Throne Room: the key to the history cupboard, and the key to the shrine.

A chill went up Gamel's spine. Friedrich! Gamel gasped – seeing the knife again plunging into his brother's chest.

"I don't want to go back there," he whispered to Lidya, "Into the Palace? I don't want to go."

Lidya stood before him, now – her face serious and sad. "I know, Gamel."

"I love the Heartland! But I don't love the Palace."

"I know."

"I could spend all my days in the valley – you know that, Lidi! And yet..."

"Yes?"

"...I know I must do this thing."

Gamel clenched his fingers into a fist around the keys of the Throne Room – he clenched his teeth. A wave of hatred swept through him for Soutar – he closed his eyes.

*Help me, Atua.*

*Submit to me.*

*I submit.*

Peace flowed through him – love flowed through him. But now there was another.

*I still see you.*

Gamel shivered. Soutar was still there! Still there...

Pain took him: a memory of exhilaration with Soutar – and then the sudden shift into torture.

*I had you,* Soutar said.

*You have me no more.*

*I will take you again.*

Gamel shifted on his feet. *You have no access.*

*I will take you anyway.*

Gamel stood straight now, grasping the Stone of Atua around his neck.

*Yeshua has defeated you.*

*Yeshua is dead.*

Now Gamel laughed. *Yeshua is dead?* He said. *Is that all you have: a denial of his new life? I saw him with my own eyes! I saw your stones melt away under the authority of Atua.*

Soutar's voice was silenced. But now, suddenly, Lidya gasped.

Gamel looked at her: watched her face. The light was dim – her eyes were distant.

"Atua," she whispered – and Gamel reached for her hand.

"It's all right," he said – and felt her trembling. "It's over."

"Not yet."

"No – but soon."

She looked at him now. "We must face the Palace."

"Yes."

"Face where it all began."

"Yes, Lidi."

Gamel swallowed. He had feared leaving the Heartland Valley – feared being alone in the wilderness with the stone. But Yeshua had carried the stone – done away with it! And now Gamel feared returning.

Yet there was more than fear: there was also hope. And now there was a curious growing power he was feeling within, different from the power of Soutar. There was a purpose beyond himself – a driving force above himself.

A branch snapped. Gamel spun around – and saw another Northern warrior. Gamel stretched out a hand, while the man advanced – his sword drawn.

"I have no weapon," Gamel said. "You need not fear me."

"Who are you?"

"I am a friend."

"A friend?"

"I have no weapon."

Gamel separated his hands now, before the man, exposing his chest.

The warrior frowned at him. Then he re-sheathed his sword and suddenly disappeared between trees. Astonished, Gamel looked at Lidya. Her eyes were wide. Then Taierre appeared.

Gamel held his eyes.

"There was someone here," he said, and Taierre frowned.

"Who?"

"A Northern warrior."

"Of the Resistance?"

"I don't know."

Taierre's eyes quickly moved through the trees, keen and attentive, and then returned to Gamel.

"You should not stay here."

"He didn't attack me."

"He didn't recognise you."

Gamel swallowed, feeling Taierre's implied threat as yet another sword to his throat – a sword this time he did not want to acknowledge.

"He did not attack."

"Prince Gamel!" Taierre insisted. "Listen to me: he did not recognise you."

Gamel listened – and searched Taierre's face. Should he really fear death, as he feared it before? Was this really to be his inevitable fate?

"What are you saying?"

"The Resistance will try to kill you, Gamel."

"But why?"

"The Throne is the Threat! You know that!"

"Yes," Gamel said. "But am I a threat separate from the Throne?"

Now Taierre was silenced, while Gamel pondered his own question – and Koram also appeared to stand alongside.

"What are you suggesting?" Koram asked.

169

"I'm not sure," Gamel said, reaching a hand to his chin – furiously thinking, "Not just yet."

"Your father…"

Gamel straightened suddenly – his father! Soon he would need to face his father.

"King Maki is without the Stone of Soutar."

"But he is not without Soutar himself."

Grimacing, Gamel nodded, "Agreed. But Soutar can't override our wills without the Stone – he can only influence us."

"What is your strategy, Prince Gamel?" It was Taierre.

Gamel looked across the Ice Lake. Night had deepened – moonlight and starlight reflected off the rough surface.

"My strategy?" he said. "I have no strategy – not yet. But I do have powerful news: the stones overcome. And I am beginning to see other kinds of power also."

"What kinds of power?"

"The power of words and actions."

Gamel glanced between Koram and Taierre: Koram was looking thoughtful; Taierre perplexed. Then Gamel reached to grasp Lidya's hand.

"Time for rest," he said quickly. "We should ride first thing in the morning, if you are both in agreement."

"Yes," Koram said. "We will be ready with sunrise."

"What about the local threat?" Taierre asked.

"I believe we are safe tonight," Lidya said.

Taierre and Koram searched her face – but then Koram looked to Gamel.

"Let's continue here tonight," Gamel said. "Tomorrow we will arise with daylight."

"Very well," Taierre muttered, "As you wish."

And Gamel led Lidya back to the camp, escorted by Northerner and Southerner.

CHAPTER THIRTY-SIX: Possibility and Dissension

Lidya awoke. She was in the tent, lying across from Gamel. He was still sleeping.

Quietly Lidya lifted herself from the blankets and slipped out of the tent – creeping behind Taierre's back and then escaping beyond.

The Ice Lake was before her – lit by scattered early morning sun, between the leaves of the trees. Lidya drew her Heartland coat more tightly around her, and hastily moved between the trees to seek out the view.

The Heartland Valley was before her! With joy Lidya clapped her hands, like a child. Home! Home...She cast her eyes down the Highland Elevation, above the tops of the remaining trees of the forest to the brush-laden slope, and beyond this to the beginning of the valley itself. The farmland was drawing ever closer – the grass, the sheep and the scattered trees: the Dandes River, the cottages of Raventown and Raven Hill...Tears filled her eyes, and she longed to rush to Brena and hasten down the rest of the slope. Soon they would arrive! Soon.

The yellow early morning sun was warm on Lidya's face, rising above the Eastern Ridge – over the glistening Blue Lake. The mountains of North and South also reflected yellow warmth, though the morning air was crisp.

"Altenhine..." Lidya breathed. She had failed to realize how much she had missed her own home.

Leaning against an oak tree, Lidya's thoughts began to wander. Koram and Taierre had seen a shadow approaching the Heartland from North and South – could she see it? Perhaps. And yet somehow she felt at peace. All of the beauty before her, all of the goodness of her life, was not hers to own – it belonged to Atua: it was his to work out.

Her voice lifted in a quiet song of worship, as she looked across the mountains and the valley – a song of love for Atua: a song of trust in Yeshua.

*Watch over us, Master.*
*I will watch over you.*
*Show us what to do.*
*Stay with me, and I will show you what to do.*

Lidya sang, and rested – she fleetingly closed her eyes. Then she heard the sound of a sword unsheathed. Holding her breath, she stared out to the farmland – then closed her eyes in prayer again.

*Father...*
*Do not be afraid.*

"How can I help you?" she asked, fixing her eyes on a distant farm. "Have you lost your way?"

Now, slowly, she turned. A Southerner was before her – his white face drawn, and frowning as he cast his eyes over her dishevelled clothes.

"You are a Heartlander?" he said.

"I am."

"What are you doing here?"

Lidya hesitated. "I am camping."

"Alone?"

171

Now two other Southerners were alongside him – all tall, slim and blonde: all casting their eyes over her.

*I will have you, Princess of the Heartland.* It was Soutar.

Lidya stiffened – but made herself not clench her hands.

"I am not alone," she said. "My Father is with me."

"Your father," another chided, "Camping with his daughter, totally unaware: typical Heartlander."

"And what brings you here?" Lidya asked. They seemed surprised at the question.

"What do you know of us, Heartlander?" The third asked. "Tucked up in your warm valley, plenty of food in all seasons – what would you know of our intentions?"

"It must be difficult in the South."

"It is what it is."

"I wonder if we can help you."

"Help?" The first warrior looked suspiciously at her.

"Yes – since we have enough, I wonder if we can help you."

Now they were silenced. Lidya was surprised to see their response: they seemed perplexed. She placed a hand slowly in her coat pocket, and withdrew a piece of bread from the night before.

"Are you hungry?" she asked. "Personally, I don't enjoy roasted squirrel."

And she handed the piece of bread to the first warrior.

He took the bread on the tip of his sword – one of the others laughed. But then, suddenly, Taierre stormed in with sword drawn.

"No!" Lidya cried, and Taierre froze – looking at his fellow countrymen.

The warriors stared at Taierre – the first Southerner shook the bread off his sword in readiness.

"Taierre!" The warrior said. "We know you: right hand to the King!"

"Right hand?" Lidya said.

Taierre stared at his opponents, glancing between the three – adjusting the grip on his sword.

"Who are you?" he asked. "Speak!"

"I am Brierre," the first said. "These are my men."

"What is your purpose?"

"What is your purpose, 'Sir' – on the Highland Elevation, well away from the Southland and Heartland Valley? Do you know this girl?"

Taierre's eyes briefly met Lidya's before looking again back to Brierre.

"I met her whilst scouting the Heartland perimeter. She is of no concern to you – I ask you again: what is your purpose?"

Brierre held his stare and then grimaced. "You know our purpose, right hand to the King."

"You are Resistance!" Taierre shifted on his feet with disdain.

"And you are outnumbered, royalist – in a land not our own."

Taierre watched him. "The Law still applies to our citizens on their return."

"Only if the King remains in power."

"You speak of treachery!"

172

"No, Taierre – I speak of freedom."

"The Highland Elevation is free," Lidya quickly interrupted. "Here all voices can be heard."

Taierre and Brierre both looked at her – and then Koram appeared, with Gamel alongside.

Gamel's eyes found Lidya quickly, in concern and questioning. She shook her head slightly. Koram stood next to Taierre, his hand on his sword in readiness – and Brierre laughed.

"Now this is a strange sight: a Northerner is set to defend the right hand to the Southern King! How are we to understand this? And a young Heartlander is with him!"

"A strange thought indeed," Koram said, "Yet it speaks of new possibilities."

"New possibilities?"

"Friendship," Gamel said, "The possibility of friendship, between all our lands."

Brierre studied Gamel's face, now, frowning. He glanced back to Lidya, and stooped to pick up the piece of bread she had offered, dislodged from his sword.

"Friendship?" he said. "After five hundred years of control? Five hundred years of oppression by the King of the South, controlled by the King of the Heartland, all over our basic food supply – after all this you dare to suggest friendship?"

He broke the bread in two and threw it to the ground. "This is what I say to friendship!" he declared. "We must seize control of our own fate! The time for domination is over!"

He swung his sword in the air, and Taierre engaged him – but Koram now quickly drew his sword and flicked the others apart.

"Enough!" he said. "Enough."

Brierre tried again to swing at Taierre – Koram blocked him. Now Brierre's men drew swords – now both Taierre and Koram defended against three.

"Enough!" Gamel cried out. "Too many people have died! Enough!"

His voice seemed to penetrate – the five warriors paused, but Brierre was agitated. Lidya could see his unspent aggression: unresolved anger. Should they tell of the stones? Should they reveal their true identities?

She glanced across to Gamel – and now he shook his head slightly to her.

"I'm sorry," Gamel said. "We seem to have crossed paths at the wrong time."

"Wrong time?" Brierre said. "When would be a right time?"

"That remains to be seen."

"Who are you?" Brierre asked, frowning at him. "You speak with authority."

"I am a Heartlander – I represent the Heartland: such is my authority."

Brierre looked at him, and then looked to Lidya. He bowed slightly to her.

"Excuse us, madam – we did not mean to interrupt."

Lidya could see the intense frustration in his posture – as he bent again, picked up the bread, and this time ate from it.

"Have a good day," he said. And then, gesturing to his men, he quickly departed.

Lidya let out a deep breath of relief. Gamel joined her – he touched her arm, searching her eyes.

"Are you all right?"

"Yes," she whispered.

Taierre and Koram now also joined them.

"We must keep moving," Taierre said sharply. "They may suspect your true identities very soon."

"They are Resistance!" Koram said. "Our suspicions must be true."

"An imminent attack on the Heartland…" Gamel murmured. "Yes: the forces are gathering."

The four quickly returned to the camp – they quickly packed, and mounted their horses. Lidya sat behind Gamel, on Brena – she leaned against his back, as they sped between pines and oak.

*The Heartland is mine*, Soutar whispered to her, and Lidya shook her head.

*Your time is over*, she said back to him. *Your age is through.*

Soutar pressed into her now – she felt him smothering, she choked: yet the stone was gone.

*Yeshua has dealt with you*, she said, and she felt his fury.

*My army is stirring up war, Princess Lidya!* He hissed. *Northerners, Southerners – they will attack your precious home: they will override the Palace. If your brother will not rule, I will choose another from North or South to enslave your people. Heartlanders will kiss the feet of their enemies: my Throne will remain!*

The four broke free of the Highland Forest – and now they were riding through the yellow-green brush of the Elevation, rapidly approaching the bottom of the slope and the beginning of the Heartland Valley.

Lidya looked out, with Gamel, across the valley. The sun was high in the sky. Light clouds were gathering – and there, across the farmland, to north and south, at the foot of the foothills, warriors were moving on foot toward Raventown.

"There they are!" Lidya cried – and Soutar again was upon her.

*As I raped you, so I will rape your homeland.*

Hatred stirred within her – but she knew what to do.

"Gamel."

He brought Brena to a halt, and she slipped of his back to the ground – then she went down to her knees.

"Atua!"

*Remain with me.*

"Save us!"

*Remain with me.*

Lidya closed her eyes, murmured a few words – found her song again in Atua. Then she rose to her feet.

Gamel's face looked white: she touched his shoulder. Then she looked out across the valley: to the warriors, to the helpless and undefended cottages – and to the Palace.

*Time for me to take my prize.* It was Soutar

Lidya's heart burned now with a righteous fury she had never known.

*Strike my people, and we will defeat you,* she said within. *Rape my land, and we will crush you underfoot.*

*Crush me?* Soutar replied, laughing. *The Heartland is defenceless.*

*You are wrong.*

*You lie.*

*There is a force stronger than hatred; there is a presence stronger than rape. Do you not know? Yeshua made it known! Atua melted your stones into his purposes.*

*Yeshua has gone!*

*But love remains, Soutar! Love remains! Love rules – and love will rule.*

*"The Throne of the Heartland will be ruled by Love."*

She had spoken it out aloud.

Gamel's eyes were on her, now – and she watched them fill with tears.

"I understand," he whispered. "I understand."

His body was trembling – but he turned now and set his face to the valley. The battle was before them: the battle for their home; the battle for their lives.

*Love your enemy, and do good to those who hate you.*

It was time.

Gamel rode forward on Brena.

Behind his back sat Lidya – silent: ready. Behind Brena rode Koram, on Tenith, and Taierre, on Stiar – alongside each other.

They all now galloped together through farms, across grass, and between white woollen sheep. Wind blew through Gamel's hair – he would have laughed, if their task had not been so serious.

Ahead, Northern and Southern warriors were converging on Raventown: converging toward the Palace. The warriors were on foot, while the four rode forward at top speed. Gamel considered the conflict before him: King Maki and Queen Tali in the Palace, with the Palace Guard. Those in Raventown were unarmed – would they fight? Would the men find their natural instinct in attack? If so, they would be swiftly killed.

Gamel remembered Hana – and now they were passing the Raventown stable, to their right. On they rode – and then they saw the forces, now only fifty feet away.

Gamel looked at the Northerners first, to their left: stocky build, gathered together, striding steadily forward across the farmland – there must have been over five thousand who had gathered, and were surging ahead. Gamel had never seen anything like it – he swallowed a hard lump in his throat, glancing back at Koram.

The warriors saw them ride past – some raised a yell, and many began to run after them, but they could not keep up with the horses, and fell away.

Soon after, Gamel saw the Southerners: tall, slim – graceful and disciplined, marching in line, to their right, with swords drawn – perhaps over six thousand. The Southern warriors also saw the horses – but they did not change their tactic: simply kept marching forward.

Eleven thousand warriors. Gamel grimaced – Raventown herself only housed six thousand men, women and children. To win by fighting would be impossible: but he had known this all along – this had always been their fate.

*I will help you to defeat them.* It was Soutar. *You need me – you have always needed me.*

*What are you trying to achieve?* Gamel asked. *You have drawn all of these: from North and South. They fight you, and yet they are following your urge. What do you want from us?*

Soutar hesitated, and then he responded. *Do you not know?* He said, *Even after all you have seen in Yerim? I want your destruction, pathetic boy! I want your souls!*

Gamel shuddered at the thought. Their collective destruction: the corruption of the soul; the blackening of the human heart. Suddenly he understood: it didn't matter to Soutar who he owned, or how he came to own – only that he come to own, and that he corrupt all into his own likeness.

"You will not have our souls," Gamel whispered – and he rode on, with greater fervour, toward Raventown.

At last they approached the first cottages, of the western aspect of the town.

Gamel slowed Brena down to a walk. He called out to the Raventowners he had previously watched, under the cover of night, and now peered through their windows – but no one was there. Lidya's voice sounded out from behind him, to the Raventowners – still no one emerged.

"Are they hiding?" Gamel murmured, but Lidya shook her head.

"There is nowhere to hide."

Gamel continued along the southern aspect of the town, past Hana's farm. He could see her, in the distance, outdoors – amidst her vegetables.

"We can't leave her there," he said. "The Southerners will see her."

"Pick her up!" Lidya said – and so Gamel diverted south, and noticed Koram and Taierre following him.

Hana looked up at him, carrying a cabbage in each hand. "Prince Gamel!"

She quickly placed the cabbages on the ground and straightened to extend a muddy hand to him. "Welcome home!"

Gamel gratefully shook her hand. Hana's brown eyes passed quickly over his face, glancing to Lidya behind, and then to Koram and Taierre.

"May I help you?"

"No," Gamel said quickly. "We need to help you. Come with us now."

Hana hesitated for a moment, and then nodded. "Very well."

Gamel lowered himself off Brena then stepped aside, gesturing. Hana easily lifted herself onto Brena's back, in front of Lidya – and Koram promptly lifted Gamel up behind him onto Tenith's back.

Hana rode Brena alongside Gamel on Tenith, as he tried to explain.

"Raventown is under attack!"

"Under attack?"

"An army of Southerners and Northerners is on their way."

"Why?"

"They are resisting the authority of our Throne."

"And the Stone?"

Gamel looked at her. "It has been destroyed."

"Destroyed?" She looked astonished. "How?"

Now Gamel smiled. "I can't explain it all now, but remember our talks? It turns out I found someone much bigger than a king."

She had shared the rumours of the Heartland, and now looked fascinated by his words. Gamel longed to tell her all, but could not.

"Come," he said, "We must get to the Palace."

And Koram rode forward, with Taierre to the right and Hana and Lidya to the left.

After a few minutes, riding east along the southern aspect of the town, and turning left to ride up Main Street, they reached the Palace.

Gamel lowered himself off Tenith, and stood aside – finally standing before the Palace: standing before his home.

Three levels of greystone towered over the courtyard – but now, gathered in front, were thousands of men, women and children. It seemed all of Raventown had been assembled!

Surprised, Gamel reached to straighten his clothes – and realized he looked a mess. His white shirt was filthy, his commoner grey trousers dishevelled. Lidya was dressed in trousers and a man's shirt, also messy – her hair tangled and falling everywhere. For a moment he hesitated, and then discarded his pride. There was no time to wash or change: he was who he was – the Prince of the Heartland.

The people looked disgruntled – mothers holding hungry children in their arms, and men pacing backwards and forwards. Palace guards encircled the group, but Gamel could not see his mother or father.

"What's going on?"

A few Heartlanders began to notice Koram and Taierre – a few shouted out, pointing. Soon two guards were approaching them – so Gamel promptly approached them.

"Jamel!" he said, and Jamel started and gave a double take.

"Prince Gamel!"

"These are Sir Koram and Sir Taierre."

"Ah…"

"They are our allies."

"Our allies?"

"They have given me their allegiance."

Jamel looked at him – casting his eyes over Gamel's messy hair, dirty face, and filthy shirt – and smirked.

"We will need to hold them in custody," he said.

"Custody!" Gamel exploded. "No."

"With all due respect, Prince Gamel…"

"We are soon to be at war, Jamel."

"The King is in control."

"Listen to me…"

"You are not the King, Prince Gamel! Get back into line!"

Gamel stared at him – and rose straight up.

"That's enough, Jamel!" he said. "I may not be the King, but I am the First Prince and I am to be the future King! I'm ordering you now to allow my colleagues to stand free. We are at war, and I am going to inform the King."

Jamel flushed, and said nothing. Gamel glanced at Koram and Taierre, and muttered under his breath.

"Maybe it would be best to stay discreet."

"I'll stay with them!" Hana said brightly. "I'll introduce them to our neighbours as guests of the Prince."

"Good idea!" Gamel said – and now he grasped Lidya's hand, and strode forward toward the Palace.

They entered through the front entrance: a wide arch, watched now by ten guards. All were armed with swords – all reached for their weapons, but then they recognised Gamel and stepped back.

"Welcome, Prince Gamel and Princess Lidya," they said, and Gamel grimaced.

"Shouldn't you be out the front, protecting the people?"

"King Maki…"

"Never mind – so be it."

Gamel walked with Lidya down the corridor and up the steps to the second level. There, in the lounge, he looked out of the windows to the valley. The forces were approaching fast! He could see the mass of Northerners and Southerners now nearing the western border of Raventown. Gamel suddenly realized his father would have been watching them for some time: he had gathered the entire town in preparation for the battle.

Voices were over their head: Maki and Tali. Swallowing, Gamel looked at Lidya. Her face was pale. Up there, Friedrich had died! Up there, Lidya had been taken by Soutar.

"Courage," Lidya whispered – and both, fleetingly, closed their eyes.

*Courage,* Atua said. *I am with you.*

And now Gamel grasped Lidya's hand, and strode up the stairs into the Throne Room.

Maki was there: large, and strong. But he had a knife, and was desperately cutting himself. Gamel took a deep breath, and stepped forward.

"Father."

Maki looked up at him – his blue eyes haunted. "Gamel!" he cried, "Gamel!"

He gesticulated to the windows – the higher view: the throngs flooding through Raventown.

"They are coming!"

Gamel swallowed. "Father, I know they are coming: I saw them on my way home."

"We must appease Soutar!" Maki said. "He has sent them, because of our disobedience! We must sacrifice to him!"

And he continued to cut.

Gamel shuddered, and glanced at Tali. She was standing back, from Maki: her face white.

"Mother?" Gamel whispered – and now Lidya rushed to Tali, embracing her.

Tali began to weep. "You're alive!" she said. "You're both alive! You're alive! You're alive!"

But now Maki grasped his arms. "Where is the Stone?"

Heart pounding with fear, Gamel faced him. "The Stone has been destroyed, Father," he said, and Maki suddenly hit him across the face.

"What do you mean it's been destroyed?" he said. "It is our only hope, Gamel! You idiot! You destroyed it?"

Face stinging, body shaking, Gamel stood before him – and tears filled his eyes.

"It's destroyed!" he said. "It is destroyed."

"No!" Maki cried, towering over him. "How could you destroy it? How could you?"

And he began to beat him.

"Father!" Lidya's voice screamed. "Stop it!"

Her hands clutched at his fists, but she did not have the strength to stop him. Her figure was tiny next to his towering strength.

Gamel sank to his knees under his father's blows – face aching, lips bleeding. He closed his eyes – and the blows stopped. The beating of his father in childhood was upon him: the terror! The pain. His body trembled – but Yeshua was there.

*Am I worthless?* He breathed within.

*Atua has a purpose for everyone he has made.*

Tears filled Gamel's eyes again: but now they were tears of resolution. He grasped the new pendant around his neck: the stone of Atua.

*Father.*

And now he rose to his feet.

Maki's eyes were upon him as he spoke. "The old stone is destroyed," he said, "A new stone has been made."

And he removed the Stone of Atua and held it up before his father's eyes.

Maki stared at it, and stared at Gamel – but now Tali's voice rang out loud and victorious.

"The One across the Sea!" she cried. "It is the symbol of Atua! The Son of Atua destroyed the Stone for us!"

Gamel stared at Tali in utter amazement – she knew? How could she know? But now Maki drew back his gaze – now he was beginning to shake hard before Gamel.

"Is it true?" he asked, and Gamel nodded.

"It is true."

"How?"

Tears filled Gamel's eyes. "The One, Yeshua – he carried the Stone. He died wearing it. And then..." Now Gamel swallowed, and girded himself. "...and then I saw him alive again."

Maki looked at him. He smiled – an eerie, evil kind of smile. And then he stretched out his hand.

"Give me the keys."

Gamel clenched his teeth together. "No," he said.

"Give me the keys!"

Gamel felt the keys sitting in his left trouser pocket: the key to the shrine of Soutar, and the key to the history of the kings of Soutar – the kings who had appeased him.

"I will not give you the keys."

Gamel tucked the pendant of Atua into his right pocket, but now Maki was hitting him again.

"Give me the keys, you fool!" he cried. "Don't you understand? We are all going to die! Give me the keys!"

And Maki clutched at his trouser pocket.

180

Gamel fought him, but knew he could not win a physical fight. He removed the keys – he longed to throw them out of the window, but knew another would find them. He hesitated – and then he gave them to his father.

Maki rushed to the shrine, used the key, opened the doors – and reached into a cabinet Gamel had not noticed before.

He removed a parchment, and a silver cup with powder.

"Father," Lidya breathed. "What is it?"

Gamel glanced quickly at her – at her insight. What was she feeling? He looked at the powder.

"Soutar showed me this," Maki said, "When I last wore the stone. He showed me how to make it. He showed me how to use it."

Gamel grasped the parchment, turning his back – focusing on the writing, and the diagrams. Ingredients were mixed – powder, and liquid. A flame was added, and...

Gamel's body went cold. He stared out to the advancing warriors – and stared at the parchment in his hand.

*This is your plan*, he whispered to Soutar, *Your plan to destroy us all*.

"If we gather a little together," Maki said, "and we aim it at the warriors, and ignite..."

"This is mass murder," Gamel said tightly. "This is mass murder!"

"Self-defence!" Maki insisted.

"Lidi," Gamel said. "Tell the people to leave."

"Leave?" Lidya breathed.

"The Heartlanders, Lidi! Tell them to run!"

"But where?" Lidya cried.

"Around the back of the Palace!" Tali said. "Around the Blue Lake."

"Tell Koram and Taierre to help them, with each of you," Gamel said. "Get them out of here! Hurry!"

Tali moved toward the steps, but Lidya grasped Gamel's arm. "Gamel..."

Tears blurred his vision – he hastily cleared them. "I can't let this happen, Lidi. I can't let this happen."

She frowned at him, uncertain – he pushed her away. "Go."

She left – and now he was alone with Maki.

Maki was hastily gathering the powder together into tubes. He carried the tubes to a larger tube that was pointing out of the window.

"Father..." Gamel breathed. "Don't do this."

"Self-defence!" Maki said crossly, and he returned to the altar.

Gamel stared at his back, at his arms working steadily at evil, and closed his eyes.

*What must I do?*

*Forgive him.*

Pain stabbed at Gamel's heart – and then deep grief. He watched his father – he mourned.

"Father," he said. "I think we are all going to die."

"Not if I can help it."

"I need to tell you..."

181

"It will have to wait."

"I need to say…"

"Where is that last tube?"

"I'm so sorry."

Tears filled Gamel's eyes to overflowing – uncontrollable tears.

Now Maki stopped searching – now his body was suddenly very still, his back still to Gamel.

"What?"

Pain filled Gamel's heart – yet he continued. "Before we die, father: I'm so sorry."

Maki was silent. Gamel glanced across the town: the warriors had reached Hana's farm. Surely this was the end! Surely it was soon to be over.

In that moment, Gamel accepted death. He closed his eyes – he grasped the stone of Atua in his pocket.

*My life belongs to you now*, he breathed within. *Have your way.*

Maki turned – and Gamel saw agony in his eyes.

The sight pained Gamel more than any beating. "Oh, father…" he breathed – and now Maki began to weep. Stunned, Gamel stood before him – shakily extended a hand to him.

"Soutar!" Maki whispered. "Soutar!"

"I know," Gamel said with tears. "But Yeshua did away with him! He destroyed the stone! He gave me this one instead."

And he pulled the stone of Atua out of his pocket.

Maki touched the stone – he pulled his finger back, as though it was burnt.

"What does it mean?" he whispered.

"Forgiveness," Gamel breathed.

"Forgiveness?" Maki's body shuddered now. "Forgiveness?"

"Yeshua died for us, in our place, for our crimes."

"Your crimes?" Maki breathed.

"Hatred," Gamel confessed. "I'm sorry, father! For all of it. And…and I forgive you, for all of…of *this*…"

And he gestured around the Throne Room.

Maki's eyes were on him, steadfast. And then his expression changed.

"What happens after death, Gamel?" he whispered. "Did Yeshua say?"

Gamel held his eyes. "He said that we could reach the place of joy if we stay with him."

"What about the place of suffering?"

"You know about it?"

"Soutar threatens it."

"We are safe, father, with Yeshua. But it means giving our crimes to him. It means changing: turning away from causing harm."

Maki's eyes intensified. "Gamel," he said. "May I have your stone?"

Gamel hesitated – Yeshua had given it to him! It was his only one! And yet he had given it to pass it on…

"It's only a symbol," Gamel said. "The real connection is in our hearts."

"I know," Maki said, "But may I have it?"

Gamel handed it over – and now Maki laid a hand on his shoulder.

"Leave, Gamel."

Chills went up Gamel's spine. "What are you going to do?" he whispered.

"Leave now."

Tears again filled Gamel's eyes, and stayed. "Father…"

He shook his head, but Maki smiled slightly. "I love you, Gamel – leave now."

Weeping took Gamel as Maki pushed him toward the steps. "All of this!" he said, behind Gamel's back. "I know what to do now! I know what to do."

Gamel glanced behind him, to see Maki placing the stone of Atua over his own chest. His face contorted – it hurt him! It hurt him, to bring Yeshua into his heart! And yet Gamel also saw a glimpse of something he had never seen in his father: the beginnings of resolution – the beginnings of peace.

"Go!" Maki said, and Gamel obeyed him.

Gamel passed through the second level of the Palace – the lounge, looking across to his parents' bedchamber. He ran down the stairs to the first level – through the corridor, past Friedrich's bedchamber, the dining chamber, and past Lidya's bedchamber and his own, on the right, as he ran out of the front entrance.

Tears poured down his face.

The courtyard was empty. Gamel fleetingly closed his eyes.

*Protect them!*

Koram and Taierre were standing at the entrance to the courtyard. Gamel wandered up to them, and then saw Lidya was also with them.

"No, Lidi," he whispered. "You should not be here."

But she reached for his hand, her face flushed and wet.

"Two from birth," she whispered, and he closed his eyes tightly.

"All right," he said. "Thank you."

The Northerners and Southerners now were storming through the roads of Raventown, emerging through Main Road and Market Lane.

"The others are safe?" Gamel asked Koram and Taierre.

"As safe as they can be, at this short notice," Taierre said, and Gamel nodded.

"Thank you for helping my people."

Gamel stood straight, to face the onslaught of warriors approaching them – and Koram and Taierre drew swords. The Northerners arrived first – a short stocky man lunged at Gamel with a sword. Koram defended, another attacked, Taierre defended, a third attacked – but Lidya stepped forward, in front of Gamel.

The sword pierced her, and she fell.

"No!" Gamel cried, all of his instinct driving his strength – seizing the sword from the Northerner. "No!"

He went to attack – but Lidya's voice cried out in agony.

"No, Gamel – stop!"

183

He froze, at her words – trembled, as she continued. "'Don't hit back!' Remember what Yeshua said? 'Give love for hatred!'"

*Take the first strike without retaliation.* They were Michel's words.

Gamel threw the sword to the ground, stumbled back, and sank to his knees beside her. She reached to grasp his hand.

"Altenhine, Gamel!" she said. "Don't just fight for me! You are fighting to save all of Altenhine!"

He choked, holding her hand – he pulled out her handkerchief from his right trouser pocket, with two lanterns, and pressed it to the bleeding wound in her shoulder. And now, reaching to grasp her around the shoulders, he pulled her up alongside himself.

The Southerners had arrived. Taierre and Koram were engaging sword to sword, and bearing down on two Northern warriors.

"Stop it!" Gamel cried. "Let me speak!"

Taierre and Koram stopped and stepped back, but now the Southern warriors were pressing in.

Suddenly Brierre stepped forward – Gamel recognised him. "Halt the fighting!" he ordered. The Southerners stopped, and now the Northerners shifted on their feet – swords drawn, but uncertain.

"Who are you?" Brierre asked, and Gamel smiled sadly.

"We are Gamel and Lidya: the Prince and Princess of the Heartland."

Brierre's eyebrows shot up in surprise. "The Prince and Princess?"

"I am the future King."

"Where is your army? Where are your guards?"

"We have no defence, Sir Brierre: my sister was attacked, and I have not retaliated!" And Gamel stretched out his arms, exposing his chest.

The warriors hesitated, staring at him – and then another stepped forward.

"I know him!" the Northerner cried. "I saw him on the Highland Elevation."

Brierre cast his eyes over Gamel, and Lidya, and then over the Palace. "I also know them," he said, "from the Elevation."

Gamel watched Brierre, and the Northern warrior, keeping his arms outstretched – keeping his chest exposed. What kind of co-incidence was this? Both North and South had already been engaged, on the Elevation, in peace, before this battle had even begun! And yet the battle was far from over.

"The Palace is wide open, easy for the taking!" Another Northerner announced. "Take it quickly, before the South!"

"Wait!" Gamel called out. "There is no need for you to take the Palace."

"Why not?"

"The Palace is empty."

"The Stone of Soutar controls our kings!"

"The Stone has been destroyed!"

The Northern and Southern gaze were upon him – and Gamel looked steadily from warrior to warrior.

"It can't be," they said, but now Taierre and Koram spoke up.

"We have witnessed the fact."

"The stone of the North?"

184

"And the stone of the South," Taierre said.

"All destroyed?"

"Yes."

"For what purpose?"

"To remove the oppression," Gamel said, watching them – bowing his head slightly: smiling slightly.

Now many Southerners frowned. "Surely you are lying!"

"The Kings of North and South sent us to destroy the stones," Taierre said, his expression also brightening ever so slightly. "We are united in purpose."

"I longed to destroy the Heartland Stone," Gamel said, tightening his arm around Lidya's shoulders.

Warriors shifted on their feet, wanting war and yet interrupted.

"There is more," Gamel announced – wanting to quickly progress the talks, while he had the chance.

"What is it?"

"When I am King, I will provide free access to the Heartland for your fertilizer."

"Free access?"

"Respect our freedom, and we will respect your need for food."

They stared at him. They frowned. Gamel could see they were rather bewildered by the offer, in the setting of war. Brierre smiled slightly – but then he spoke.

"How do we know we can trust you?"

Gamel grimaced, looking at him – it was a fair enough question: rightly asked.

He sought within. *What do I do now?*

*Protect them.*

*What?*

*Protect them, as you would have them protect you: as you protected your own.*

Suddenly understanding, Gamel glanced up at the Palace.

"All right, Brierre," he said, "Here's an offering to demonstrate my trustworthiness. We are all in danger here: all of us, together."

"What?"

"There is another kind of threat – a power you have never seen. We must move."

Urgency suddenly seized Gamel, though he could not entirely explain it – he began to lift Lidya down the street.

"Follow me!" he cried. "We need to get away from here."

"Why?"

"Trust me! Follow me!"

Gamel staggered down Main Road, and turned into Market Lane, past Southern and Northern warriors. They stared at him, and then moved forward to flood the Palace.

"No!" Gamel cried. "If you go that way you will die!"

Brierre glanced at Taierre. "What is he saying?"

"I don't know," Taierre said – and Brierre smirked.

"Then it is not a preplanned strategy. Follow him!" he ordered, and Gamel and Lidya found numerous warriors following them away from the Palace.

Koram appeared at Gamel's side. "Let me carry her," he said, and Gamel gratefully agreed. Their pace picked up – Gamel strode through the very centre of Raventown, zigzagging through different streets. Northerners and Southerners gathered around him. And then he turned, and looked back to the Palace.

Maki's form was standing at the window of the Throne Room. He was looking out: he had been waiting.

With deep sorrow, Gamel watched him. Now was the moment: how would he act? Would Gamel and Lidya be the sacrifice, to uphold Soutar's reign, with all of the Northerners and Southerners gathered together?

Gamel fleetingly closed his eyes – and then jerked them open. There was an explosion. Lidya was again by his side, grasping his hand. Was it toward them? Was it all over?

His fear was realized: the reason he had fled the Palace at his father's command.

The Throne Room now exploded – grey stone flung out in all directions. The top layer of the Palace was decimated – then the second layer collapsed, and then the first layer. Dust was flung out everywhere – and then the dust settled.

The Palace, the three towering levels, was reduced to rubble. The Throne Room was gone. The shrine was gone. The cabinet of history was gone. The keys were gone.

And Maki...Maki was dead.

With deep grief, Gamel sank to his knees. Northerners and Southerners were staring at him – he had just saved their lives! And...and the Palace was gone.

An eerie silence pervaded the town: the dust of the Palace settled on the cottages, and across the grass – across all of the people present.

Gamel stared at the fragmented remains of his home, and began to weep. Lidya was crying, next to him. Some Heartlanders were running forward now, through the rubble, into the town, trying to grasp what had just happened.

Hana was there. Gamel looked up at her, to see the compassionate understanding in her face.

"The King is dead!" she cried to all. "Long live King Gamel!"

Her words filled his heart with pain. She offered her hand to him, and helped him up – he swayed on his feet, and turned to face the masses from North, South and Heartland.

"Hear me!" he cried. "The Heartland will not engage in war! I will conduct meetings with the Resistance of the North and South – I will also conduct meetings with the Kings of the North and South. Change is afoot, but leadership remains! From now on the fertilizer will be made available for free trade with no conditions except the expectation of mutual respect and consideration."

The warriors were still staring at the decimated palace.

A piece of parchment floated down with the dust. A Northerner caught it. He began to read – his eyes began to light up.

186

"The formula for the explosion!" he said. But Gamel quickly grasped the parchment and reduced it into tiny pieces, scattering it on the wind.

Suddenly extremely tired, burdened with grief, Gamel buried his head in his hands. An arm came around his shoulders – he glanced up erratically to see who it was.

Koram was kneeling next to him. Gamel glanced at him – and he smiled sadly.

"Your father," he said, and Gamel felt his face contort.

"Yes."

"He would be proud of you," Koram said gently – and Gamel again looked at the remains of the palace: the tomb of his father.

"Proud?" he whispered – and for a moment he remembered Maki looking out. At that moment they had worked together! At that moment Maki had handed on leadership to the next King.

"Proud," Gamel breathed. And then he buried his head again in his arms, and cried.

CHAPTER THIRTY-EIGHT: Death, Life and Love

Lidya stood amongst the rubble of the Palace.

In front of her, in Main Street, Gamel stood amongst the Northerners and Southerners. Heartlanders flooded past her in their haste to reach their new King – what had happened? What would happen now? What did this all mean?

They barraged him with their questions – and his face was drawn with strain. There was no time to work through his own grief – now all of these needed him: now, instantly, he must perform as a king.

He glanced up at her – she smiled sadly at him, and then fixed a strong gaze of love upon him: her gaze of support. He also smiled, transiently, with deep sadness. And then he returned to his role.

The broken stones of the Palace were at Lidya's feet. She stood now in the place of her Bedchamber – the shape was still preserved a little, the broken walls still outlining the room. Her bed was gone, her royal clothes destroyed – her trinkets scattered in the dust. She reached down to lift a tiny doll that had survived: her favourite doll from childhood. She grasped it to her chest – and now she began to wail.

Her parents' room should have been above her head! Now it was gone. Swaying on her feet, she gazed into the space where it had been – and then beyond, into the space where the Throne Room had been.

The Throne…What had happened in those last fateful moments? What had Maki felt? What had he done?

"Oh, Yeshua…" she breathed in agony. "He killed himself! He is dead!"

*I took his life*, Soutar whispered. *He belongs to me.*

The thought plagued her: had it been suicide – a last act of desperation and escape? Yet something drew her closer to the scene – there was something more to understand.

For a moment she saw, in her mind's eye, the Throne Room – for a moment she heard the words exchanged:

*"I forgive you for all of this…"* Gamel gestured around the Throne Room.

*"Forgiveness?"* Maki shuddered.

*"We are safe with Yeshua – but we must turn away from causing harm."*

A reflection caught Lidya's eye: a polished stone was poking out undamaged, amidst the rubble of Gamel's room. She reached down to it: the symbol of Atua! The Stone of Atua! With tears she lifted her eyes again to the vision of the Throne Room.

*"May I have your stone?"* Maki asked.

Gamel handed it over. *"There is a place of joy with Yeshua."*

*"Leave, Gamel – I love you."*

Now Maki was wearing the Stone of Atua! Now he was clutching at his own Throne, peering out of the Palace window at Gamel and Lidya, safely away.

*"Yeshua, Atua,"* his voice whispered, *"I don't want to die – but I must! To undo all of this, I must."*

And now he was igniting the powder, falling to his knees in readiness for the explosion…

Lidya's hand trembled on the stone in realization – with this symbol had come her father's last act! Not personal suicide, but a king's martyrdom!

Lidya lifted her voice to the sky in victory. "Love has won!" she cried out to Soutar. "No more oppression! The Throne of the Heartland will be ruled by Love!"

All eyes were upon her – the crowd silenced by her words. Lidya looked at each one – men, women and children from her home, and men from the North and South. She met Gamel's gaze – his eyes were suddenly intense with renewed passion in purpose. She walked up to him – and now she lowered the Stone of Atua over his head: over his heart.

"Behold!" she cried out, "The new King of the Heartland! Soutar is defeated! Freedom has come."

Tears filled Gamel's eyes, looking at her. Then he turned to the crowd.

"As king," he cried, "My first act will be to bury the stones of the Palace in the Blue Lake. The time of oppression is over! The time of Soutar has gone. And then…" Now his eyes found Lidya again. "…then we will rebuild."

"What will you build?" Hana called out, stepping forward out of the crowd. "What will be the new king's bidding?"

Lidya watched, as Gamel cast his eyes over all the people – the Heartland, the Northland, and the Southland. Koram and Taierre were close at hand – standing straight, listening carefully.

"In the place of the Palace," Gamel announced, "We will build a new home for the royal family: a cottage! A home the same as your homes."

Tears of understanding filled Lidya's eyes as he continued.

"Alongside the cottage, to the south, we will build a Ruling House: there all the leadership decisions will be made for the Heartland."

Some shifted on their feet, but Hana was beginning to smile as Gamel continued.

"To the north of the cottage, we will build a Fellowship House."

"A Fellowship House?" Koram asked, his gaze astute.

Gamel looked at him, smiling, as he continued with strong voice. "In the Fellowship House, I will share the Good News I bring from Over the Sea: a new Ruler! A King of the heart – and a Kingdom of the heart. He destroyed our Stones of Soutar! I will share all this news in the Fellowship House."

"And will these meetings be a matter of Law?" Taierre asked, his gaze fixed with expectation on the Heartland King. "Will this Good News rule all the proceedings of the Heartland? Will the Fellowship Hall be inextricably linked to the Ruling House?"

Gamel's eyes were shining as he responded.

"Hear me," he said, his voice lifting across all Heartlanders, Northerners and Southerners. "Never again will the matters of the spirit, the matters of the heart, be forced upon my neighbours! Each will be free to choose – each will carry their own responsibility: each will need wisdom."

"A Law will remain!" Gamel continued, "The Ruling Law of the Land. But within the realm of choice, in the Fellowship Hall, we will offer what we have learned of Yeshua – within the realm of choice we will offer what we know of Atua, and of wisdom. Within the realm of choice, we will offer Love."

His eyes were on Lidya again. She smiled widely, and he nodded to her then turned back to the crowd.

"Understand!" he announced. "I rule today as a king – but the time will soon come, when all are ready, when I will offer you a kingly gift."

"What will it be?" Hana asked.

"Your own rule."

Lidya watched Hana's face light up. Other Heartlanders began to protest, still others were silent – but a shout of joy went up amongst the Resistance of the North and South.

"Gamel!" Koram whispered urgently, with Taierre alongside. "We are royalists! Your words may incite civil war in our lands!"

"Hear me!" Gamel quickly added. "I still respect the Throne of the North and South!"

Now the jubilation of the Resistance rapidly faded.

"A king may still rule well, if he is a good king!" Gamel continued. "This choice is out of my hands. The stones of Soutar have been neutralized, understand: the Kings of North and South sought to overcome evil – we are unified in purpose!

"But in this land, the Heartland, there will be only one King."

Gamel's eyes shone again. "My kingship I lay down," he said with joy. "Not yet! But soon. I lay it down for another kind of Kingship – a Kingdom of the Heart, between each man, woman and child, and Yeshua. Understand: I am still a royalist! But I know that we, ourselves, are only really brothers and sisters."

Gamel took Lidya's hand. "Equality, in the Heartland!" he cried. "Soon we will all choose our human leaders to rule in the Ruling House: soon the Ruling House will become Governance. The leaders will rule to serve the people! The leaders will be chosen by the people. Not yet, but soon.

"And when all is done, and Governance is in place," Gamel said, "then I will begin to share of Yeshua, the true King, with our neighbours."

Now Gamel's eyes were upon Koram and Taierre – now his face broke into a wide grin.

"Behold!" he said to his friends. "The Second Prince hides amongst his people."

"Behold," Koram replied in conclusion, "The king has come of age."

The crowd began to disperse. Heartlanders joined in excited and perplexed chatter, as they returned to their cottages. Northern warriors began to tentatively talk with their Southern neighbours. Brierre drew alongside Taierre, and began to speak of King Faier. Koram listened with interest.

Lidya watched them all, with joy – and then Gamel was before her, reaching to move her handkerchief.

Her shoulder hurt – the handkerchief was soaked with blood. Astonished, Lidya looked at it – she had forgotten the pain! And then she looked at Gamel.

He was smiling: a wide, bright smile.

"We did it," he whispered, and she squeezed his hand.

"Yes," she said. "We all did it."

"Soutar is defeated!"

"Yes – he is defeated!"

Lidya could no longer hear Soutar's voice.

With relief, she squeezed Gamel's arm – and then she noticed Tali standing behind Gamel.

Her mother was quiet – her face thoughtful, and sad: her green eyes insightful.

"Soutar is defeated," Tali murmured – and Lidya rushed to her.

"Father!" she gushed, and Tali embraced her.

"It's all right," Tali murmured over her. "He is at peace now – finally at peace."

"At peace?" Lidya asked.

"He is alive." It was Gamel.

Lidya trembled as Gamel moved to their mother to grasp her hands.

"Father is alive," he said. "Do you see it? At the last moment he overcame Soutar, though it cost him his life. And now..."

"Now...?" Tali asked, her expression lifting.

"...now is the time for all of us to live."

Lidya smiled at him – and then suddenly clapped her hands.

"Yes!" she cried at the top of her voice. "Soutar is defeated! It's over! It's done. And now is the time to celebrate!"

And she raised her hands high up to the sky.

Gamel's eyes were widening, now, and deep blue – Lidya saw him, and rejoiced in what she saw. He was young again! He was free again, as a child.

"Yes!" he shouted with glee, rubbing his hands. "It is over! It is done. He has gone! And now is the time – for true life to start."

## CHAPTER THIRTY-NINE: A New Beginning

Raventown was sleeping. A quiet township of six thousand, she was the crown of the Heartland. Built along the western shore of the Blue Lake, and along the edge of the River Dandes, she stood charming and inviting, surrounded by the majestic mountains of the North and South.

All was still.

A small figure gazed out across Raventown's oak and pine cottages. He stood in an open courtyard, outside the front patio of a new oak cottage. His home was small but inviting, warm and endearing. The Blue Lake was quiet, behind: two graves were set in the backyard.

The figure suddenly moved – and now he thrust himself up Raven Hill.

Gamel emerged, gazing expectantly east – to find Altenhine spread out before him. Below his feet, at the foot of the hill, was the still dark water of the Blue Lake – the stones of the Palace buried in her depths. Beyond the lake's distant shore, up the remote Eastern Ridge emerged the deep blood red beginnings of sunrise. To his left and right beckoned the mountains of the North and South: majestic peaks, lit with the faintest hint of pink as the new day began to dawn.

Gamel drew in a deep breath, drinking in the pure delight of the land. Chest full, heart pounding, he stood – and then he exhaled, and turned.

A slim figure sat on a flat rock, a few feet from him: her face fully exposed to the rising sun – radiant in its light.

Gamel smiled. "Lidya!"

She turned to him – she smiled at him. Gamel grasped her hands and lifted her to her feet. He turned her to look south and then west: beyond the sight of their new home, alongside the lake, to the stirring cottages of Raventown, and beyond these to the farmland of the valley. Sunlight now fell across the land, revealing tents from North and South – their neighbours settled temporarily in peace, side by side, in their valley.

"Today is the day," Gamel said, "When everything begins to change."

"Today is the day," Lidya responded, "When victory begins."

The warriors had returned, representing Resistance and Kings – and now they awaited discussions with Gamel regarding the Stones of Soutar: discussions regarding access to the fertilizer.

"Koram will be there," Gamel said, smiling, "And Taierre."

"And yet the Kings remain on their Thrones," Lidya said, "in the North and South."

"They do remain in their lands, Lidya – but I long to visit them."

Now Gamel turned away from the valley – back again to the mountains of North and South, lit with pink.

Lidya was quiet, by his side – and Gamel smiled widely.

"You know what I am thinking," he said whimsically.

"I do know," she said.

"Koram and Taierre would guide us. I must tell them, Lidi! I must tell the Kings everything we have seen."

192

Now Lidya looked at him – now she took a deep breath.

"You want me to come with you."

"Of course!" he said. "Two from birth, Lidi: remember? Two from birth!"

And he pulled out the handkerchief from his pocket – now stained from blood.

Lidya reached for the pendant around her neck. "Loyalty?" she said, eyes shining. "Last time you were trying to get me to stay away!"

"Last time I was a fool," Gamel said wryly.

He watched Lidya cast her eyes back over the valley – over their new cottage, the Fellowship Hall, the Ruling House: over the Blue Lake, and the mountains beyond.

"Leave home...?" she murmured to Atua. "Leave home again, after everything that has happened?"

She fleetingly closed her eyes, and Gamel silently prayed – but then, with a smile, Lidya opened her eyes again.

"My home is with Atua," she said, "And my place is with you. Very well, my brother: I will come with you! When all is done here – when the Northerners and Southerners are appeased – we shall travel to our neighbours."

Gamel grinned, and reached gladly for the Stone of Atua around his neck. The sun had risen, now, well over the Eastern Ridge. The Blue Lake sparkled in the bright light – the Palace remains were hidden: unseen.

Soutar had been defeated – and now it was time to spread the good news.

"Victory!" Gamel proclaimed to the mountains of North and South. "Victory!"

The Heartland was secure; but the North and South were still lingering in conflict.

*Don't keep great treasure to yourself.*

It was time to pass it on.

www.ingramcontent.com/pod-product-compliance
Lightning Source LLC
Chambersburg PA
CBHW031111260626
47172CB00001B/315